I0627576

Also by Joan Byrd

From Indigo Sea Press

The All My Tomorrows Series:

A New Beginning

Love Finds a Way

Today, Tomorrow and Always

The Seed Has Been Sown

The Shadow of the Moon Rider

Lost Stories of Jesus

The Box in the Attic

The Good Seed—the Bad Seed

The Devil's Revenge—God's Victory

Sunset Over Dixie

indigoseapress.com

Keeping Watch Over You

Book Four of the

All My Tomorrows Series

By

Joan Byrd

Deep Indigo Books

Published by Indigo Sea Press
Winston-Salem

Deep Indigo Books
Indigo Sea Press
PO Box 26701
Winston-Salem, NC 27114

This book is a work of fiction. Names, characters, locations and events are either a product of the author's imagination, fictitious or used fictitiously. Any resemblance to any event, locale or person, living or dead, is purely coincidental.

First Deep Indigo Books edition published
May, 2021
Deep Indigo Books, Moon Sailor and all production design are trademarks of Indigo Sea Press, used under license.

For information regarding bulk purchases of this book, digital purchase and special discounts, please contact the publisher at indigoseapress@gmail.com

Cover design by Pan Morelli
Manufactured in the United States of America
ISBN 978-1-63066-520-3

I dedicate this book to all my loyal 'All My Tomorrows' fans!

I hope you enjoy this exciting new adventure,

as Gene & Susan's story continues.

—Joan Byrd

Chapter One

Africa, 1976

Gene and Susan, along with Jobi Andrews, stood staring up at the shabby sign "Taboo Village." Gene Scott chuckled.

"Some things never change!" Gene felt someone tugging at his arm. Glancing down, he saw a young black boy whose eyes were wide with uncertainty. "Hey, kid, what do you think you're doing?"

"Are you Rev. Scott?" he said, shaking with fear.

"That's me, kid. Did Rogers send you?" Gene realized the boy was frightened of him, so he smiled and patted his short black hair. "It's alright, buddy, I don't bite."

"A…no, sir, Dr. Rogers did not send me." He relaxed and pulled out a white envelope. "I work on the docks and I was supposed to give this letter to you when you arrived. I about missed you. I was relieving myself, sir."

"Understand! Can't stand in the way when Mother Nature calls." Gene took out a dollar and exchanged it for the first-class envelope with "open immediately" written across the side in bold letters. "Thanks, kid." Gene watched the boy return to the docks, then looked down at Susan who'd walked over to have a closer look at the letter in his hand.

"Who's it from, Gene—Granddad?" Susan noticed the American seal on the return address. "On second guess, it looks official."

"There's one way to find out." Gene smiled down at her as he tore open the envelope and started reading out loud, "Rev. Scott, my name is Jack Reeves, the head of Foreign International Affairs in the U.S.A. My sources tell me that you're just the man I've been looking for, praying for. Your reputation is at the top of our list and you've helped us in the past. Rev. Scott, we need your expert help again." Gene chuckled as he winked at his wife. "They think flattery will get them anything."

"Gene darling, you are the best!" Susan pulled his head down to whisper in his ear, so Jobi wouldn't hear. "The best at *everything*!"

Gene kissed her nose, smiled, then continued reading, "My men in Texas were impressed with the job you and your group did there. I need your help again, Scott, right where you are. I know you've come to Africa to assist your wife's grandfather, Dr. William Rogers, who's somehow involved in this case. I'm not saying he's a suspect. Dr. Rogers may be one of the diamond gang's targets. My men, Vance and McLeod, will fill you in on our plan and what these evil people are doing to innocent landowners like Dr. Rogers. As you see, Rev. Scott, your interest is at stake here and with your invaluable help, we can bust this crime family. You'll recognize my men by the following: they'll be driving a solid black Ford, wearing black suits, white shirts with black and white bow ties. Stan McLeod will be smoking a pipe, and Herbert Vance will be smoking a cigar and walking with a cane. They should be easy to spot."

"I haven't met a clown yet I couldn't spot!" Gene chuckled and placed the disturbing letter in his pants pocket. "I hope those clowns don't expect me to dress like them."

"Then we're going to do it?" Susan picked up her small suitcase and hurried along beside her husband as he made his way toward the trading store.

"I don't think we have a choice, Susan. If something's happened to your granddad, that may be the only way we can find him." Scott walked inside the store and rang the bell as he gazed down at his wife. "Nothing ever changes in this place! Hello! Is anyone awake around here?"

With quick little footsteps, the owner rushed from the back room, brushing a hand through his shaggy hair.

"Do you have to make all that noise?" He stopped suddenly when he recognized Scott and the kids. "Hey, it's you, that preacher and his two kids!"

"Yeh, that's us alright and we're back for more supplies." Gene slapped the counter and smiled broadly. "We need one Jeep, water, a few snacks and directions to Dr. William Rogers' ranch."

"Old Bill's place? You're the second one to ask for directions there." The owner of the supply store started pulling out snacks and water. "Of course, you and your kids look a lot more regular than that other fellow."

"What the shit does that mean—more regular?" Scott's voice grew loud and the owner started shaking. "Look, pal, I don't have all day to try and figure out just what the hell you're referring to! Just tell me who this other man was and why he was asking for directions to Rogers' ranch?"

"Don't know exactly—he didn't say." The man jumped when Scott hit the counter. "Reverend, he looked…a…very rich. Dressed in real fancy clothes and smoking one of them English pipes. You folks, on the other hand, look like hard-working, God-fearing, everyday people."

"Directions—the easiest and fastest route!" Gene was losing his patience with the shop owner.

"There's only one way from the village, Rev." His voice shook when Gene stared down at him angrily. He walked to the door and pointed down the street. "Straight out of town there. You will come to a crossroad. Take the right. Bill's entrance is about ten miles down that road. Simple!"

"Why didn't you say so?" Gene held out his hand. "Keys!"

"Keys, yes, sir! Take the Jeep parked out front. It's full of gas and ready to go." He took Gene's money, smiled and handed him the keys. "When you see Bill, tell him to bring Kata and come see old Freddy real soon."

Without another word, the small group walked quickly to the rented Jeep and loaded their luggage and the box filled with snacks and water, climbed in and took off down the dusty road. About a mile from town, Jobi leaned up from the back seat.

"Susan, who's Kata? Does Granddad have a dog?"

"I assure you, brother, I have no idea." Susan looked out at the underbrush growing on both sides of the narrow road. "I can't see what Granddad sees in this wild place."

"Remember, sis, Granddad's place is beautiful compared to the rest of this wild jungle. He has trees, a rose garden, a vineyard on a hill and lots of olive trees!" Jobi coughed and sneezed from the dust flying up around the Jeep. "Those twin mountains standing behind his house have names, remember?"

"Yes, I do. Granddad called them Frick and Frack!" Susan giggled. "You're right about Granddad's place; it was surprisingly beautiful for the jungle." Susan turned around and handed Jobi a tissue when he sneezed again. "It's probably a dog, Jobi. He must get lonely with just a field hand around. Kata—what a cute name. I wonder what kind of dog it is?"

"You two beat all!" Gene laughed out. "Why does it have to be a dog? Why not a cat or a woman?"

"Gene Scott—a woman?" Susan slapped his arm playfully. "Don't you think Granddad would have told us if he'd gotten married?"

"There you go again, assuming he's married." Gene smiled to himself. "William could be shacking up with Kata!"

"Rev. Scott, you're terrible!" Susan laughed at the notion her granddad would be having sex at his age. She spotted the crossroads up ahead and sat up pointing. "Our turn. So far old Freddy looks right. This road does look familiar, don't you think, Jobi?"

"Can't say for sure, sis." Jobi looked around at the passing scenery. "You were twelve and I was only eight the last time we paid Granddad a visit."

"I do remember a sign over the entrance to Granddad's ranch. It was called 'The Lazy Lizard.'" She sat up, her eyes bright as she visualized the long drive going to her grandfather's house. "Olive trees lined the long drive, and the surrounding countryside was covered with grapevines!"

"I remember now! I thought we'd never get there. Then all of a sudden you round a curve and there's the big ranch house!" Jobi raised his shoulders. "Well, it looked big back then."

"And standing at the door, wrapped in each other's arms, would be Kata and William, greeting their family!" Gene's eyes fell on the sign over the entrance, a big green lizard with the words in bold print, "The Lazy Lizard Ranch." Gene chuckled as he slowed down for a better look. "The Lazy Lizard! I've known a few of them in my time!"

Susan frowned at her husband and turned to enjoy the peaceful long drive as she spotted the trees lining the road up ahead.

"There are those olive trees, and I can't believe how much they've grown in seven years."

"Just like my little Susan." Gene squeezed her hand as he looked out across the vineyard loaded with big clusters of grapes. "Does William make any wine with those grapes?"

"Oh, I remember grown-ups having wine, but I was only twelve so Jobi and I enjoyed the grape juice Granddad also put up." Susan grew quiet when she spotted the large ranch house and noticed immediately how still everything was. Gene climbed out and looked around.

"No dog barking. The place looks deserted."

"Oh, Gene, something's not right! Granddad should have been coming out to meet us when we drove up!" Susan looked around worried, then up at her husband. "You don't think that rich creep did something to him?"

Without a word, Gene made his way quickly to the front door and knocked loudly. "William, open the door! It's Scott with Susan and Jobi!"

"Granddad, please open the door!" Susan clutched her husband's strong hand as she felt tears sting her eyes. "Gene, where can he be?"

Jobi walked up between them and tried the doorknob. It turned, so the young man opened the door and looked inside at the big empty room. Jobi called out as Gene and Susan stepped up behind him,

"Granddad, where are you? It's Jobi. I've come with Scott and Susan to help you!"

Gene stepped past him into the empty room and tried to keep his voice calm as he called out, "Kata, if you're here, please come out. We only want to help you. William asked us to come, said there was some danger involved."

Gene could feel Susan watching him closely as he made his way around the room speaking, "You have nothing to fear from us, Kata. I know you're in here."

"Are you sure she's here, Gene?" Susan whispered and watched Gene nod his head in a positive.

"Please, Kata, we came to help Granddad, just like Gene said." Susan's eyes grew wide when a light-brown native woman walked out from a secret door behind a huge cabinet. "Kata?"

"Yes, Miss Susan, I Kata. Prapa tell me you and your brother come." She walked slowly over to Gene and looked up at the tall handsome preacher. "And you, Rev. Scott, he need your help much!"

Chapter Two

Gene and Susan led the frightened native over to a big sofa to sit down as Jobi raced off to the kitchen to get her a glass of water. Seeing her hand shaking, Gene reached over and took it gently.

"Kata, you call William 'Prapa'. Is that his name in your language?" Kata stared down at her hand and nodded. Then he continued, "Do you live here with Prapa?"

Kata looked up as tears began to fall from her eyes. "Prapa and Kata much in love, Rev. Scott. This my home now, by my love one." A frown creased her brow. "Bad men, they take Prapa! I much afraid they hurt him, even kill my Prapa!"

"Kata, why would these men want to hurt Granddad? His heart is good and he helps people when they're sick." Susan looked to Gene and he patted her arm and turned back to the scared girl.

"What did those bad men want, Kata? I can help you, but I must know what those men were after!"

"They want Prapa to sell his land! My man tell them, 'NO! My land, no can buy! It not for sale!' They give him papers and tell him he must sign or else!" Kata pulled out the document and handed it to Scott. "Bad men try to steal land for nothing! Prapa not sign!"

Gene began reading the agreement out loud, "I, Dr. William Rogers, agree to sell my entire ranch containing one 2,000-square-foot house and 200 acres of land for"—Gene's eyebrows flew up as his voice grew loud—"$50,000!" Passing the legal-looking letter to Susan, Gene stood up and started pacing the floor. "That's downright disgusting! Those low-life thieves!" His eyes met Susan's. "They were pushing your granddad into a corner, threatening him to sell it to them for almost nothing, damn it!"

Susan looked down at the threatening agreement as she tried to fight back her tears, her heart pounding with fear.

"Kata, when did those evil men take Granddad? How many days ago?"

"Bad men take my Prapa away four day ago, Miss Susan." Kata moved around nervously. "When they come first time with agreement, they tell him he have one day to read it, then they return! Prapa got his shotgun and hunting rifle and wait for them. He make me hide in big cabinet after he give me papers to hold till you arrive. I think Prapa know they too strong for him. My love one so brave, Rev. Scott."

"Yes, William's very brave, Kata." Gene took hold of her trembling shoulders. "You said they took him four days ago, so we have no way of knowing how far they took him. We won't give up, Kata, until we find him."

"Oh, Gene, four days ago?" Susan looked up into Scott's blue eyes as tears ran down her cheeks. "We were getting ready to take the youth on a hike at Camp Lookout! We were laughing and having a great time when Granddad was..." She burst into tears. Gene pulled her into his arms and hugged her gently.

"My darling, we had no way of knowing William was in danger." Gene looked over Susan's head to find Kata observing them lovingly. "Kata, did you hear those men say when they might be returning?"

"The big man—Mr. Blackwell—he did all talking. He tell men they take Prapa, lock him up, then get supplies need for mining. He laugh and say we see this dump two weeks!" The young native covered her face with her hands as she remembered the day they took William away. "Then Kata hear door slam and loud Jeep drive fast away...like cheetah!" Kata stood up and stepped up in front of the tall preacher. "Then Kata wait for you, Scott, Miss Susan and young Jobi, to warn you!"

The young native pulled a cloth bag from one of the drawers in the cabinet and began placing clothing inside it. As she packed, she continued talking, "Yes, Kata wait and watch! Hope you get here before bad men return. I hide in cabinet with no food! Kata go now! Go stay with my people till you bring news about my Prapa!"

"Kata, are you and Granddad married?" Susan walked over to help the nervous woman.

"Kata's people no let marry Prapa. Just stay with him. They say white man grow tired of Kata and send away."

"Kata, I don't think my granddad would send you away. If you're here, then he must really love you."

"You right, Miss Susan. Prapa love Kata and Kata love Prapa." She took a firm hold on Susan's arm and began telling her why her village elders didn't trust white men. "My dada was white man, hunter of wild game. He fall in love with my mama and she love him deeply. Tribe leaders no let stay after find he had white wife in America. His leaving break mama heart, and she leave life at early age with broken heart after she had me." Kata looked from Susan to Gene, then smiled.

"Miss Susan, you young wife to older man, but it love, I tell. I young, yes, and Prapa older man, but it true love."

"Kata, if there's one thing Gene and I understand, it's that age doesn't matter when you're really in love." Susan felt Gene's arm slip around her waist.

"Susan's right, Kata, but we'll see about you two getting married when I find Prapa and bring him home to you." Gene smiled broadly as he held down her bag so she could fasten it. "I'll make your people understand."

"Much thanks, Rev. Scott." She looked down shyly as she tossed the bag behind her back. "You the reason why Prapa no tell Miss Susan family about me. He say Scott no like us shack up."

Gene and Susan tried hard not to laugh as she walked to the gun cabinet.

"Do you need me to go with you through the jungle, Kata? William wouldn't want you to make the journey to your people alone."

"You much kind to offer, Rev. Scott, but my brother Rafa, he wait for me at river just down jungle path. Kata be fine." She slipped a hunting rifle over her slim shoulder and gazed back at the preacher. "Scott bring Prapa home! I know it!" Kata turned and walked proudly out the door.

Glancing at his watch, Gene pulled out the feds' letter to finish reading as Susan and Jobi walked over to listen.

"My men will be arriving in Taboo Village sometime Monday morning and get directions to Rogers' ranch at the Taboo Trading Store. When they arrive, they'll fill you in on our plans. Your wife and her brother will have a big part to play in this big performance. Good luck, Scott! Lieutenant Jack Reeves."

"So our well-dressed F.B.I. men will be here sometime tomorrow to give us the scoop!" Gene laid down the letter and walked outside to the Jeep, Susan and Jobi right behind him. "We'll take these things inside, settle in for the night and see what food is in the house so we can stir up a quick supper."

"Let me do the cooking, sweetheart. I've tasted your cooking, and I know why Pogo does all the cooking for us." Susan carried her bag upstairs and laid it on the big bed in the guest bedroom, turned and headed back down to the kitchen, Gene right behind her.

"So you don't think your old man can cook?" Gene watched Susan going through the shelves and food pantry. "You're probably right, but…I'm good at something else!" Gene grabbed her breasts, laughing.

"Gene Scott!" Susan looked around for her brother and let out her breath when she saw they were alone. "Good, not here!"

"Now, Mrs. Scott, do you think for one minute I'd grab my sexy wife's breasts in front of an impressionable kid?" Susan hugged his neck and laughed.

"Gene Scott, you're impossible! Sexy, but impossible!" She opened the freezer and smiled. "Perfect! A frozen pizza!" Taking it out, she switched on the oven and opened the container as she called out to her husband, "Look under that big cabinet for a large pizza pan, darling. You're really good at looking!" She winked as he laughed and bent down to check.

"You know, speaking of Pogo, I wonder who his mystery date was? He wouldn't even give his old pal one clue."

"Maybe Pogo's just trying to be mysterious like we were, remember?" Susan walked over and took the pan from his hand as he stood thinking. "Pizza in twenty-five minutes! Grab three small plates down from the cabinet next to the sink while I check and see if Granddad bought any beer." She smiled over at Gene when she noticed the refrigerator was well-stocked with both beer and homemade wine, not to mention plenty of soft drinks. "Good old Granddad!" Susan took out a beer and thought some more about Pogo's date. "I wonder if it's one of the girls from church? He's always got one cornered."

"More than likely, sweetheart. Pogo has had his eye on three of them: a blonde, a brunette and a redhead." Gene set the table and grabbed the beer from Susan's hand. "That little redhead's a doll. I can't think of her name."

"Beth Riggins! She just moved to TarSa a few months ago to attend college." Susan looked out at the growing darkness. "Where's that brother of mine? He usually can smell pizza a mile away."

"Jobi said he was having a look in the barn; something out there was real cool. Yep! Those were his very words!" Gene took a big sip of the cold beer. "Mumm! William did good with this beer!" He chuckled and looked around when the back door slammed. "I think Jobi's nose finally caught the pizza breeze, little darling."

"Do I smell pizza?" He ran over to the sink and washed his hands. "Good find, sis!" Jobi grabbed a Coke from the refrigerator and joined Scott at the table. Gene reached over and playfully rubbed his head.

"Find anything interesting out there, buddy?"

"I sure did!" He licked his lips as he watched his sister pull the steaming pizza from the oven and motion Gene over. "I guess you get to slice the pizza, sir." Jobi marveled at his perfect slices, then sat up when he brought it over and set it down. "I bet Granddad bought these pizzas just for us!"

"Probably so, pal. Had them shipped in along with the beer when he invited us to come over." Gene reached out and got a slice, then carefully took a bite of the steaming pizza. Susan set another beer down in front of him, then carefully set her red wine down as she joined the hungry guys.

"Hey, you two, save me a couple of slices!" Laughing, Susan laid two on her plate as she looked over at her brother as he crammed the pizza in his mouth. "You didn't say, Jobi—what did you find out there in that old barn?"

Jobi tried to wash his pizza down with a big sip of his Coke so he could answer. "Oh yeah! I found some really cool stuff! There's this box filled with arrowheads from the Bauta Barga tribe! Granddad had shown me all his collection when I was eight and told me the tribe members were real savages! Some of the arrows are really sharp! Some have slits in the head where the natives put poison inside to shoot their victims—could be animals or people who came too close to their village!"

"Let's hope we don't have to tangle with the Bauta Barga tribe this round. Those diamond thugs will be enough to deal with." Gene reached for the last slice of pizza before Jobi could finish the ones he'd grabbed. Thinking the pizza had cooled, he took a bite and burned his tongue. "Shit! Burned my tongue! Remember what Lincoln said when he heard Canada had threatened him with war during the Civil War? He said, 'One war at a time!' So first the diamond thieves, then if we have time, the dangerous natives with the poison arrows!" Gene took a big sip of beer after trying to blow the heat off his tongue.

"Just watch burning that tongue, mister! You might need it later!" Susan blushed when Gene and Jobi laughed. "The way you fellows are devouring that pizza, I should've baked two! I'll see what Granddad has for dessert." As she checked the cabinets, Gene cleared his throat to get her attention. When she glanced over, he looked at her with an innocent expression on his face and said, "I thought you were my dessert, little darling!" Gene winked at Jobi who burst out laughing as Susan shook her head.

"I just can't win with you two!" Susan set a bag of chocolate chip cookies on the table. "Here you go, boys! I'm grabbing another glass of this wine and heading upstairs for a nice warm shower."

Gene watched Susan as she made her way up the stairs. He stood up stretching as he smiled to himself. "Jobi, have some cookies, watch a little television and you can lock up before you get sleepy. Then get your butt to bed. We've got to be ready for those clowns tomorrow." Gene walked over to the refrigerator and pulled out a bottle of wine as he whistled their song, "Chances Are". He grabbed a wine glass and headed for the stairs.

Jobi opened the bag of cookies as he called to the preacher, "Hey, where are you going, Rev. Scott? Don't you want a few of these cookies? They smell great!" Jobi pulled out four cookies, never taking his eyes off the big guy, who had turned around, his eyebrows arched.

"I'm following my wife up to our bedroom, sport, and if you ask me why, I'll kill you!" Gene chuckled and headed up the steps while Jobi watched him disappear behind the bedroom door. Jobi snickered as he bit down into one of the chewy cookies and jumped up to lock the door. Grabbing the bag of cookies and another Coke, he went up to his bedroom to read.

Chapter Three

Gloria Ann Weber stared at her reflection in the mirror. She hardly recognized the girl looking back at her with her long red hair pulled up in a simple ponytail.

"I almost look younger without so much makeup on!" She smiled once more at her reflection before pulling the plain pink t-shirt over her head and tucking the tail inside her slim blue jeans. Pushing her heels aside, Gloria searched inside her big closet and found her single pair of sneakers. As she put them on, she whispered, "I think I like you better this way, Gloria Ann Weber!" She stood up and walked to her floor-length mirror and twirled around, laughing happily. "Just think—me and Pogo all alone in that beautiful farmhouse!"

Gloria walked over to peek out at her bedroom door. She looked up and down the long hall for any sign of life. Feeling the need for a fast getaway, she slipped quickly down the winding staircase. She tiptoed into the entrance hall and pulled out a writing pad, as she thought, *I hope Mother and Father don't see me leave. They'll ask me a dozen questions about where I'm going and why I'm dressed like a common peasant instead of my usual glamorous self.* She quickly wrote a note to her parents and laid it on the hall table. She made her way to the large front door, hoping Johnson or another staff member wouldn't see her. The bishop's daughter walked quickly out the door and straight to her sports car. After she climbed in and locked the doors, she said softly,

"I almost wish I had a regular little car like a Ford or a Chevy." Gloria giggled at the thought as she started the motor and the expensive red sports car roared to life. She drove swiftly down the long driveway and through the high rock entrance, grateful that the iron gates were open. She drove quickly through the wealthy neighborhood. Once on the open highway, she drove until she came to the Scotts' farm entrance and, smiling with joy, turned to go up to where Pogo was waiting. She slowed down as she thought about how lucky she was.

I feel just like a schoolgirl going out on my first date. Oh, Pogo, my darling, I still remember our first date and how after a bumpy start, we declared our love to one another. We talked all night in that little pub on Fifth Street over beer and pizza. The next night we shared popcorn at the movies. I can't remember what was showing that night because I was caught up in your warm embrace as you chatted away about a lot of silly things you and Scott did back in North Carolina.

Gloria smiled in her rear-view mirror as she remembered Pogo inviting her over for a cookout and telling her he wanted her to try some of his great cooking. She'd written in the note to her parents that she was going over to a friend's house and might be spending the night. Earlier in the day, Gloria had slipped an overnight bag out to her car in hopes that Pogo would ask her to stay the night. Gloria became anxious when she saw the farmhouse approaching. Soon she'd be in Pogo's arms.

Pogo looked pleased with the two fresh salads sitting in front of him. He wrapped them up and placed them inside the refrigerator next to the marinating steaks he'd grill later. Pogo smiled at the big assortment of beer and wine, then removed his apron, tossed it on a chair and headed for the hall to wait for his beautiful redhead. The big mirror hanging on one wall caught his attention as he checked himself out. Standing back, Pogo admired the way he looked in his blue, long-sleeved turtleneck t-shirt and tight jeans. He would be the perfect cookout host, he thought and smiled as he remembered telling Gloria to dress comfortably since it was going to be just an old-fashioned cookout, nothing fancy.

Looking around the room, Pogo suddenly broke out in a cold sweat. He could almost see Scott standing at the top of the stairs shaking his head and yelling at him, "Pogo! What the shit is wrong with you? Did you take an overdose of stupid pills after I left? What the hell are you thinking—Gloria Ann Weber?"

"Oh, shit, Scott! I'm sure glad you're in Africa instead of here! Can I help it if I fell in love with your reject? Why can't your old pal Pogo have a little romance in his life?" Pogo stopped talking when He heard the sports car pull to a stop in front of the house. His stomach suddenly got butterflies as he hurried to the front door and slung it open. With quick footsteps, Pogo reached her car and opened her door to help her out.

"Welcome, Miss Weber, to your very first Pogo cookout!" He fell silent when Gloria stepped from the car smiling as his eyes grew in wide circles of disbelief. "Gloria! I thought you were a knockout before, but Lord, woman, look at all that beauty you've been hiding under all that war paint!"

"My eyes are getting a treat too, Pogo! You just get better every time I see you!" Gloria checked him out from head to toe, then took his hands. "Darling, it gets harder and harder to leave you."

"I know what you mean, sweetheart." He reached up and flipped her ponytail. "Love it! And your jeans—some kind of hot!"

"I hope you haven't been slaving in the kitchen too long, darling." Gloria stood on her tiptoes and kissed him. "The only dessert I need is you, my dearest."

"That sounds very tempting, beautiful." Pogo took her hand and pulled her inside the farmhouse, then shut the door. "To get started on our first-ever-alone date, how 'bout an ice-cold beer and a stroll in the backyard before I start the grill. There's a great swing out there with room for two."

"It sounds perfect! I love the idea!" Gloria squeezed the hand of the young man she'd fallen in love with. "A cold beer with my man, sitting close on a garden swing! What a great way to start our evening together."

After the wonderful cookout, Pogo and Gloria walked from the kitchen laughing. Gloria looped her arms around his neck and smiled into his handsome face.

"Can you believe Gloria Ann Weber doing dirty dishes? The truth is I really enjoyed it, Pogo." She kissed his cheek. "You make everything enjoyable and loads of fun!"

Pogo rolled his eyes up innocently and teased, "It must be true love! My woman, who's never had to lift one pretty little finger before when it came to household chores, now enjoys washing dirty dishes with her man! Tell me the truth, did you enjoy your steak as much as you did doing the dishes?"

"Did I enjoy your mouth-watering, tender and tasty steak?" Gloria's eyes sparkled. "Pogo, I absolutely loved every tempting flavorful mouthful! Trust me, darling. I've eaten at some really classy restaurants in New York City, Paris, England, Italy—you name it—and not one of those chefs are as good as you! Any fine restaurant here, any big city in America or abroad would love to hire you for their head chef, my wonderful darling."

"I never knew I had a gift for cooking until I started trying out new recipes. When Scott lost Faye, his first wife, it was up to the two of us to do the cooking and housework." Pogo thought back about how he and Scott barely got by doing women's work around the parsonage, but their friendship grew stronger because of it. "Scott and I'd take turns cooking, but after a while, he put me in total control of that job because his cooking was poor to pitiful." Pogo laughed as he remembered how the preacher would open the lid over the boiling potatoes and after sampling it, add more salt.

"Then Scott married the girl of his heart, and Susan didn't know much more about cooking than her devoted husband. Thank heaven, she's great at cleaning and doing laundry because I remained the cook for the Scott household."

"Susan and Scott are lucky to have you, darling. I hope they appreciate you." Gloria laid her head over on the man she loved.

Pogo smiled at her as his hand ran over her head. "They say I'm irreplaceable. Scott pays me a good salary and gives me my own bedroom and bath. I'm just one member of the happiest family on TarSa."

"You're irreplaceable to me too, Pogo! Of all our dates, this one's my very favorite." Gloria looked into his eyes. "Just the two of us, alone. No one watching our every move. I belong here, my darling, in your arms."

Pogo pulled her up close and kissed her with passion, then spoke just above a whisper, "I don't want this night to end, Gloria. I want to keep you here with me all night!"

"Pogo, I want you too, darling." Gloria looked down shyly at her hands, not sure how young Pogo would respond to her next statement. "I was hoping you'd ask me, so I packed an overnight bag, just in case. Am I bad?"

"Bad? Why? Because you desire me as much as I do you?" Pogo pulled her closer to him, the need to have her growing stronger. "I just know I want you, Gloria, to feel your body next to mine. I can't wait!" He kissed her as he picked her up into his arms, then carried her up to his bedroom.

Gloria pulled his blue shirt over his thick brown locks and smiled down at his tanned chest as he pulled off her pink t-shirt. Pogo looked down at her black bra and swallowed as his fingers nervously undid the snaps in the back. For the very first time in his young life, Pogo stared at a woman's perfect breasts. He could feel himself growing with desire and closed his eyes seeing Scott shaking his head in disgust at his weakness. Gloria could tell Pogo was nervous as she kissed him and heard him whisper as though someone was listening,

"You're so beautiful, Gloria."

"Pogo, is this your first time, darling?" She gracefully unzipped his jeans and slipped them down. Her gaze fell on his huge swell inside his underwear and she touched it with her fingers. It seemed to come to life under her touch. Pogo started breathing heavily as she pushed his boxers down and whispered, "You've got a good start, darling!"

Pogo kicked the boxers to one side as he watched Gloria pull her shoes off and slip out of her jeans. He stared down at her panties, wide-eyed. Gloria smiled up into his nervous eyes and said softly, "Take them off, sweetheart, and I'm all yours."

Pogo throbbed with passion. He wanted to rip off her delicate underwear, but he gently pulled them down and tossed them across the room, unknowingly over a picture of Scott he had on his dresser. His attention was totally on the seductive redhead as she laid back on the bed and held out her arms for him. Pogo didn't hesitate this time; he was ready and for the first time in his life, he knew what it was like to make beautiful love.

Pogo breathed deeply when he felt the powerful explosion escape his private part as he let out, "My god! Oh my god!" Never had he felt anything that wonderful as he whispered, "Gloria, I love you!"

"I love you too, my darling Pogo." Still breathing heavily, Gloria held him tightly as she spoke softly, "That might have been your first act of making love, darling, but this was my best time ever!"

Pogo sat up and pulled on his boxers as Gloria reached for his hand, concerned about his actions, not sure about how he felt about their making love.

"Hey you? Where do you think you're going? Are you already leaving me?"

"No way, beautiful!" Pogo bent down and kissed her. "I'm going out to get your bag, grab two glasses and a bottle of wine; then your man will be right back!"

Gloria plumped up the pillows behind her and sat up, placing her hands behind her head. "Hurry back, handsome! I'll keep our bed warm!"

"You bet!" Pogo blew her a kiss and danced out the door smiling as he thought to himself, *Damn, that was good, making love to Gloria!* He stopped briefly and looked in the hall mirror. *Scott will kill me! Well, he would if he knew, so I won't share this activity with my best pal.*

Brushing it from his mind, Pogo dashed out into the growing darkness and retrieved Gloria's overnight bag, then ran back inside and locked the door. His eyes fell on a portrait of Gene and Susan and he felt as though they were watching him. *Scott will never understand about me and Gloria. He'll demand I tell him who my mysterious woman is. What can I tell him?*

Pogo got the wine and glasses, then with Gloria's overnight bag draped over his arm, made his way back to the bedroom. Gloria was sitting up in bed, the covers pulled up over her naked body and her long red hair hanging down over her smooth shoulders. Pogo smiled down at the beautiful redhead as he held out the items he'd brought up.

"I have your bag, madam, wine, two glasses and me!"

Gloria laughed and patted the bed. "Pour us a couple of glasses and get your sweet butt back in this bed beside me, minus the boxers!" Taking the glass from his trembling hand, she noticed the serious look on his face. "Alright, Pogo, what's bothering you? Are you worried about Gene?"

Pogo climbed into bed and laid his head back. "Gloria, Gene will want a name when he gets home. What can I tell him? He'll never understand about you and me falling in love!"

"Pogo, I've been thinking about this too, sweetheart." Gloria took his free hand. "My parents will never understand our love either. You told me Gene and Susan call themselves Samson and Delilah, so I've come up with some Bible names for us." She took a sip of wine and winked at him. "How do David and Bethsheba sound?"

"David and…Bethsheba?" Pogo frowned, unsure. "I can't tell my best friend I'm dating Bethsheba! He'll know I'm making it up and will laugh at me first, then slap me crazy!"

Gloria giggled. "No, you won't tell Gene you're dating Bathsheba, darling. We'll be using nicknames for them, Bath and Dave! What do you think, Dave?"

Pogo laughed, trying to picture Gene's face. "Bath, my love, I can see it now. Gene will be checking out all the girls and women from church who are named Bath but he'll be thinking B-e-t-h! Priceless!"

Gloria relaxed and leaned back against the headboard, knowing Pogo finally felt alright about what to tell his best friend. Taking a sip of the wine, Gloria casually asked,

"Pogo, why didn't Gene ever tell you about having sex with a girl?" She set her glass down and snuggled up next to him. "You know, the birds and the bees."

"Gene taught me everything I know." Pogo bent down and kissed the top of her head. "As far as the speech about the birds and the bees, he told me when it was time for me to make love to a woman, I'd catch on fast and be an old pro before I knew it!"

Gloria looked up and smiled. "Was Gene right, darling?" She ran her hand down his chest and stopped just above his privates. Pogo took a deep breath as he felt himself getting aroused again. He reached down and took hold of Gloria's firm breasts.

"As always, he was right!" He slid down to kiss her breasts and Gloria laid her head back, feeling passionate again. Her mind began to wander as she thought,

I've never gone twice so close together, but something tells me, this time will be different. The more Pogo kissed her breasts and let his tongue run around her nipples, the more turned on she became. Her fingers ran through his messed-up hair and her voice came out softly and seductively, "Pogo, my love, make love to me!"

Pogo smiled up lazily and pulled her under him as they made love again until they both cried out in sheer delight. Exhausted, the young lovers fell asleep in each other's arms, and Pogo never even noticed Gloria's black panties covering the good reverend's eyes.

Chapter Four

Gene Scott stood staring at the black Ford as it flew to a stop in front of William's ranch house, leaving a trail of dust behind. He walked over to the staircase and called up to Susan and Jobi, "Hey, kids, the well-dressed fed clowns are here!"

They came down laughing and continued laughing all the way down to where Gene stood frowning.

"Hey, you two, get quiet! Haven't you ever seen clowns before?" Gene chuckled to himself as he opened the door and smiled at the oddly-dressed men standing on the stoop, looking serious. Trying not to laugh, Gene motioned for them to enter. "Gentlemen, I've been expecting you. Come in and shake off the dust!" He could hear the Andrews' siblings trying to stifle their laughter as he smiled broadly when the feds looked their way. Gene cleared his throat to get their attention.

"Gentlemen, I hear you've got some orders for me and the kids here."

"That's correct, Rev. Scott! It's a pleasure to finally meet you, sir." Stanley McLeod reached out his hand and shook the strong hand of the preacher. "Our men in Texas can't say enough good things about you and how you and your group operate."

"If rounding up diamond thieves is as easy as rounding up drug-pushing prostitutes, this assignment should be a breeze!" Scott chuckled as he winked at Susan. "They all like flashy things!"

Susan and Jobi giggled and quickly covered their mouths, trying to compose their behavior. The two F.B.I. men turned to see what the two young people were laughing about as Gene chuckled and slapped their backs, pushing them forward.

"Gentlemen, you must excuse the children's behavior. It appears these two woke up this morning with their giggle boxes turned upside down!" Gene pulled Susan over in his arms and hugged her lovingly. "This one—I can handle her box, but my little buddy over there is on his own." Susan looked up at her husband, feeling embarrassed as the feds smiled at one another.

"Gene!" Susan turned and smiled sheepishly. "Mr. McLeod, I'm truly sorry for laughing, but my witty husband is always saying funny things and well, sometimes, like the 'box' statement, it comes out personally—his way of calming me down."

McLeod smiled at the beautiful young woman. "You follow directions very well, Mrs. Scott. You knew I was McLeod from my pipe." He reached out and patted his partner's back. "And, of course, the man with the cigar is Herbert Vance, my sidekick!"

"Now that the formalities are over and the two of you have noticed my wife's smarts and looks, would you care to fill us in on what our job will be?" Scott squeezed his arm protectively around Susan's waist. "Are we diamond thieves too, out to rob the robbers?"

Vance and McLeod looked at each other and laughed. Vance almost swallowed his cigar stub as he said, "That was very good, Scott, but not the least bit close!" He pulled out a notebook filled with information. "Scott, you're a rich diamond buyer, recently moved here to Africa from the U. S."

Gene smiled down at his wife. "I must do *rich* well! It didn't come from real-life experience though, right, beautiful?"

"Money's not everything, Rev. Scott!" Susan leaned her head on his chest. "Sharing your bed with the one you love is ten times better!"

"More like a billion times better, Mrs. Scott!" Gene noticed the feds smiling at each other so he stepped between them. "How does my wife fit in with this rich man?"

"Scott, your name is Julien Armstrong. Susan's name is Jessica Armstrong, nicknamed Jessi. She's your daughter." Vance looked up from reading when he heard Susan clear her throat loudly. "Mrs. Scott, is there a problem?"

"Yes, there is, Mr. Vance. Why can't I be Julien's wife? It would be nice to play that part for once! Believe me, fellows, I'm very good at that role, right, darling?"

"Susan's absolutely right, fellows! We don't have to make it look convincing because we're madly in love with one another." Gene playfully patted her head. "And she does the part of my wife *very* well!"

"I've no doubt about her making you happy, Rev. Scott. Susan's young, sexy and beautiful! I'm certain what the two of you have is very special, but, kids..." Vance noticed how seriously the handsome couple was staring at him, so he knew to choose his words carefully as he continued, "This is only a job. It needs to be convincing! It's like play-acting."

"We're aware of that, Vance! We've done this before, remember, in Texas!" Gene's voice grew loud. "What's so wrong with Susan acting out the role as the rich man's wife?"

"Scott, for someone who does not know you and Susan—let's face it—Susan would be more convincing playing the part of your daughter. Might as well face it. Rev. Scott, you're thirty-nine and your pretty young wife's only twenty. She could easily be your daughter in real life." Vance stepped back when Gene stepped toward him, his hand in a fist. "Look, man, I mean nothing personal here! I for one think it would be great being married to someone as young and beautiful as your wife!"

"Relax, Scott, Vance is right! If Susan goes in as your wife, the diamond thief will be suspicious from the start and you might have a hard time pulling this off!" McLeod tried to sound upbeat as he continued, "Who knows? It might even be fun for you, pretending to be father and daughter."

Susan remembered when other people had mistaken them for father and daughter and she looked up into Gene's beautiful blue eyes.

"What do you say, *DAD*?"

"That's my girl! Daddy's little pet!" Gene winked at the two men watching the loving couple, and they seemed to relax as the preacher said, "You gotta love my girl!"

Jobi stepped up, feeling left out of the loop. "Hey, gang, who am I? The rich man's kid too?"

"Very good, son! Yes, you'll be Richi, short for Richard." McLeod patted Jobi's dark hair and laughed as he added, "Richi, the rich kid! Pretty catchy, right?" He continued laughing at his corny joke as Gene bent down to Susan's ear and whispered,

"Funny like a clown too!" Gene could see a laugh coming from his beautiful wife, so he covered her lips with a kiss to hide her giggle. Hearing McLeod clear his throat, Gene pinched Susan's cheek and turned to the red-faced man. "Tell me, fellows, is Julien married with two kids or divorced with two adorable kids?" Gene squeezed his arm around his wife.

"Julien is very much married." Vance jumped back when Susan pulled away from her handsome preacher and took a step toward the nervous man. She stopped and stomped her foot in defiance.

Vance continued, "It's just an act, Mrs. Scott! We have to make it look convincing. The man we're dealing with is a big family man, and we thought it would be more fitting if our man was too."

"Then would you mind telling me just who's going to be Julien's wife, Mr. Vance?" Susan gritted her teeth angrily.

"Why, your mother, Jessi—yours and Richi's—who else?" Vance smiled until Gene Scott practically shouted,

"Shirley Andrews? My mother-in-law? Are you kidding? She thinks we're here in Africa having the time of our lives on a safari with her father!"

Stanley McLeod burst out laughing. "Shirley Andrews? Heavens, no! You misunderstood Vance! He didn't mean Susan and Jobi's real mother. Vance was referring to the undercover actress taking on the role as Mrs. Armstrong! You can relax, Mrs. Scott. You both know her well. She's worked with you before."

"Good lord! You've GOT to be kidding me—Jackie or

Ali?" Susan wasn't sure she could trust either of her *good* friends pretending to be her hunk's wife.

"Yes, that's her name…Jackie! She'll play the part of Judith Armstrong. Her boyfriend will be Christopher Adams, nicknamed Chris, Julien's bodyguard." Stanley noticed the sudden obvious question written on the preacher's face. "Is there anything wrong, Scott? You seem to have a question?"

"You said Jackie's 'boyfriend'. Did she and Michael break up?" His eyes fell on Susan. "Are they getting a divorce? We were just with them at a cookout and they seemed very much in love!"

"Relax, darling, Jackie and Michael are still together." Susan glanced up at the F.B.I. agent and forced a smile. "I'm sure Mr. McLeod meant to say Jackie's 'husband' instead of 'boyfriend', didn't you, sir?" Susan's eyes were pleading.

"Husband! Yes, I did mean to say 'husband'!" The federal agent realized Rev. Scott presumed the two couples helping were married, and he didn't want to cause friction before the case started. "I get so excited handing out parts that I get the characters mixed up with the real people. I meant Michael, Jackie's devoted husband, will play your bodyguard. Mr. and Mrs. Tabor will be helping as well. Ali will play the head house maid, Megan Ward, and James will be your ranch foreman, Tom Ward, called Stretch."

"Stretch?" Scott laughed, feeling better about his friends. "The name suits Tabor—thin with long legs!" Scott got serious as he asked, "Who'll play our butler and please don't say George Martin!"

"Martin, no! The butler will be called Edgar Henning, played by an undercover agent, and your head chef will be Tony Sorvino, a famous Italian chef whose fine cooking and acting skills have helped us in the past." Vance looked up from his notes. "Are there any questions?"

"What about the Armstrong's mansion? Does it reflect Julien's great wealth?" Gene Scott looped both arms around his wife's waist and pulled her closer. "Ah shit! If it's really huge, Ali will kill us!"

McLeod laughed. “Relax, Scott! Your friend won’t be cleaning up the extremely large house alone. She’ll have plenty of help, many of whom are already there preparing things for you. It’s really quite charming. An old southern Charleston-style plantation mansion we rented right in the Kilarama valley. You’ll be riding in style, Scott, in a brand-new black Bentley!”

“Damn, I am one rich dude!” Scott squeezed Susan as he chuckled. “Horses—do I own any horses to ride over my huge ranch and check out all my land?”

Susan laughed as she enjoyed her husband’s merry-making antics, but the feds didn’t understand he was just joking around. Susan teased him,

“Gene Scott, do you think Julien is as lucky as Lucky? There’s one thing you won’t have, buster—Foxie Roxie!”

“Shit! My little Foxie Roxie! Now she was one HOT hooker!” Gene noticed McLeod and Vance were staring with their mouths open. The preacher chuckled loudly as he playfully slapped them on their back, causing them to stumble and cough out. “What do you say, boys—horses?”

“Yes, of course! There’ll be horses if you must have them, Scott!” McLeod looked over at his partner and shook his head. “This isn’t a summer vacation retreat, Rev. Scott!”

“Scott? No, Armstrong friend! The name is Armstrong, Julien Armstrong!” Gene winked at their smiling faces. “I want everything money can buy, especially diamonds! Do you know where I can find a good deal?”

“Oh, yes sir! Hal Blackwell. He’s the big wheeler-dealer of the sparkling rock, and he’ll stop at nothing to get what he wants!” Vance narrowed his eyes as he thought of the corrupt man. “Blackwell’s a sick, depraved devil.”

Gene held Susan close when he felt her tremble as she heard the name of the man who’d kidnapped her grandfather. “We’ve heard that name before, Mr. Vance! He’s the same jerk who took my grandfather against his will because he refused to sell the thief his land! He has met his match! Julien Armstrong will stop at nothing to get not only the diamonds but also this corrupt diamond salesman himself."

Then Gene looked into Susan's worried eyes and said, "We'll get this morally debased jackass, little darling. You have my word."

Looking back up at the feds, he asked, "You said this Blackwell's a family man, so does that mean he's married with kids or does he just have a group of demons helping him destroy people's lives?"

"Blackwell has a wife named Katherine and one son, Toby, about Susan's age. You might say the only people this evil man loves are his family." Vance turned to his partner. "Would you agree, Stan?"

"What little love that black devil heart can muster goes to his wife and that spoiled son!" McLeod frowned. "Others you want to look out for are his thugs, Harvie Flint and the very worst, Nick Barrow, whose nickname is Tuffy. That heavy slob's the meanest snake in the jungle." Vance folded up the list as Gene chuckled.

"I've tangled with some pretty mean snakes before, Herbert, and I lived to tell about it! Right, Susan?" Gene winked at Susan, who remembered the box of deadly snakes Gene had to lie in because of her and his telling her about the big snake that tried to choke him.

"Don't remind me!" Susan made a face at him and turned to the agents. "When do we leave and who'll look out for Granddad's place while we're gone? Those diamond thieves are coming back and Granddad's house could be destroyed if it's left to them!"

"Don't worry, Mrs. Scott. We'll have our men stationed around Dr. Rogers' home and property. They'll make sure no one destroys anything he owns. You have our word!" McLeod motioned for his partner to hand over the list of names to Gene. "Your Bentley will arrive tomorrow with Baxter, your own personal driver. He knows the way to the Armstrong plantation. We'll keep in touch. Good luck!"

Chapter Five

Pogo woke up and noticed the bed next to him was empty. Sitting up, he stretched his arms and yawned as he looked around for any sign of the redhead. His eyes fell on Gloria's black panties hanging over Scott's face. He dove from the bed, bumped his toe on the nightstand and grabbed his mouth to stifle the painful "shit" that flew from his mouth. With speed, he yanked the silk underwear off Scott's smiling face.

"I'm sorry, man! I was in somewhat of a hurry to get my prize that was wrapped in these little panties!"

Making a face to himself for feeling guilty for being too weak to fight off his lust for Gloria, Pogo slumped to the shower. He perked up when he spotted the note in Gloria's handwriting pinned to a towel,

"Pogo, darling, I woke up early and felt terrific and alive, so I slipped out of bed quietly and took a shower. You looked so peaceful lying there asleep, I decided to let you rest a little longer after the wonderful night you gave me. I'll meet you downstairs and have a pot of coffee waiting. Not to brag, but the one thing I can make is a terrific cup of coffee! I'm not completely lost in the kitchen. I'll be waiting and never forget how very much I love you! Your Bath!"

Pogo smiled at his reflection in the mirror, expecting to see a change in himself after having sex for the first time. He was still the same ole Pogo Goings, Gene Scott's best friend. He mumbled to himself as he climbed in the warm shower,

"What did you expect, dummy? A glow on your *angelic* face?"

After brewing the good-smelling coffee, Gloria carried a tablecloth and two china cups outside and put them on the patio table. Looking across the backyard, she spotted the rose garden and walked out to break off one single rose to place in a white vase she found on the kitchen counter. After carrying the tray with the coffeepot and some sweet rolls out to the table, Gloria went back inside to wait for Pogo.

Looking around, she noticed a family portrait of the Scotts. She carefully picked it up and looked at the smiling faces: Gene, Susan and their twins.

"Gene, all those years I thought I loved you, only you. How blind I was! How terribly wrong! Look at the love between you and Susan. It's everything I thought I wanted." She replaced the framed picture and picked up one with Pogo's picture. "And then Pogo came into my life and everything changed. I'm not the same selfish little snob, thinking my daddy could get me anything or anyone I wanted." Gloria wiped her green eyes as she looked down at the face she now loved and hugged the portrait of Pogo against her chest. "I've never really known true love until now. Pogo, I love you so much."

Pogo stood listening quietly on the bottom step and closed his eyes in relief as he said softly, "You really do love me?"

Gloria turned, tears still in her beautiful green eyes.

"Gloria, my darling Bath, I'm in love with you too!" he said.

They met each other in a warm embrace as his lips parted over hers in a passionate kiss. Pogo smiled down at her, knowing now in his heart that Gloria loved him, and all her past feelings for Scott were gone. He lovingly took her soft hand.

"So let's try some of that terrific coffee. It certainly smells wonderful!"

"And it tastes as good as it smells!" Gloria laughed softly as she pulled Pogo out to the patio table. "It was such a beautiful morning, I thought coffee would be perfect out here." Pogo agreed as he pulled a chair out for her, picked up the coffeepot and started pouring coffee before sitting down next to the woman he loved.

"Just being with you, Gloria, is perfect!" Pogo tried the coffee and looked surprised to find it better than his. "My goodness! Woman, this is the best coffee I've ever had! Far better than mine!"

Gloria's eyes sparkled with delight. "Don't look so surprised, dearest. I'm not completely helpless." She grew serious as she reached over and touched his handsome face. "Pogo, I need to tell you something. Then if you still want me, I'll be here for you forever!" Gloria's eyes fell to her hands, now resting on her lap. "If you ask me to get out of your life, I'll walk out that front door and never bother you again because I love you so much."

"Gloria, darling, I…" Before Pogo could say more, she touched his lips gently, her emerald eyes sparkling with fresh tears.

"Please let me say this, Pogo, while I still have the nerve. Before you, before us, I've slept with several men, none of whom I loved. I suppose it was just the need for someone to want and desire me. Not one of those men ever satisfied me, and after they used me to satisfy their own needs, they'd leave and I'd take a shower to wash away their unfeeling love." Gloria kept her eyes down, too ashamed to look at the one she loved. "I'd climb into bed and bring myself to complete satisfaction, pretending I was in the arms of Gene. Then I'd cry myself to sleep." She heard Pogo clear his throat to speak and once more, she touched his lips to silence him. "Shhh, sweetheart, let me finish. There's still the issue of my age, Pogo. I've never told anyone my age. Vanity, I suppose." Gloria finally looked up at him as a tear ran down her face. "I need to tell you, darling. I am…thirty-three years old."

"Are you finished now?" Pogo reached over and took her hands. "Gloria Ann Weber, I love you! We all have a past. Yours breaks my heart, never finding love and having to get it through your imagination. I have no reason or right to judge you, Gloria. I've used my imagination with pretend girls before. Does that make us bad? No! We're only human and we all have needs." He lifted up her hands and kissed them. "Gloria, you're the first women I've slept with, and it was with the one I love. Now I understand what you meant by 'twice'. Last night was the first time having sex with a man brought you to total satisfaction—not just once, but twice."

"Yes, darling. I was surprised! Once, I was overjoyed, but to go twice in the same hour. I knew then the man I loved more than myself could give me complete love!" Gloria reached over and kissed him, feeling relieved that her past was finally out in the open and her Pogo still wanted her. "What about our age difference, Pogo? I'm six years younger than Gene."

"Age…what is age?" Pogo stood up to rub Gloria's tense shoulders. "Look, Gene's my very best friend. The two of us are real buddies and the age difference has never been an issue. Then Susan came into his life and there's nineteen years difference between them, but I've never seen two people that much in love before. Even after being together for two years, their love is still strong and growing stronger with each passing day." Pogo bent down and kissed Gloria's silky neck as he whispered in her ear, "I love you, Gloria Ann Weber, and I do not give a fig about age! I want you in my life! I need you in my life!"

Gloria jumped up and threw her arms around his neck. "God's given me a second chance! He gave me you and your great love. You, my darling Pogo, have brought out the hidden Gloria who lived inside a once selfish, rotten person! I love you!"

"I'll not deny that fact. You were a spoiled little brat, but love has worked wonders on my beautiful redhead!" Pogo lifted her up in his arms and carried the woman he loved back inside and up the steps. Breakfast would have to wait.

Chapter Six

Gene, Susan and Jobi were driven in front of the columned plantation house. They all sat staring out the big car's windows. The three-story mansion had a wrap-around portico with stately round pillars dancing around the huge house. Directly in front of the mansion was a cobblestone courtyard almost the size of a football field. If the city of Charleston could boast such a stately manor, so could Kilarama Valley.

Susan finally broke the silence as she gazed from the Bentley. "It's like stepping back in time! I can almost imagine a southern belle stepping through those massive doors in a long-hooped skirt, then disappearing behind one of those massive columns! Isn't it breathtaking?"

Gene chuckled as he climbed out and stretched, then helped his wife out and motioned for Jobi to follow. "Breathtaking? No, little darling, you are breathtaking! What I see in front of me is one enormous mansion! Damn, ole Julien's one rich dude!"

Jobi followed them up onto the massive porch and looked around with his big eyes.

"And I'm one rich dude's kid! I bet they have one swell swimming pool here!"

Gene rubbed his head playfully as he walked back to the car to gather their bags the driver had set out.

"You and your swimming pools! I just hope this pool is heated after that iceberg in Texas." Memories of the Lucky-C Ranch filled his thoughts as he laughed.

"A heated pool in Africa? You've got to be kidding! I say the colder, the better!" Jobi laughed and took one of the suitcases from Gene's hand. "Yeh! A nice cool pool—that's what we need here in this hot country, Rev. Scott!"

Gene chuckled as he gently pushed the young man toward the front door.

"I'm sure you're right about that, buddy." Gene's attention focused on the massive front door as it opened and a man with thin grey hair stepped out, smiling. Gene returned the smile as he asked, "Henning?"

"That is correct, sir—Edgar Henning, your loyal butler." He clapped his hands together, and two young African men came out in an orderly manner, each dressed in white pants and a plain shirt. They bowed to Gene when Henning introduced them, "This is Rata and this is Makata, Mr. Armstrong. They will be your luggage carriers, horse exercisers and waiters when you and your family dine." The butler turned to the two black men and introduced the family they'd be serving. "This is the Armstrong family: Mr. Armstrong, his daughter Miss Jessica and his son Richard. Please see to it that their luggage is taken to their rooms. Mrs. Ward is waiting upstairs to show you where to put them."

"Yes, sir, Mr. Henning." The young natives looked at the new owners as Rata said, "Welcome to Kilarama, Armstrong family." Both young men smiled at Susan as they retrieved the luggage and hurried back through the big doors.

Gene tried not to let the two young men's flirting with Susan bother him, although he was glad to see them dash off away from her. "You mentioned Megan Ward's already here, so I take it Stretch is somewhere around?"

"Yes, sir, Tom Ward is down at the stables." Henning led the way back onto the porch, glancing over his shoulder as he spoke, "Mrs. Armstrong arrived about the same time as your bodyguard, Christopher Adams. He was a big help in seeing your wife got here safely." Looking around to make sure they were alone, the fake butler leaned in toward Scott and whispered, "This place is so big that when we arrived, we had to hire outside people to make it work. We didn't have time to check them all out, so there may be a spy among them."

"I see! I'll inform my children." Gene looked around for the brother and sister and spotted them standing at the far end of the front part of the porch, their attention focused on something around the side of the house. He chuckled to himself before turning his attention back to the phony butler. “Then tell me, Henning, who else besides you, Megan and Tom Ward, my bodyguard, Adams, my wife Judith, Sorvino, the chef and Baxter, the driver, who are not possible spies are working here?”

“We already had a team of our people come in and get the house ready. They include six women who help with the cleaning and do all the laundry for both the Armstrong family as well as all the staff. Four of our men are here to take care of the grounds and run errands to get supplies for the mansion and to send constant updates and other information back and forth to the head agents stationed close by.” Checking to make sure no one was listening, the secret agent continued,

“The new people and would-be spies include Wanda Gaston, the upstairs maid; Pansy Holder, the downstairs maid; Max McCoy and Laura Rite, assistant chef and kitchen helper; two ranch hands, Harvie Flint and Nick Barrow, who appear shifty and suspicious. Then that leaves William Henry III, who is the head gardener and the two young blacks, Rata and Makata. I think we can rule out these young men from the valley. I honestly believe they just needed the job and they’ve proven to be prompt and efficient.”

“So we keep our eyes on seven of our employees. I take it everyone working undercover knows to stay in their roles at all times, correct?” Scott heard the siblings laughing and waved them over. “I hate to spoil your fun, kids, but I need to fill you in on a few details.” Gene repeated all the suspects’ names and told Susan and Jobi to stay in character at all times. Then he had to know what had them so intrigued behind the mansion. “See anything interesting behind the house, kids? Maybe a big beautiful pool?”

Susan punched his arm when he chuckled, then turned her attention back to the fake butler.

“Mr. Henning, I take it we have a big wardrobe waiting for us in our walk-in closets!” Her eyes sparkled with mischief as she winked at her handsome husband, who stood smiling. "I'm sure my loving dad gets me anything I want, and I don't think the clothes we brought with us will do for Jessica Armstrong nor for my brother Richard, for that matter."

"And you would be correct, Miss Armstrong!" Henning laughed softly. "Your father saw to it that your very large walk in-closet has the latest fashions for a young debutante such as yourself."

Even knowing this beautiful young lady was really married to the handsome preacher, her acting almost convinced him Rev. Scott was truly Julien Armstrong, her father. "If there are no more questions for now, permit me to show you up to your rooms, perhaps to freshen up after your long journey and get into something, shall we say, more appropriate." His eyes fell down on their casual clothes.

"By all means, Henning, lead on. I am dying to see inside my new mansion!" Scott took Susan's hand and followed the well-dressed man through the massive doors and into the large entrance hall with very high ceilings. Jobi held the back of his neck as he gazed up to the top and stared wide-eyed at the gigantic crystal chandelier hanging down in the middle.

Suddenly remembering one other person he failed to mention, Edgar Henning turned around and held up one finger.

"Begging your pardon, sir, there is one more employee I failed to mention. You have your own personal doctor on the estate to take care of you and your family—Dr. William Fields—also from the States." The fake butler noticed Scott's eyebrows arch up. "Sir, it is befitting for a man of your wealth to have a live-in doctor, especially here in the valley. It is a jungle, after all, and this doctor"—Henning got up close and whispered—"is a real doctor."

"That name sounds very similar to another doctor I've had the unfortunate choice to work with," Gene whispered back. Then he looked at Susan and immediately Dr. William L. Danfield came to mind.

"Let's hope his name is just a coincidence, Dad." She made

a face, remembering the flirty doctor who'd helped Gene on his first mission in Africa. Susan turned around in the huge hall and noticed the massive open arm staircase with the rich red carpet gracing the middle of what appeared to be cypress. Her eyes met Gene's as she pulled his head down and whispered, "Shit! Dad, you're rich!" He laughed softly and squeezed her hand.

"Mr. Henning, you may show us to our room now." Gene hadn't noticed some of the staff peeking at the new family through the dining room doors, but the fake butler did as he cleared his throat to correct the preacher,

"You do mean 'rooms,' sir, correct?" He motioned with his eyes to alert the fake family, and Gene chuckled as he shook his head.

"I guess I've been traveling too long, Henning! The private jet had a single room and the train from Tatoo Airport had one very small room for the three of us to share." He chuckled again. "Pure luxury!"

"Yes, sir, planes and trains can be close quarters, especially when someone of your high standing is used to state rooms everywhere you live or stay." Henning stopped at the first door and whispered as he patted the tall preacher on the back, "You catch on fast! Two of our suspects were checking the Armstrong family out downstairs." He reached up and knocked on the big walnut door. "Mrs. Armstrong, your family has arrived."

Jackie opened the door and smiled up at the handsome man towering over her.

"Darling, you've finally come home. It seems like ages since we parted from home and traveled our separate ways to get here!" She reached up and touched his face. "I hope the trip over went well." Jackie looked down and noticed Susan staring at her with a frown. She reached out and patted her head. "My dear child, you look so upset. Why the sad gloomy face? Surely our new home is big enough for my darling little angels." She tried hard not to laugh when she heard Gene chuckle under his breath.

A slightly overweight redhead walked out from behind her

carrying a bucket loaded with cleaning supplies. Jackie stepped out in the hall and touched Gene's shoulder in a very friendly manner as she looked at the upstairs maid. "My dear, may I introduce Mrs. Wanda Gaston? She'll be helping us upstairs."

"Mrs. Gaston, we really do appreciate any help you give us." Gene's smile was contagious as the maid curtsied politely, then smiled up at her new employer. "I know it must take some getting used to cleaning a new house, especially one as large as ours." He noticed the maid kept staring at their appearance. "Wanda, I hope our attire doesn't offend you, my dear." The handsome preacher chuckled at her sudden embarrassment. "We always travel this way so we won't get pounced on by thieves or heckled by people with their hands out for help."

"Oh, gracious me! Please forgive my inappropriate behavior, sir. I'm certain you must get hit on all the time by charities after your money."

"Don't get me wrong, Mrs. Gaston, there's nothing wrong with giving to a charitable cause." Gene patted her shoulder as he smiled broadly. "But I think my cause eats up most of my fat profits!"

The maid laughed out. "It's your money, sir. You're most gracious to your staff, though." Mrs. Gaston kept observing how Gene continued to hold Susan's hand. Jackie followed her intense staring and quickly put her arms around Gene as she smiled warmly into his confused eyes.

"Julien darling, why don't you let Mr. Henning take Jessica and Richard to their rooms to get settled?" Her eyes fell down at his hand, clutching his wife's tightly. Gene glanced down at the warm embrace and laughed mischievously.

"Of course, Judith, my darling. It's hard to let my little girl go, even if it's just down the hall." Gene patted her long silky hair that fell down her back, then pinched her cheek. "She is her daddy's girl, right, Jessi baby?"

"Oh Dad!" Susan reached up and kissed his cheek. "Yes, you're right! I am Daddy's girl! We love playing games together, right, Dad?"

"The more the merrier, beautiful girl!" Gene's eyes twinkled playfully. "What say we pick a good game for tonight. What do you say?"

"Sure, that sounds cool, Dad!" Susan smiled up at her husband, then looked down at her brother who was almost as tall as his sister. "Are you ready to check out our rooms, Richi?"

"Sounds cool, sis!" Jobi looked up at Scott seriously, trying not to laugh. "Hey, Dad, what about me? Do I get to play that really good game with you and Jessi?"

Gene frowned down at the young rascal. "Richi, my boy, I think your mother has something lined up for you tonight, buddy, right, my beautiful darling Judith?" He was glad to see Jackie smiling at the situation. She looped her arm around the blushing young man.

"As a matter of fact, I do. How would you like to break that pool in tonight? A little moonlight swim under the lights. I'm told it's very beautiful and the perfect place to wind down an evening." Jackie put her arm around Gene's waist as she avoided looking toward his jealous wife. "Darling, a lighted pool can be very romantic right before turning in. Perhaps you and Jessi could join us. I'll ask Mr. Adams to join us since we'll be going out after dark."

"We might take you up on that very romantic invitation, darling." Gene winked at Susan. "You can try on one of your new swimsuits, baby girl."

"Sounds cool! I can't wait to pick one out." Susan faked a smile and took Jobi by the arm. "Come along, brother, let's check out our rooms and closets!"

The fake butler listened to the make-believe Armstrong's chat about swimming as he watched the upstairs maid dusting her way down the hall so she could listen to their conversation. He turned to speak to Gene,

"We dine at 7 p.m., sir, if that is alright with you and your lovely wife."

"That'll be perfect, Henning. Please see that the pool lights are on tonight. My family's going for an evening swim later." Gene watched the undercover agent go downstairs before stepping inside the large master bedroom he'd have to share with Jackie. He immediately noticed the two king-size beds placed close together. He swallowed when he felt a hand take his arm. Looking down, he saw Susan peeking past him at the two beds. He lifted her face up to meet his handsome smile.

"Back so soon, sweetheart? Did you forget something?"

"I was wondering when Richi and I should be down for dinner, Dad."

"We dine at 7 p.m., Jessi, so tell Richi to wear something nice. I have no doubts my little Jessi will look beautiful in whatever she decides to wear." Gene touched her face lovingly. "We'll change into our swimsuits for our moonlight swim after dinner." Noticing Wanda, the maid, had moved closer to them, Gene casually bent down to kiss Susan's cheek and whispered, "You can trust me, Susan. You're the only woman I desire."

Susan smiled brightly, feeling reassured by the man she loved, and watched Jackie walking toward them.

"See you at dinner, Dad. I love you." Glancing at Jackie with a big smile, she said, "I love you too, Mom. I've got to start looking through all my beautiful clothes and pick out my dinner dress and my swimsuit I think will look best under the lights." Susan turned, waved over her head and walked back to her room, knowing she had nothing to worry about as far as her husband's faithfulness was concerned.

Chapter Seven

Michael and James smiled as they watched Gene escort Jackie down the wide staircase. All the staff in the area stopped to admire the handsome couple, whose choice of attire complemented each other so well. Jackie wore a long, white silk dress, adorned with a gold necklace sporting a sparkling blue diamond. The preacher looked extra handsome in his white silk suit with a royal-blue polo shirt underneath.

Smiling broadly at his friends below, Gene felt safe after learning he and Jackie had separate dressing rooms and baths. He still hadn't sorted out the sleeping arrangements, but the good reverend's loyalty to Susan would help him come up with the perfect solution. Michael winked at his lover when she smiled into his blue eyes.

"You're just in time for cocktails, Mr. and Mrs. Armstrong. Mr. Henning has laid out a wonderful selection. What may I fix you, Judith?"

Jackie looked over the selection as she drew close to Michael and whispered, "I'll take you, lover boy, later."

"At your service, Mrs. Armstrong. The whisky sour is one of your favorites. Allow me to fix you one." Michael's blue eyes sparkled as he fixed the drink and handed it to her slowly, letting his fingers slide over hers. "It is your favorite, correct?"

"Yes, Mr. Adams, you know me well," Jackie answered in her silky British accent, then turned to speak to James, who'd been observing his two friends. "Good evening, Mr. Ward. I trust you've invited your lovely wife to join us for drinks and dinner?"

"I have and it was very thoughtful of you to invite us, Mrs. Armstrong." James waved Ali over and she stepped into the big room wearing a simple, but elegant, black dress. Ali smiled at the handsome couple in white as she took the drink James handed her.

"Mr. and Mrs. Armstrong, thank you for inviting us to join you this evening." Ali took a sip of her cocktail and added, "It's a joy to work for people who look after their employees."

"My dear Megan, we consider you and Stretch family." Scott noticed everyone in the room had their full attention, so he added, "As we do all our hard-working staff. Please, everyone, enjoy a drink." Gene smiled as the staff each happily got a drink, then noticed James pulled an ice-cold beer from a tub of ice. "That looks refreshing, Stretch; toss me one." As he popped the cap off, Gene noticed Susan and Jobi making their way down the staircase. She was wearing a long emerald-green dress with a gold chain ending in a heart-shaped rare red diamond.

Rev. Scott's heart began to beat faster as he watched her and knew he was growing excited and hoped it didn't show. As she stopped in front of him, his eyes fell on her full bosom, part of which was revealed from the low-cut top. Remembering the interested party of workers, Gene reached for her soft hand as his eyes wandered to her beautiful face.

"You look beautiful, baby girl. What can Dad fix you to drink?"

"You may fix me a glass of sherry, Dad." Susan smiled briefly down at his bulging pants, then looked into his serious blue eyes. "I'm glad my dress pleases you. Might I say, you and Mom look very handsome this evening as well." She smoothed out the front of her dress as her eyes twinkled with mischief. "So you really like this dress, Dad?"

"Who the hell wouldn't!" Gene chuckled as he handed her the glass of sweet wine and whispered for her ears only, "Damn, Susan, you're killing me here, woman!"

"Good!" She patted his cheek. "I'm glad you like it as much as I do." Susan took a small sip and whispered back, "I just wanted to remind you what you own, darling."

Gene laughed out as he grabbed another beer and smiled over at all the interested party.

"You gotta love this little gal!" Noticing Jobi for the first time, Scott reached in the ice and pulled out a root beer and held it up. "How about a root beer, son?"

"Sure, Dad, sounds cool!" Jobi caught the cold can when Gene sent it sailing his way. "Sis says she really loves all her clothes, Dad! Mine are pretty heavy too!"

Scott's gaze fell down on Susan seriously. "Are all your clothes this entertaining, Jessica?"

Before Susan could answer, Edgar Henning stepped into the room and announced dinner was ready to be served. Gene took Jackie's arm and led the group of diners behind the fake butler to the exquisite dining room with a long table capable of seating twenty guests.

After pulling out a chair for Jackie, Gene motioned for Susan to sit on his other side. Susan smiled up at her husband when he slid her chair in and took his seat at the head of the table.

"Thank you, Dad. I hope the man I marry someday will have the same graceful manners as you." She ignored his growl as she bent forward to speak to Jackie on his other side. "Mom, isn't this a great room? It's a little bigger than our dining hall at Newport."

"Yes, Jessi dear, this is such a warm southern estate. Every room is beyond beautiful. The only thing more pleasing to look at is your handsome father." Jackie smiled at Susan's frown as she continued, "I'll take you on a tour in the morning if you like." Jackie laid her hand over on Michael's leg when he took a seat next to her. With her left hand, she caressed Scott's face. "You too, precious, if you care to join us on the tour." Gene chuckled below his breath when he felt Susan squeeze his knee under the table and smiled at James, Ali and Jobi as they found their places next to Susan.

Gene watched as the young men brought in fresh salads for everyone and filled wine glasses with white wine. He sat up when he noticed the other place setting and the servers filling the glass sitting in front of the empty chair and placing the last salad down. His eyes fell on the butler and he motioned him over.

"Henning, I notice another place setting next to Mr. Adams. Is someone joining us?"

"Yes, sir, that would be Dr. Fields. He appears to be running a bit late." Henning checked his watch as the doctor made his entrance into the dining room and slid into his seat.

"Please forgive me. I am running a tad behind." The doctor noticed Gene Scott's eyes blazing on him as William Danfield forced a weak smile for his comrade.

"Dr.….Fields, how do you like your accommodations? I trust they are suitable." The reverend watched his ex-friend closely when the doctor's eyes drifted over to Susan and a big smile came to his lips. Gene's memory flew back to Africa as he remembered Danfield always flirting with her back then.

On the other hand, as the doctor's eyes took in the beautiful young woman, his memories from Africa were about how the good reverend had tried to resist her. He turned to Scott to answer his question.

"Mr. Armstrong, my rooms are most pleasing like Judith, your beautiful wife, and Jessica, your lovely daughter." Danfield's eyes fell on Susan's revealing neckline, but he avoided looking at Gene Scott's burning glare. "My goodness, Miss Armstrong, you've become quite a little lady."

"Why, Dr. Fields, are you flirting with me?" Susan felt Gene's strong grip take a tight hold on her knee.

"Let me just say, my dear, nature has been good to you." He knew for his health he'd better change the subject before his old adversary lost it and came after him. "Judith, I'm sure Jessica gets her good looks from you, my dear lady. Julien's more a man's man."

Danfield was saved when Rata and Makata came in with the second course. The small group ate the delicious meal with just light conversation. After the diners had finished, the fake Armstrong family made their way upstairs to change for swimming.

Jackie walked from her dressing room wearing a well-fitting black swimsuit. Gene smiled down into her lovely green eyes as he opened the door for her and whispered, "I hope Susan isn't wearing one of those string-up-your-ass bikinis!"

Jackie laughed softly as she led the way to Susan's and Jobi's rooms. Hearing the tap on his door, Jobi stepped out wearing navy-blue trunks. When his eyes fell on Jackie, he let out a whistle. "Wow! Mom, you look real hot!"

"Watch that talk, son!" Gene playfully rubbed his head and looked up when Susan opened her door wearing a one-piece leopard bathing suit which accentuated all her curves. She shut her door smiling, then took Gene's hand.

"I had a hard time choosing, Dad. You really found a great shopper to buy all our new clothes. I have ten beautiful swimsuits, three more than I have back home."

"I'm really glad you like them, baby girl. I'm liking your new clothes pretty well myself so far." Gene wanted to pull his young wife into his arms and kiss her, but the maids were coming down the hall with fresh towels. So instead of the needed kiss, Gene pulled her out the sliding glass door that led to the second-floor balcony, and the group made their way down the steps to the lighted pool area. He chuckled as he stretched. "Let's go break in this big pool!"

The lights around the pool plus the bright moonlight made the pool glisten. Gene tightened his grip on Susan's hand as they walked out to the pool.

"Now, that's what you call a romantic pool!"

"I couldn't agree more, Dad! Just enough light to see but dark enough to have a little fun." Susan made her way down the pool steps into the refreshing water. She smiled up at her handsome husband, who stood admiring his beautiful wife. "Come on in, Dad, the water feels great!"

"You bet, baby girl!" he called out in case they were being watched, then made a dive off the side of the pool. Coming up to the surface, Scott slung his head from side to side to shake off the water. "Hey, not bad! How about a game, sweetheart?" The preacher's strong arms lifted his shapely wife up over his head. He smiled as she laughed. "How's the view up there?"

"Great, Dad!" Susan stretched out her arms and legs, feeling safe in her husband's hands. "I feel like a bird! No, I'm an airplane, ready for take-off, Mr. Launchpad!"

"Can I get a ride on your plane, little darling?" Gene's strong arms held her up with ease as he kept his eyes on her shapely body. Susan smiled as she tried to steady herself.

"You can ride on me anytime, handsome. First class, just for you! Just get a reservation!"

Gene mumbled to himself, "Shit! Somehow, someway tonight!" Then he sent her flying into the air until she landed gracefully back in the water and came up laughing. They swam out to meet one another. Taking her in his arms, Gene pulled her to the dark side of the pool. His lips parted over hers in a passionate kiss as his tongue slipped inside her sweet mouth. They began breathing with desire as Susan whispered,

"Gene darling, I need my husband tonight!"

Gene looked into her eyes as a mischievous grin spread across his face. "I'll come to your room tonight, darling, after everyone's gone to bed. Tell me, do I need to make a reservation to ride you?"

"Just pay me right now with a hot kiss, and you'll be riding in first class all the way!" Susan looped her arms tightly around his strong neck as he kissed her again.

Gene was so caught up in Susan that he jumped when someone touched his back. He swung around and looked down at Jackie and Michael, who had swum out to warn them.

"Gene, we really hate to break up this romantic kissing, but we came out to warn you we aren't alone out here. There's someone hiding in the bushes over by the pool chairs," Jackie whispered.

"You may be hidden over here in this dark area, Scott, but the interested party may be growing suspicious as to what father and daughter are doing for so long." Michael's blue eyes glistened in the moonlight that filtered through the trees overhead. "If you remain here, the spies may move to another spot to see what you're up to."

"Gotcha!" Scott gazed down at his wife and whispered, "Tonight, darling!" Then he took Jackie's hand, and they swam out together as he whispered, "Play along with what I say." After reaching the ladder on poolside next to the mansion, Gene chuckled, "Judith, I hate you missed that strange bird! It was the weirdest-looking crane I've ever laid my eyes on! It kept dipping its long neck in the water, looking for a damn fish. I assume it thought it was at a marsh with those willows hanging down over the pool."

"I'm sorry it flew away when we came over, darling. I did see it swoop down about the same time you and Jessi saw it and swam over to see what it was." Jackie held out her hands for Scott to lift her out of the pool; then they watched Susan and Michael swim out of the dark area of the pool.

"The bird didn't exactly fly away, dear. It flew up into the tree overhead when he saw you and Chris." Gene then called out to Michael, "Did you see the bird, Chris? When you and Judith swam over, it got spooked and flew up in the tree overhead."

"I'm afraid I didn't spot it, Julien. Jessica tried to find it and point it out, but that tree and the dark made it impossible to spot." Michael shook his head.

Susan picked up the farce quickly and said, "Dad and I saw that big bird swoop down and heard all the splashing, then slipped over in the dark to investigate!" She giggled, "Boy, were we surprised to find that unusual jungle bird trying to find a stupid fish in a swimming pool!"

"Hey, what did I miss?" Jobi swam up as Susan was telling about the bird, not knowing it was a fantasy to fool the snooping spies. "I've been practicing my dives and I missed out on all the excitement! Darn!"

"Well, it's over now, sport!" Gene hugged Jackie, knowing if they could fool Jobi, they could fool anyone. "It's time we all say good night to the pool and go up to shower before hitting the sheets."

"Are we going up just to go to bed, darling, after our swim

in this romantic pool?" Jackie smiled as she heard Susan and Michael grunt; then she picked up her towel and wrapped it around her shapely body.

"Not on your life, my beautiful wife! You're far too tempting to resist. Let's shower, then hit the sheets...together!" Gene chuckled, as he thought, *I'll hit the sheets with my woman*!

"I thought you'd never ask, you sexy devil!" Jackie smiled down in the pool at Michael, Susan and Jobi. "Good night, my little angels. Mr. Adams, good night." She walked over next to Gene. He took her hand as his eyes met Susan's.

"Alright, kids, time to get out and have your bath." He watched his wife climb out and start drying off. His eyes remained on her as he spoke, "Jessi, get your sweet butt to bed." Gene lifted his eyebrows with mischief. "Then it's sweet dreams! Maybe we'll dream about jungle birds or…airplanes!"

"Alright, Richi, get a move on!" Susan walked up next to Gene and hugged him as she whispered, "I'll leave the door unlocked." Then she spoke out, "Good night, Dad."

Gene squeezed her tightly and whispered, "Good night, little darling. I'll be there!"

Chapter Eight

Gene peeked out into the dimly lit hallway and found it completely deserted. He checked his watch and assumed everyone else would be in bed by now. He heard Jackie laugh softly and turned to see her propped up in her bed, ready to read a book while she watched him closely.

"Gene, if the coast is clear, go on to Susan. I'm sure she's waiting and wondering where you are."

"What about Michael? Is he coming to you tonight?" Gene pulled at his silk pajama bottoms, trying to keep them up.

"You may leave the door unlocked. He'll be here soon." Jackie fluffed up her pillows. "Mike is down the hall waiting for you to leave and he'll slip back out before sunrise around 5 a.m." She recognized Scott's uncertain frown. "Don't worry, darling, Mike knows to be careful as I know you will. Now scoot while there's still time for lovemaking and don't worry, Mike will lock the door when he gets inside."

"Alright, just make sure Mike leaves by 5 a.m. I'll be returning then and don't need to find hot lovers in bed!" Gene laughed softly as he pulled the door closed behind him and made his way quickly to Susan's room. He turned the doorknob, stepped inside and locked the deadbolt as well as the door lock. With nosy people around, one couldn't be too careful. Gene tried to focus in the dim light and barely made out the empty bed with the covers pulled down.

"Susan, sweetheart, where are you?"

"What kept you so long, Rev. Scott?" Susan had slipped up behind him and circled her arms around his waist. "Nice pj's, Mr. Scott!"

Gene twirled around quickly and grabbed his young wife in his arms. To his pleasant surprise, all he could feel was her soft skin.

“Susan, what are you wearing, darling?” His eyes finally grew accustomed to the dim light, and he could see her standing there with nothing on but a brilliant smile.

“I thought I’d save you the trouble of undressing me, so we could get right at it—as soon as we get you out of these sexy pajamas.” Susan started undoing the buttons on his silk top as she continued, “I’ve been waiting for my wonderful husband to come and make passionate love to me.” She pulled the silk against her breasts and sighed, “Mmm, pure silk! Nothing’s too good for my ‘dad’! The top slipped from her fingers as Gene’s hands cupped her full round breasts, then closed his eyes.

“Susan, my Susan, god, you feel so good!” His blue eyes opened slowly and landed on hers. “Of all the possessions your rich ‘dad’ owns, you, my darling girl, are the best!”

They both breathed heavily as Gene continued to caress her young breasts. Gene’s lips parted over hers as her fingers undid his pajama bottom and helped it slide to the floor. Her eyes fell on his naked aroused manhood. Susan smiled as she gathered her prize in her hand. “My heavens! Rev. Scott, so big, so long, so ready!”

“It goes with the frame, sweetheart.” His strong arms lifted her with ease as their eyes met. “Ah shit, it’s all yours, girl!”

“Then carry me to bed and make love to me, my darling.” Scott’s lips burned over hers as he laid her down and climbed on top of her. Susan felt hot all over as her body moved under his weight. She was lost in their fiery passion. Their night of love was total and complete.

Susan and Gene lay exhausted in each other’s arms, the passion and desires still sweeping through their tired bodies. Gene pulled her close to him, knowing what they had was special and wonderful.

“Susan! Oh god, my Susan, how I love you! You’ve made me so happy and complete, my darling. I realize now, I was living like only half a man until you came into my life! Thank God you were on that ship going to Africa! Thank God you didn’t give up on our love!”

Susan was still trying to catch her breath after all the hot passion between them. She took a deep breath as she held on to the man she loved.

"Oh, my darling Gene, you make me happy and complete as well! I wasn't looking for romance or love when I climbed aboard that ship going to visit my granddad, but love and romance found me. I'm still amazed that I'm married to Rev. Gene Scott and that you finally took me seriously."

"I just thank God I had the common sense to stop you from running away from me the day I told you I loved you." Gene pulled the covers over them, then switched off the lamp next to the bed. After pulling her in his warm embrace, he whispered, "Better get our rest. Good night, sweetheart. I'll have to get up before daylight so no one will see me leave your room."

"As long as we have the nights together, I can get through this act." Susan yawned and snuggled up close to her man and fell asleep.

Gene Scott opened his eyes and saw that the room was still dark. Something had awakened him or maybe he'd been dreaming. He glanced over at the bedside clock…4 a.m. His attention fell on Susan, still in his arms, fast asleep. Then he heard the noise again and sat up slowly to listen. Gene recognized the sound of a doorknob rattling and knew someone was trying to get into Susan's room. The alert husband put his hand over his wife's mouth as he shook her awake.

"Susan, sweetheart, there's someone at the door. They're trying to get in," he whispered. Then the sound came again and Susan sat up, her eyes wide with fear. "It's going to be alright, Susan. Just get up quietly and put your gown on while I find my pajamas." Gene climbed slowly out of the covers and searched the floor for his silk pajamas until he found them and slipped them on.

Susan walked up behind him and whispered, "What are we going to do, Gene?"

"I want you to climb back in bed and pretend you're asleep. I'll say that you had a nightmare and came to our room. I came back with you to calm you down so you could fall back to sleep. Being tired myself, I fell asleep in the chair."

"What chair, sweetheart?" Susan looked up into Gene's serious eyes. "The only chair I have is inside my dressing room at my vanity."

"Alright then, Dad fell asleep on the side of your bed, watching over his precious young daughter." He bent down and kissed her, then patted the top of her head.

Susan reached up and hugged him before climbing back into the big bed. Gene tenderly pulled the covers over her, letting his hand touch her breasts.

"Damn, you're so tempting lying there."

"Just don't get a hard-on, 'Dad'!' Susan giggled as she quickly covered her mouth. "Now start acting like Dad while I get my sleep."

"A hard-on? Shit, that's all I need, to open that door and some nosy person notices a hard-on!" Gene mumbled to himself as he walked over, unlocked the deadbolt and slung the door open. Wanda Gaston jumped back and tried to muffle her scream with her hands.

"Good lord, sir, you scared the willies out of me!"

"Mrs. Gaston, what the devil are you doing out here so blasted early in the morning and why are you trying to get inside my daughter's room?" Gene Scott stepped out in the hall and quietly shut the door, pretending not to wake his daughter, Jessica. "Just explain why you were trying to get inside her room."

Suddenly, it dawned on the nosy maid…what was this father doing in his daughter's bedroom at 4 a.m.? Mrs. Gaston held her head high, thinking she might have caught a pervert molesting his young daughter. She narrowed her eyes as she picked her words carefully,

"I could also ask you what you're doing in your young daughter's bedroom at such an ungodly hour? It seems strange to find you in there with the door securely locked!"

"Madam, are you accusing me of something obscene with

my daughter? If you hadn't been so nosy to start with, we wouldn't be out here in the dark hall at this hour and I wouldn't have the need to explain why I was in my daughter's room!" Gene eyebrows flew up. "Would you like to keep your job here?"

Susan had heard the maid accusing Gene of doing something to her so she peeked out the door, rubbing her eyes.

"Daddy, did you fall asleep again in my room?" she asked innocently.

"I'm afraid I did, baby girl. It took you longer to fall asleep this time, honey." Gene put his arms around her in a fatherly hug. "Shouldn't you try to get some more sleep after that nightmare?"

"Probably, but…I heard you talking to someone and it woke me up." Susan looked over at the upstairs maid, whose face was flushed with embarrassment. "Mrs. Gaston, did you have a nightmare too?"

"A nightmare? Me? Oh, no my dear. It's just that Laura Rite, you know, the lady that helps in the kitchen, well, she fell asleep last evening in the dining room while folding napkins for the week, and she didn't wake up until midnight. Laura and I share the same quarters, and she swore she heard sounds coming from Miss Jessica's bedroom."

"My little girl had a nightmare, Mrs. Gaston. Sometimes she talks in her sleep while having them." Gene took Susan's hand, as he looked on her in a fatherly way. "Jessi knows she can always come to me or her mother whenever a nightmare wakes her up. If it's in the middle of the night, I usually go back to her room with her and sometimes I fall asleep."

"My dad's the best! He's so patient, the gentlest man I've ever known." Susan smiled up at Gene with innocence. "Some nights it takes me longer to go back to sleep and poor Dad nods off. It may sound childish, but I just feel safe when Dad's in the room with me."

"That's a relief." Wanda smiled sheepishly up at Gene, after accusing him of bad behavior. "After Laura woke me and told me she heard something, I couldn't go back to sleep worrying about the poor kid. So after tossing and turning, I decided to get up to check on her. I'm truly sorry I jumped to the wrong conclusion, Mr. Armstrong. I never meant something was going on between the two of you."

Gene laughed softly. "I guess I did look a little suspicious coming out from my daughter's bedroom at 4 a.m. and how someone might get the impression I was up to no good." Gene put on one of his winning smiles as he said, "No harm done, Wanda. It's good to know you care about my daughter's welfare when you hardly know us."

"Well, I did hear you tell Mrs. Ward your workers were like family, and it made me feel wanted and appreciated, Mr. Armstrong." The master bedroom door opened briefly, then closed, causing the maid to look down the hall. Scott closed his eyes in dismay as he thought, *Michael, stay put or our great performance was all for nothing.*

Aloud, Gene said as he smiled down at the busybody maid, "Excuse me, Mrs. Gaston, I just saw Judith look out into the hall for me. She probably woke and found my bed empty and got up to check." He avoided her stare as he kissed Susan's forehead. "I'm off to have a shower after I relieve your mother's worries, then it's down for an early breakfast. I'm wide awake now and starving! See that the cook gets a move on, will you, Wanda?"

"I'm wide awake too, Dad. I'll meet you and Mom in the breakfast room." Susan smiled at the bewildered maid. "Oh, and thank you, Wanda, for your concern." She disappeared behind her bedroom door and laughed softly, knowing their act had been a success.

Gene made his way quickly to the master bedroom and found Michael waiting just inside, his face draped with concern.

"Good lord, Scott, what happened out there in the hall? Did that woman catch you in bed with Susan?"

"What do you take me for, Mike—a stupid idiot?" Gene

stormed passed him. "I can think fast on my feet!" He chuckled when he remembered waking up with Susan in his arms. "Or to be more exact, I can think fast on my butt!"

Michael shook his head and glanced down, noticing Scott's hard-on showing through his silk pajamas. He looked up laughing. "Shit, Gene, let's hope that busybody didn't get an eyeful of that boy!"

Gene looked down and mumbled, "Damn! How long does that thing stand at full attention?"

Michael couldn't control his laughter. "Another hot night, Daddy-o?"

"By the looks of Jackie's bed, I'd say your night wasn't any cooler, Mike ole fellow!" Gene slapped Michael on the back and chuckled, "And with my 'wife', of all things!"

"I just couldn't control myself, Julien. She looked so lonely without her devoted sexy devil of a husband!" Michael laughed softly and turned when he heard Jackie's sleepy voice,

"What the devil are you fellows talking about at 5 a.m.?"

"I'll fill you in later, baby. I'd better make my getaway while the coast is clear." Michael opened the door and looked right into Max McCoy's eyes. He swallowed nervously after being caught leaving the master bedroom so early. "Max, what are you doing out here standing right outside Mr. Armstrong's private quarters?"

Gene walked casually out of the door and pulled it to, then turned and gave the morning cook a stern look, "Did you forget the way to the kitchen, McCoy? I hope you're headed down there now to fix my breakfast I ordered thirty minutes ago!"

Max McCoy looked from Gene to Michael, trying to make sense of the odd situation.

"Excuse me, young man, are you hard of hearing or are you trying my patience at the break of dawn?" Gene took a step closer as the frightened worker stared up and blinked. "Are you going to have that breakfast ready when I get down there?"

"A…yes, sir, Mr. Armstrong. Miss Rite has already gone down to start the ham. Mrs. Gaston informed us you would be having your breakfast early, sir."

"And the dear lady told you correctly, young man. Mr. Adams will be joining me as soon as he's showered and dressed." Gene chuckled as he slapped Michael's back, causing him to stumble forward, but he quickly caught his balance. "When Armstrong can't sleep, Adams can't!"

"You never did tell me what woke you up so early, boss." Michael's eyes twinkled with mischief as Gene narrowed his eyes.

"My little girl had another bad dream last night and came to her old man so he could sit up with her until she fell asleep again." Gene gritted his teeth when Michael laughed softly. "I'd had a long day and was really exhausted, so I fell asleep sitting up with her. I was awakened when I heard Wanda Gaston trying to open the door."

"Good lord!" Michael looked surprised. "She didn't just walk in, did she?"

Scott squeezed Michael's shoulder as a warning, causing him to grunt in pain.

"No! She didn't get in, Mr. Adams! The dream made Jessi afraid and being in a strange house made it worse, so she asked me to lock the door like she did when she was little and believed that spooks would open her door and slip in."

"Spooks?" Michael lifted his eyebrows. "How terrible for the poor kid. Maybe I should set up a rollaway bed in her bedroom and protect her from spooks!"

"I'll protect my daughter, Mr. Adams!" Gene's voice grew loud. "You just take care of my family when I need help, got it?"

Mr. McCoy had been frozen in his spot observing the two men's exchanges and felt uncomfortable and somewhat nervous, knowing he should have already gone downstairs to the kitchen. He started backing away as both men noticed his movements.

"I will…go now…and help fix your breakfast. Your permission to leave, sir?"

"By all means, McCoy, go and get that breakfast finished while Adams still has teeth to eat with!" Gene threw open the bedroom door and walked in, catching Jackie standing there naked as she was putting on her robe.

"Good Lord, Gene! Shut that door before someone sees me!" Jackie smiled at his blushing face. "Relax, it's not like you've never seen a woman's naked body before." She waved over her head as she walked back to her Bathroom. "See you after a long hot shower, darling."

"Damn!" Gene mumbled to himself as he made his way quickly to his shower so he could hurry, get dressed and get out of that bedroom. He stared at his reflection in the mirror. *Susan would kill me if she knew I just saw Jackie's body.*

Gene walked quickly down the steps and noticed a telephone just inside an office. He slipped in and dialed his home number.

"Alright, Pogo, answer the phone. I don't have all morning." Gene waited, but got no answer. "Pogo, it's Friday morning! Where the shit are you?" The preacher counted the rings as he counted the hours' differences between Africa and TarSa. "It's 9 p.m. in TarSa." The answering machine picked up. "Pogo, this is Scott. Where are you, buddy? I'll try later when I get a chance." Gene hung up the receiver and made his way out the door unseen.

Chapter Nine

Pogo and Gloria lay wrapped in each other's arms, still breathing heavily after making love. Pogo ran his hand over her large breasts and took a deep breath.

"I love you so much, Gloria. Did you go twice again, darling?"

"Pogo darling, my heart's still pounding." Gloria turned on her side and found his lips. "Yes, my love, I did go twice!" Her gaze fell on the telephone. "Do you think whoever called left a message?"

"Could be, I'll check." He pulled her into his arms and smiled. "I wasn't about to answer that phone when we were about to reach our second fireworks!"

"We?" Gloria laughed softly. "Are you saying…?"

"Shit yes! I came twice too!" Pogo ran his fingers through his hair. "Hot damn, that was good!"

Suddenly the phone rang and Pogo sat up. He stared at the phone for a moment, then slipped from the covers and placed his finger over his lips.

"It might be Scott…shit!" He nervously picked up the receiver. "Scott residence." He heard Gene's voice on the other end.

"Pogo? Where were you? I called you twenty minutes ago, buddy. Did you get my message?"

"Scott! Shit, man, it's good to hear from you." Pogo was still breathing heavily as he continued, "Sorry I missed your first call."

"Pogo, what have you been up to? You sound like you're out of breath. Are you alright?" The preacher was concerned for his friend.

"I'm good, man. I just got out of the shower and heard the phone ringing. I threw a towel around me and made a dash for the phone." Pogo made a face over at Gloria who was trying to cover her giggles. Gene scratched his head as he tried to make out the background sound.

"Do I hear someone laughing behind you, pal? It sounded sort of muffled."

"Laughing? Oh yeah!" Pogo tried to sound upbeat. "I have my television on. You know how Johnny Carson keeps the audience in stitches. I'll go over and cut off the set." Pogo walked heavily across the wooden floor and pretended to cut it off when he said, "Click. Can you hear me better now?"

"A television?" Scott sounded relieved. "For a minute there I thought you had Beth in your bedroom."

"Now that's funny, Scott!" Pogo laughed sheepishly. "Sounds tempting, but funny."

"Say, Pogo, when did you get a television for your bedroom?" Gene knew the only television set in the farmhouse was in the family den. It had been Susan's when she lived at the Andrews' house.

"A…it's just…well, it gets lonely around here when you guys are gone. The department store on Maple Street had a terrific sale on their old store display set, so I bought it."

"I figured you'd be so busy with all the house and yardwork, plus dating that girl of yours, you wouldn't have time to get lonely, pal." Scott chuckled. "I'll check it out when I get home."

Pogo knew he was getting himself in deeper so he quickly changed the subject back to why he was out of breath when he answered the phone.

"Sure thing, Scott." He made a face of discouragement. "Well, anyway, the reason I was out of breath when I answered was because I thought it might be you calling and I didn't want to miss your call."

"How are things back home, pal? Are the kids alright?" Gene kept his voice down so the staff couldn't hear him.

"Things couldn't be better around here, Scott. All is calm and peaceful. The twins are being spoiled by Mildred, and I'm keeping the home fires burning." Pogo blew a kiss to Gloria. "I'm keeping the grass mowed, weeds pulled, the house is spic and span." He forced a laugh. "Not to worry, Scott, I have everything under control."

"That's great! One less thing to worry about because we're in hot shit here, pal," Scott whispered. "I can't talk too much longer. Another house full of spies, if you catch my meaning."

"Be careful, Scott." Pogo grew serious. "Are Susan and Jobi alright?"

"I'm taking good care of my girl, and Jobi's his usual outgoing teenager." Scott smiled to himself as he added, "Speaking of girls, how are you making out with Beth?"

"Funny you should ask. I'm making out with Bath every chance I get." Pogo heard Scott make his distinct familiar sound that meant dangerous territory. "Scott, you're breaking up. The connection on this end seems to be fading. Call me back when you can."

"Sure thing, buddy. Take care of yourself and, Pogo, don't do anything stupid." The phone went silent and Pogo fell down across the bed, still holding the receiver in his shaking hand.

"Pogo, that was priceless!" Gloria climbed out of bed to take the receiver and replaced it on the telephone, then walked back to the Bathroom, calling over her shoulder, "Could you imagine his face when you said you were making out with Bath every chance you get?"

"I didn't have to imagine Scott's face. I could hear it in his fierce growl he gives when something rubs him the wrong way." Pogo followed Gloria in the Bathroom and grabbed her around the waist, then pinned her up against the wall. "Let the big man wonder what I'm up to. Maybe he'll stop with the girl-scout jokes and the watching out for wholes ribbing." Pogo kissed her nose and moved his body up against hers. "My best friend doesn't know his buddy's had sex with one beautiful redhead!"

"The same redhead who was a thorn in his side all those wasted years." Gloria dropped her head in remorse. Pogo lifted her face and his lips parted over hers with a warm tenderness. He whispered,

"The same beautiful redhead I fell madly in love with."

"Oh, Pogo, I love you so very, very much!" Gloria freed her arms to hug him around the neck, then said in a teasing manner, "Would you care to have a shower with your redhead?"

"That, my darling, is an invitation I cannot pass up!" Pogo took her hand and pulled her into the shower.

Gene was sitting in the breakfast room when Susan and Jackie walked in and filled their plates at the breakfast bar, then joined him. Susan leaned over and whispered, "When is this diamond salesman going to show up, Gene? Granddad could be in serious danger."

"Henning said Mr. Blackwell's coming for dinner tonight, along with his family. They wish to meet the Armstrong family, check us out." Gene took a bite of toast as he watched the two young servers walk from the kitchen with more ham, eggs, toast and hash browns. Rata stopped next to Scott.

"Would boss like more breakfast? Fresh ham, eggs, hot toast, potatoes?"

"You know, I'd love another piece of that ham between two slices of toast." Gene noticed Susan was frowning up at him, and he returned it with his big smile. "And, fellows, if you could round up some jelly to put on this toast, it'd really make me happy."

"Jelly! Yes, sir, Mr. Armstrong!" Rata gave a pleasing smile and walked back through the kitchen door.

Makata refilled their coffee, then smiled down at Susan after she thanked him.

"Can I get missy anything else?"

"I'd love a small glass of orange juice, please. Thank you." Susan smiled and felt her husband's strong squeeze on her knee. Glancing his way, she gave him a smile.

"Much happy to get pretty lady the orange juice." Smiling

broadly, the young man handed her the fancy glass. "Can I get you anything else?"

"Just that jelly, Makata! We have everything else we need. So you may return to the kitchen and put a rush on Rata bringing me that hard-to-find jelly!" Scott frowned down at his wife as she laughed softly, then took a sip of her juice.

"Say, Dad, is Blackwell's son coming? I think he and I might have a lot in common."

Scott could see the two young blacks had left the kitchen door open so they could hear everything that was being said. Gene reached under the table and took Susan's hand.

"Jessi, just eat your breakfast before I spank your butt!" Susan looked up into his serious blue eyes as he whispered, "Don't try and make me jealous; I might lose it!"

Jackie could see the cooks hiding just behind the door, so she laughed softly.

"Julien, Jessi's only playing with you, darling. Daddy's little girl wants attention, just like your wife did this morning. Remember, darling?" Jackie looked away to keep from laughing at Scott's expression.

"What's that supposed to mean?" Susan stared over at Gene. "What did your 'wife' do this morning, Daddy dear?"

"Nothing, precious, she did nothing." Gene frowned over at Jackie as she sipped on her coffee, unconcerned over his dilemma. Jackie reached over and patted Susan's hand when she noticed Rata was bringing a tray of jellies out.

"Jessi dear, just eat your breakfast. You have nothing to worry about." Jackie took two hot pieces of toast and replaced the cold toast Scott had on his plate, before getting a piece of toast for her jelly. Rata returned to the kitchen, leaving the door open. As she spread jelly over her bread, she smiled at Susan. "Daddy still loves his little girl." Jackie took a bite and continued, "Julien dear, when should we expect our guests? I need to inform Henning to prepare the staff."

"The Blackwells will arrive around 2 p.m. so I can show him around the estate." Gene kept his eyes on Susan. "Stick with your old man, baby girl, and don't get too friendly with Toby Blackwell. Understand?"

"Alright, Dad, whatever you want." Susan stood up and stretched. "Until then, I think I'll go round up Richi so we can play a round of tennis before our guests arrive." She bent down and kissed Gene's cheek. "You may join us if you're not too busy, Dad." She gave him a beautiful smile and walked quickly from the room.

Chapter Ten

The Blackwells pulled up exactly at 2 p.m. and made their way to the massive front door. Looking down at his wife, the diamond magnate smiled his approval at what he saw. Armstrong could prove to be one of his best buyers and with those happy thoughts, his smile met the butler with total delight when he opened the door.

"You must be Henning. We talked on the phone." Blackwell took his wife's hand and waited for the man to speak.

"That is correct, sir; I am Henning. Welcome to the Armstrong's plantation. Do come in." The undercover agent stepped to one side to allow Hal Blackwell, his wife Katherine and their son, Toby, to step inside the large entrance hall. "Mr. and Mrs. Armstrong are expecting you and should be down shortly." Henning smiled down at Katherine. "Mrs. Blackwell, I am sure you can understand Mrs. Armstrong's delay. She has to have everything perfect before she descends the grand staircase."

"Of course, Mr. Henning. We ladies take pride in the way we look, especially for first impressions." Seeing movement, Katherine Blackwell glanced up and noticed the handsome couple descending the wide staircase. Her attention was drawn to Scott, wearing white satin pants and a black shirt pulled out at the waist. Taking a deep breath, she thought, *My god, that man is handsome and dashing.* Aloud she managed to say, "My, what a lovely couple you make."

"Thank you. You must be Katherine." Jackie put out her soft hand. "I'm Judith Armstrong and this is my husband Julien."

"Julien Armstrong…finally we meet." Hal was impressed by Gene's strong handshake. "That's quite a handshake, neighbor. You and your lovely wife have a beautiful place here."

"We like it. May I call you Hal?" Gene chuckled as he thought, *I'd rather call you thieving jackass.* He reached over and patted the 5'8" tall man's back. "Looks like we might be doing business."

"Please call me Hal, Julien, and yes, I have a hunch we will be doing a lot of business together. My people tell me when it comes to diamonds, you want nothing but the best." Blackwell took Jackie's hand to admire her diamond ring. "I'd guess…four carats?"

"You do have an eye for exquisite jewelry, Mr. Blackwell." Jackie's smile was charming, and she looked stunning in her white satin gown and black pearls to match Gene's outfit. "Katherine, that's a lovely shade of green you're wearing."

"Thank you, my dear. It's a new shade called soft moss, one of the latest fashion colors." Katherine's attention kept going back to the handsome preacher. "With a name like Julien, I had you pictured handsome, but I wasn't expecting such a dashing man." Hal laughed at his wife's brazen remark.

"My dear wife admires men with good looks, my friend. By her actions, I'd say she ranks you at the top. Nothing personal, Mrs. Armstrong; Katherine is quite harmless."

"I certainly understand her admiring Julien's good looks. Most women find him irresistible." Jackie smiled. "I'm very pleased with my husband, Katherine. He's very dashing, as you described him. He's also a great father to our two children, Jessica and Richard, and an excellent lover." Jackie noticed a silent young man looking around the room, seemingly bored with the conversation. "You must be Toby. I understand you're about our daughter's age."

Toby's demeaner seem to change as his eyes lit up with interest. "Yes, Mrs. Armstrong, I'm twenty-one and I believe your Jessica is twenty. Correct?"

"That's correct, son." Gene watched him closely. "I'm sure a good-looking fellow like yourself must have plenty of girls on your arm."

"I suppose I could have my pick from several acquaintances, Mr. Blackwell, but I'm looking for the perfect girl." Toby kept looking up the steps. "I hear your daughter's not only beautiful but also very smart."

"Yes, Jessi's quite the beauty. She gets her good looks from her mother. Her smarts she gets from her old man." Gene did not smile as he watched the young man staring up the stairsteps. He felt an instant dislike for Toby Blackwell. "Jessica's my little girl, Toby, and she'll always be daddy's little girl."

The fake butler noticed the tension building in Rev. Scott, so he stepped forward, a little ahead of his planned schedule. "The drinks are ready to be served, sir. If you and your guests would step over to the bar, we can get started."

"Very good, Henning." Gene patted Blackwell on the back as he waved his free hand toward the bar. "What's your pleasure, Hal, and you two ladies?" As their drinks were being fixed, Gene walked out into the entrance hall to find Toby standing at the staircase, gazing up. "Jessi will be down soon, son. Come and get yourself a drink."

"Thank you, sir." Toby made his way to the bar and poured himself a glass of straight scotch, then moved back out of the way and took a seat near the door.

Everyone had a drink and were making small talk when Gene saw Toby rise to his feet and gaze up at the stairs with dreamy eyes. Gene instantly looked up to see Susan and Jobi coming down the steps. His heart began beating faster as he watched her making her way down, dressed in a red jumpsuit. Susan's eyes were fixed on her husband's, and her smile for him was brilliant. She stopped right in front of him.

"I'm sorry we're late, Dad. I couldn't decide what to wear." Gene chuckled and took her hand protectively.

"Like mother, like daughter." Gene leaned down and kissed her cheek, wishing it could be her lips. He turned to his guests. "Hal, Katherine, Toby, I'd like you to meet our beautiful daughter, Jessica, and our son Richard."

Katherine studied their faces closely and wrinkled her brows.

"To be perfectly honest, Julien darling, Jessica doesn't look anything like her mother, and I can't see any family resemblance in your son either."

"Judith and Jessica are more alike than you know, Katherine." Gene couldn't help but notice how Toby Blackwell kept staring at Susan. He clinched his teeth tightly, then turned to his young wife. "Would you care for a drink, sweetheart? And can I get you a Coke, son?" Gene ran his free hand over Jobi's hair.

"I'd love a Coke, Mr. Henning!" Jobi smiled up at the patient agent. "I never turn down a Coke, sir!" Then Susan's brother turned his attention back to the flirty young man as he wondered how long Rev. Scott would keep his cool.

Susan reached over to punch her brother's arm for staring from Toby to Gene. Then she said sweetly, "Nothing but water for me, Dad. I'll wait and have a drink before dinner." Susan found a seat after Hal Blackwell came over to speak to Gene about diamonds. She looked up when Toby sat down beside her.

"Jessi, do you play tennis?" His eyes fell down her shapely body. "I noticed you have a beautiful"—his eyes met hers—"court."

Jobi had been listening and meandered over. "My sister's a champ at tennis." Jobi sipped on the Coke, feeling the tension building in Scott. "I wouldn't bet with her if I were you."

Everyone had been drawn into their conversation and laughed at the young boy's statement. Everyone that is, except Gene Scott, who was watching Toby Blackwell's every move. Walking over to the vacant seat on Susan's other side, Gene sat down and gathered her hand in his. Toby was too busy looking at her to notice the dark cloud in the preacher's eyes.

Toby remarked, "Perhaps we could play a set sometime in the near future. I'd *love* to *play the game* with you, Jessi. I'm pretty good myself. I know we can make a great match."

"That sounds heavy, Toby. Perhaps, the next visit." Susan glanced over at her husband whose attention was solely on the tanned young man with the blond hair. She could read Gene well and knew he wanted to lay a fist in the flirty man's face. Silently she thought, *Gene Scott, this is no time to get jealous!* Out loud she said, "Dad and I play all the time. Don't we, Daddy?"

Gene gazed down at the woman he loved most in the world and smiled mischievously. "You bet we do, sweetheart, and we always love playing together!"

Jackie made her way over to try and calm down the situation as she laughed. "That Jessi's her daddy's pet! Tennis, swimming, horseback riding, hiking, you name it; those two are never separated, right, Richi?"

"They definitely enjoy playing together!" Jobi smiled broadly over at the loving couple. "But Mom and I have a great time too; and many times we all do things together as one big happy family, right, Dad?"

"Can't deny that, son. Like going out in our fishing boat on our private lake in Wyoming or flying into Jackson Hole and taking a raft ride down the Snake River, then having dinner at the lodge." Gene rubbed the top of Jobi's head. "And sport here and I throw, catch or make the hoops occasionally."

Susan looked over at Gene in wonder. "That was some trip we took, Dad! Bringing back all those lovely memories. I do wish we could go back there again." She smiled at the listening visitors. "That's our dad! He's the best!" Susan suddenly felt Gene's hand on her leg and it began to move up, a frequent habit he often did when they were alone. She reached down to stop him and smiled up into his eyes.

Realizing at once what he'd been doing, he quickly noticed everyone watching him with interest. Gene chuckled as he patted her leg playfully.

"As you see, I'm always the protective dad. She's my little girl."

"I guess we fathers always see our sons or daughters as

children. It's good to see such a close family." Hal smiled, feeling more at ease with what he'd just witnessed. "I too am very proud of my family, Julien, and if I had a daughter as lovely as yours, I wouldn't let her out of my sight."

"Mr. Armstrong?" Ali stepped up behind Gene. "Mr. Ward would like a word with you, sir, whenever you have the time. He says there's no hurry."

"Thank you, Megan. I'll go and see what Stretch needs. It must be something important or he wouldn't have sent for me." Gene stood up and pulled Susan to her feet. "Want to come with your old man, darling?"

"Sure, Dad. I need to check on Champ anyway." Susan looked down at her admirer. "I'll see you for cocktails, Toby."

Before the young man could respond, Gene quickly led Susan out the sliding glass doors and began walking down the path to the stables. When they were halfway down the path and out of view from the plantation house, Gene looped his arms around his wife and pulled her up close. Susan let her fingers run through the curls on the back of his neck.

"Gene, darling, you'd better watch your familiar habits in front of guests who think we're father and daughter. If I hadn't stopped you, you would have slid that sexy hand between my legs."

"Shit, I can't keep my hands off you. You look so beautiful and tempting in that sexy jumpsuit." Knowing they were alone, Gene lowered his head to kiss her. "Oh, Susan, I love you so damn much! If that Toby tries anything with you, I'll strangle the punk!"

"Sweetheart," Susan laughed. "We're just acting, remember? I can't act cold toward that punk. We need answers to where Granddad is and Toby might have the answer."

Gene pulled her into his arms tightly as he whispered in her ear, "Just don't lead him on, darling. Remember the last time we were in Africa a certain young native named Rama? Promise me, Susan?"

"Gene darling, I promise! I won't give Toby Blackwell any false hopes." She returned his hug; then they continued toward the stables. They stopped to listened to James as he gave last-minute instructions to the two workers.

"Be sure the new boards are put on the fences in the south pasture. They're made to keep wild animals from attacking the horses. They'll be moved there tomorrow morning, and Mr. Armstrong would prefer his fine horses not to become a free meal!"

"Sure thing, Mr. Ward." Harvie Flint climbed inside the truck next to Nick Barrow, who was mumbling to himself as he drove away, leaving a dust trail. Gene walked up, waving the dust away from his face.

"James, you got something?"

"Yeh, man, I think so." James smiled at Susan as she walked over to a black horse and started rubbing its nose. "Ali and I were sitting on the top balcony last night, having a great bottle of wine, while we watched you guys enjoying the swimming pool. We noticed Pansy Holder and Laura Rite were also watching with interest as they hid behind some bushes."

"So that's who Michael and Jackie saw." Gene gazed over at his wife, still enjoying the beautiful black mare. "What about those two hired hands? Any news there?"

"I did catch them talking this morning behind the feed shed and caught some of the conversation. Harvie Flint called Nick Barrow 'Tuffy.' Then Barrow told Flint to keep his eyes open but not to get caught."

"The feds are already onto Barrow and called him the meanest snake in the jungle." Gene chuckled, "Too bad he's not the smartest or the strongest! That makes four spies for sure, and I have my suspicions about Wanda Gaston as well. That nosy maid tried to get into Susan's bedroom early this morning when I was with her. If I hadn't put that deadbolt on, the unwanted intruder would have walked in and found me in bed with my 'daughter' naked!"

"Shit, Scott! That was close! What happened?" James noticed Susan was still interested in the mare as she curried her shiny black coat.

"I got up quietly after warning Susan, dressed and made my presence known to Mrs. Gaston. The snooping woman fell for my explanation after I told her my daughter had had a nightmare, and I was sitting up with her until she fell asleep again." Gene felt Susan take his arm.

"Sweetheart, did you say Wanda Gaston tried to unlock our door this morning… with a key?"

"All the staff probably have a set of keys to all the rooms so they can clean them when we're out. That's one reason I put the deadbolt on. When I went to unlock the door, the deadbolt was the only one locked, and I'd locked them both." Gene gazed down into Susan's luminous blue eyes. "I guess you heard the rest of my conversation with Stretch here."

"Yes, four spies, maybe Mrs. Gaston makes five." Susan turned her attention on their thin friend. "James, could you or Ali see what Gene and I were doing on the dark side of the pool last night?"

"No, but you were there for several minutes before Jackie and Mike swam over to warn you." James's eyed twinkled with mischief. "I can assure you those two snooping women were wondering what a father and daughter could be doing that long in the dark. They even moved to another hiding place." He laughed as he added, "I know Ali and I were wondering what you might be doing too, and we were pretty sure what."

"Okay, so we have to be more careful from now on." Scott frowned at James, who had a big grin on his handsome face. "At least you and Ali are playing a married couple, like in real life."

"Yeh, man! Happily married!" James laughed. "It does make things easier to play ourselves, just a different name. I guess being a worker has its benefits! Real hip!"

"Don't rub it in!" Scott patted his back, nearly knocking him over. "Let me know if you see or hear anything else. I've got to get back to that diamond thug."

"Just watch yourself, Scott!" James gave a sneaky smile before adding, "And watch getting so excited it shows!"

"Just get back to work, Stretch, before I fire your sorry ass!" The preacher took his wife's hand and headed toward the house as Susan started giggling.

"Gene, you didn't? You really had a hard-on when you stepped out to confront that woman?"

"So shoot me! You do something to me!" He grabbed her around her waist and chuckled. Suddenly, remembering Jackie's comment at breakfast, she pulled away, placing her hands on her shapely hips.

"By the way, mister, just what did Jackie mean this morning about wanting attention? Gene, spit it out!"

"It was an innocent accident, Susan. I…walked in on Jackie putting on her bathrobe."

"Bathrobe? In the Bathroom?" Her eyes grew wide with concern.

"Not the Bathroom, darling. We have our own Bathroom. She was putting her bathrobe on after she got up from bed." Gene swallowed. "She was…well…she was naked."

"Naked? You saw…Jackie without her clothes on?" Susan narrowed her eyes, trying to picture the situation. "So you just walked into the bedroom and Jackie was naked! Did you stand there dumbfounded and stare?"

"No! For god's sake, Susan!" Gene took a firm hold of his wife's hands and looked her in the eyes. "Jackie was putting on her robe so quickly when I opened the door, I barely saw anything. She was naked because Michael had been there with her all night!" He looked so innocent, Susan looked down and smiled, knowing it had surprised and embarrassed her husband catching Jackie. "I was a total wreck while Jackie was so ho-hum about the whole incident. I was scared shitless you'd find out and kill me."

"Me? Kill you? Gene Scott, I could never hurt you but I don't like the situation!" Susan started walking up the path as she shook her head. "I just hate you sharing a room with her! You wouldn't want me to share a bedroom with some man, even if you knew it was just an act!"

"You're absolutely correct, little darling. You I trust, but some man in the room with my woman will never happen." Scott pulled her around. "Susan sweetheart, you're the only woman I want, the only woman I need! I love you, damn it! You're my beautiful sexy wife and I won't share you with anyone."

"I know, my handsome sexy husband!" She laughed, "I just like to see you sweat! Are you coming to me tonight?"

"Susan, my love, I'll come to you every night. But to play it safe, I need to leave right after we make love." Gene patted her behind. "Those eavesdropping battle-axes are getting too nosy."

"That means you'll be sleeping in the same room with Jackie! Darn!" Susan started pacing back and forth. "I trust you, darling. It's Jackie I'm not sure of. She loves to be flirty!"

"Sweetheart, it takes two to make whoopee, and I'm completely devoted to you." Gene looked up when the big house came into view. "Listen, Susan, I'm ten times bigger than Jackie. I can handle her. Besides, Jackie's happily married to Michael."

Susan rolled her eyes, knowing that Jackie was single, beautiful and advanced in the art and experience of female charms, not to mention extremely sexy with her British accent. She took a deep breath and said, "Jackie's a big cut-up and she loves to tease me. I know she deeply loves Michael and I can trust her." Susan reached for Gene's hand. "I believe you, Gene. I know I can trust you. I'm sorry I got so upset. Shoot me!" She giggled for using Gene's cute remark. "Well, we have guests waiting and I need to go pick out what I'll wear for dinner."

"Why change, darling? You look beautiful. Just keep this on for dinner." Gene saw Toby standing at the double glass doors, looking out at them. The preacher mumbled as he waved at him. "Whatever you decide to wear, don't look so damn sexy. Toby's already in heat."

Susan laughed and took his hand as they walked on to the house.

Chapter Eleven

Gene Scott showed Hal and Toby Blackwell around the grounds on the massive plantation, while Jackie gave Katherine a tour of the manor house. Susan and Jobi decided to change into their swimsuits and go for a swim. They were playing in the pool when Gene brought his guests around back. He stopped short when he heard the brother and sister splashing around and laughing. It was too late for him to change directions for Toby spotted them as well and walked quickly past Gene over to the side of the pool. He stopped and smiled down at the shapely young woman.

"So you're an expert swimmer, too, Jessica Armstrong?"

"I've been swimming all my life, Toby…my brother Richi and I." Susan was relieved when Gene stepped up beside the flirty young man. "Hi, Dad! I wish you were in here. We could play airplane."

Gene gave her a winning smile and prayed she'd stay in the water.

"We can play airplane tomorrow, sweetheart."

"Jessi, what kind of game is airplane? Maybe we can play the game together next week." Toby could feel the big man's eyes burning on him, but he couldn't care less what dear old Dad thought. He had his sights set on Jessica and he'd get her one way or the other. Right now his eyes remained on her and wished he could see more. "Jessi, are you going to stay in the pool all day? It's not good for your beautiful soft skin. Why don't you come out?"

Susan looked up at her husband who was shaking his head NO, so she quickly patted her brother on the arm.

"Later, Toby, this is my brother's time."

"Yeh, Toby, Jessi promised to throw the water ball with me." Jobi swam over to retrieve the big rubber ball floating at the far side of the pool. Rev. Scott took the fresh boy's arm.

"Come along, Toby, you'll see Jessi for cocktails before dinner. Let the kids play. It's bonding!"

"If you don't mind, Mr. Armstrong, I'd rather stay here and watch them play." Toby pulled free and started to sit down but was yanked back up to his feet by Gene Scott, who was forcing a chuckle.

"Toby, Toby! I do mind! You're going with us!"

Hal looked at Scott and noticed his arched brows, then turned to find both Scott's children had worried looks. He stepped up between the two tense men.

"Toby, son, I think you need to come with us and respect Mr. Armstrong's wishes." Hal pulled his rude son out of Gene's grip and took a firm hold on his arm. "Let the kids play. You'll see Jessi soon enough."

"Sure thing, Pops." Toby looked back at Susan and winked. "I'll be counting the minutes, Jessi." Turning to see Scott's angry stare, Toby faked a smile and started up the path calling, "Are you old men coming?"

At 6 p.m. everyone met in the drawing room where Max McCoy and Laura Rite were serving drinks and appetizers. Rev. Gene Scott sported black silk pants and a royal blue silk shirt to match Jackie's royal-blue full-length gown, a diamond necklace gracing her beautiful neck. The Blackwells wore black while Toby showed off his tan in a white suit.

Jobi came down with Ali and waved happily at the interested party watching.

"Dad, Mom, I'm going to have a cookout with Megan and Stretch this afternoon, instead of sitting around listening to adult conversation and a lot of business chat!"

"That's very sweet of you and Stretch, Megan." Jackie smiled at her best friend. "I'm sure Richi will enjoy having a cookout with you and Tom instead of getting all dressed up for a fancy meal."

"Thanks, Mom!" Jobi hugged Jackie as he sniffed her

perfume on her neck. "Wow, Mom, you smell great!" The young teen glanced down at Scott's frowning face and smiled innocently. "See you, Dad!" He took Ali's hand and followed her out the door, both laughing at the remarks he'd made to upset the serious preacher.

Susan slipped up behind Gene and reached around him to kiss his cheek as she whispered, "Hi, handsome."

Gene's hand went up and took the back of her neck.

"Come around here and let me take a look at you, baby girl." Susan took his hand and walked around in front of his chair. She was a vision in her long silver dress with a gentle scoop neck just above her beautiful bosom. Gene smiled his approval. "Damn, you look good!" He squeezed her hand and their eyes spoke love.

Toby walked over, all of his attention on the beautiful woman in silver.

"Your father's right, Jessica, you look beautiful. The wait was worth it."

"Thank you, Toby." Susan felt Gene's warning when his fingers bit into her hand. She moved her attention around the room and smiled. "Everyone looks quite stunning tonight."

"What would you like to drink, Jessi? Please permit me to get it for you." Toby reached for her free hand. "Please excuse me, sir, but Jessi did tell me we could talk over cocktails. I have a dozen questions to ask her."

"I'm sure!" Gene moved nervously in his seat. "Just stay in here; there's plenty of chairs sitting around." He looked around for the two chairs sitting the furthest apart and smiled when he spotted the perfect set. "The two chairs over by the fireplace look like the perfect place to have a quiet conversation."

"We'll stay in this room, sir, but those chairs are miles apart." Tobi faked a smile at the serious preacher. "I consider myself capable of choosing the right seating arrangement for us." He turned to avoid any more conflict with the possessive father and took Susan to a love seat at the far end of the large room.

Gene Scott felt his temper starting to boil when he spoke to the brazen young man, "See that you stay in this room! We don't want to send out a search party for you when we get ready to go in to dinner."

Susan turned her body to face Gene's chair as she pulled her hand free to get a glass of merlot from one of the servers, then smiled over at her handsome husband who was observing them closely.

"Dad, we'll sit right here until dinner's called. I have a few questions of my own for Toby."

"Me first, beautiful." He pulled her face around to look into her blue eyes. "Will you be attending college after the summer is over?"

"My father's a professor, Toby. He used to teach at Harvard University. Now he teaches me at home, like he will Richi when he graduates from high school." Susan took a sip of her wine as she let her eyes wander over at her husband, whose stare made her nervous. "Boy, that's really good wine." She sat up on the hard bench and glanced at the flirty man. "What about you, Toby? Which college do you attend?"

"I attend Cambridge in England, lovely old college." Toby's eyes fell on Susan's neckline. "Your mother and father were kind enough to invite us for a few days next week. I hope we can get to know one another, Jessi."

"I can always use another friend, Toby, but I must be honest. I have a boyfriend in the States and we're practically engaged." Susan glanced down at her hands as she thought what she could add to that statement. "He's very special to me, and I don't think he'd appreciate my flirting with someone else."

"What he doesn't know won't hurt him, Jessi." Toby laid his hand on her knee and that act drove Gene to his feet, and he walked quickly over to the love bench.

"Jessi, could I get you to run up to my bedroom and see if I left my wallet up there. I feel lost without it." He pulled Susan to her feet. "You don't mind, do you, sweet girl?"

"Sure, Dad. Do you think you left it on your dresser?" She noticed Gene was not smiling but maintained his serious expression.

Toby stood up, the need to stick by her side eating into his soul.

"I'll be glad to help you look, Jessi. Two sets of eyes are better than one."

"You're absolutely right, son." Gene pushed Toby back down on the bench. "You can keep your seat warm while I go up and help my daughter look. My bedroom's a private place, Toby, and forgive me, son, but I don't know you all that well."

Hal joined the group after hearing the conversation. He reached down and patted Toby on the back.

"Son, just sit still and wait for Julien and Jessica." Hal smiled up at the tall preacher. "Julien, I guess it's hard to remember what young love is like."

"Love?" Gene's eyes shot fire. "Let's hope that's just a loose-lip expression, Hal! These kids just met!"

"Yes, that's true, Julien darling, but haven't you ever heard of love at first sight?" Katherine spoke softly as she looked up at him with dreamy eyes after walking over. Susan could see the woman was opening flirting with Gene, and she took a firm hold on his hand and pulled him toward the door.

"Come on, Dad, let's get that wallet before they call dinner!" She remained quiet until they reached the master bedroom and closed the door behind them. "The nerve of that woman!" Susan walked over to the dresser and looked around. "Your wallet's not here!"

"No, it's not! It's in my pants pocket!" Gene turned her around. "Susan, you're sitting beside me tonight at dinner, woman!"

"Of course, I'm sitting next to you, mister!" Susan slung her hand to his back side and felt the wallet safe in his pocket. "Did you bring me up here to preach to me, Rev. Scott?"

"That shit boy can't keep his eyes or hands off you!" Gene's strong fingers bit into her soft skin, causing her to close her eyes in pain. As soon as he realized he was hurting her, he pulled her lovingly into his arms. "Susan, sweetheart, forgive me for taking my anger out on you. That spoiled brat just makes my blood boil!"

"Gene, my wonderful loving husband, you know you're the only one I want. It's all a big act, remember?" Susan's hands ran down his chest. "I told Toby I had a boyfriend in the States and we were practically engaged, hoping he would back off."

"Susan, you're just so damn beautiful. I'm always having to watch younger men run after you." Gene put his arms around her and pulled her closer. "You are mine, Susan Scott, all mine."

"All yours, Rev. Scott, so stop thinking these younger men can turn my head." Her luminous eyes held his. "Gene, the day you yelled those five beautiful words, 'I love you, damn it' was the best day of my life. You're the best part of me, and I'll love you for all my tomorrows!"

Gene pulled Susan into a warm embrace as he kissed her with passion. They were totally locked in each other's arms when a light knock came on the door. They pulled apart, breathing heavily.

"Yes? What…who is it?" Gene smiled down at Susan as she wiped her lipstick off his mouth and whispered, "Sorry, Dad." She took Gene's hand when the fake butler whispered loudly, "It's Edgar Henning, sir. Your guests are wondering what's keeping you. Did you find your wallet?"

Gene opened the door, still clutching Susan's hand.

"Cool it, Henning," he whispered. "I needed to get my wife away from that wolf until I calmed down. I was about to deck the little punk."

"Good heavens, Scott! Control your jealousy before you blow your cover!" The federal agent frowned at the preacher. "Just make sure that punk, as you put it, doesn't get your little wife alone." He looked down the hall to make sure the coast was clear before continuing, "Now get the rest of your wife's lipstick off your face and get back to your job!"

"Don't push me, Henning, or whatever your name is! Just get your ass back down there and tell them I'm on my way down!" Gene pulled a tissue from a box Susan was holding up for him, and started wiping off his lips as he winked at her.

Henning laughed, "Alright, Scott." He looked down at Susan. "I can't say that I blame you. If she were mine, I'd be possessive too." The agent disappeared down the steps as Gene shut the bedroom door and pulled out his wallet.

"I'm ready, sweetheart. I'll do better, I hope." Susan laughed and took his hand as they walked down the staircase. Everyone waiting was staring up at the couple and noticed Gene was holding up his wallet, smiling broadly.

"Finally found it after a frantic search. How it got in the Bathroom drawer is beyond me."

"Julien darling, you must have slipped it in there when we were in a hurry to climb into the shower." Jackie took his hand in hers and smiled at a frowning Susan. "Our dinner's ready. Shall we go in?"

"By all means, beautiful." Gene chuckled as his spare hand grabbed onto Susan's and his contagious smile played on the guests. "Everyone, let's enjoy a great meal together."

Gene sat at the head of the table between Jackie and Susan. Toby hurried to take the seat next to Susan and moved his mother's place card to his place. He looked over at the beautiful young woman he wanted so desperately.

"I was beginning to think you'd gotten lost, Jessica. Who found the missing wallet—you or your dad?"

"Dad found it. He had me searching in the bedroom." Susan moved her hands so Makata could ladle soup into her bowl. "I'm sorry it took so long, but Mom and Dad's rooms are large and there are quite a few hiding places."

"Interesting." Toby's eyes took in Susan's shapely body and spoke softly, but Gene's full attention was on the flirty boy's actions and words. "I say as long as there's a bed, there's no need for anything else."

"Not if your wife has a dozen boxes of jewelry." Gene

smiled at Hal and Katherine. "Over half of them are loaded with diamonds, like the one my beautiful Judith is wearing around her silky neck tonight."

"I hope she has room for more, my friend." Hal Blackwell took the salad from Rata so he could remove the empty soup bowl. "My supply is never-ending. The good stuff keeps coming in and my mines are growing as we speak."

"Sound good, Hal! I can't get enough of those pretty shiny rocks, my friend." Gene chuckled, "They say a diamond is a girl's best friend, but hell, they're my best buddies!"

"Then I'll bring some of my very best next week for you to check out." Hal smiled over at Jackie, who sat quietly listening to the men chat. "A little business with pleasure, my dear."

"Julien takes pleasure in doing business, Mr. Blackwell." Jackie ran her fingers over Gene's curls. "Julien takes pleasure in many things, right, darling?"

Gene pinched Jackie's cheek lovingly. "You bet, beautiful, but I stack up my pleasures! First sex, then diamonds, then sex, then good food, then sex, then fun, loads of fun!"

"Dad, where do I fit in that line-up?" Susan smiled over at her handsome husband.

"Trust me, pretty girl, you're right at the top. Like I was saying, my little Jessica is first!" Gene reached over and kissed her.

The Blackwood family looked at each other in confusion and finally Toby spoke as he stared at his host,

"Armstrong, you said sex was first and now you just said Jessica's first. So, which is it, sir—sex or Jessica?"

"Exactly what you said, sonny boy." Gene laughed as he forked up his pasta and winked at Hal. "Now that the pleasure matter's cleared up, is Monday through Thursday alright for your visit next week?"

"Yes, I do believe those days are free." Hal glanced at his wife, who still looked confused. "Aren't they, my dear?" Hal Blackwell wasn't exactly sure what had just happened, so the quick change of subject suited him; and his wife relaxed, knowing she would be spending four beautiful days with Julien Armstrong. Katherine smiled warmly up at Scott.

"Those days are perfect, dear. The more, the better."

"Good, it's settled." Blackwell cut into his tender steak. "This steak's excellent, Julien, and the pasta makes it very different but yummy."

"That's our Italian chef, always lots of good pasta!" Gene took a sip of his wine and relaxed when everyone grew quiet as they enjoyed the great meal.

The remainder of the evening went well; then the pretend Armstrongs were seeing their guests to the door. Toby stopped and gathered Susan's hands in his as his eyes feasted on her body.

"I had a lovely time, Jessi, at least those moments I spent with you." The bold young man ignored the big man standing next to his daughter as he continued, "I hope we can have some alone time when I come over for our next visit."

"There's plenty to do around the plantation, Toby: tennis, swimming, horseback-riding." Susan avoided making eye contact with Gene, for fear of his reaction to her acting.

"That's a start." Toby kissed her hand, his thoughts dreaming of more, much more. "Until Monday, farewell, my sweet dove." Smiling, Toby Blackwell walked to his parent's big car.

Gene waved as he faked a smile until they drove away. He mumbled loudly, "Farewell, my dove! Shit!" Then he turned back through the open door and noticed Pansy Holder and Laura Rite observing him closely. "Aren't you ladies supposed to be cleaning up the dining room or something I pay you to do?" Jackie noticed the friction between the preacher and the nosy workers so she stepped up beside Gene.

"Julien's very much his little girl's daddy, ladies, and he doesn't fancy fresh boys flirting openly around him. If you ask me, it was very disrespectful."

"You're exactly right, Mrs. Armstrong. Young Toby Blackwell was completely out of line. You can't blame Mr.

Armstrong for getting upset, ladies." Edgar Henning had overheard the conversation and was there to help. "This young man just met Miss Jessica, and he's moving a bit too fast."

"Yes, sir, it does seem that way." Laura Rite smiled. "Not to worry, Mr. Armstrong. I'm sure Miss Jessica can handle poor Toby Blackwell."

"Yes, sir, Laura's right about Miss Jessica; but begging your pardon, sir, I think it's Mrs. Blackwell who needs watching." Pansy Holder looked sympathetically up at Jackie. "It's way too obvious that woman has a crush on your husband."

"You think so?" Jackie smiled at Gene, then over at Susan, who had narrowed her eyes at the remark the downstairs maid had made. "Jessi, did you notice Mrs. Blackwell flirting with your father?"

"As a matter of fact, Mom, I've been watching that bimbo ever since she arrived!" Susan put her hands angrily on her hips as she stated, "Katherine Blackwell's been openly flirting with my hu…dad, and I do not like it!"

"It sounds like your daughter is just as protective of her father when it comes to flirting." Laura Rite turned to leave, shaking her head. "And it's alright to say what you were going to say, child."

"And what might that be, Laura?" Pansy followed her friend.

"Miss Jessica was going to say 'hunk of a dad' and she's absolutely right."

Gene and Susan looked at each other and laughed as they made their way up the stairs.

Chapter Twelve

As Gene, Susan and Jackie reached the second floor, Jobi came rushing past them, beaming from ear to ear.

"That was a blast! J…Stretch and Megan are the best!" Jobi looked around, then whispered, "Harvie and Nick joined us and sat around whispering and watching our every move. We played it real cool so they left early, claiming they needed a little shut-eye 'cause 5 a.m. comes early." Jobi leaned in closer so no one else could hear him as he added, "I saw them hiding in the shadows, still watching us. I told James and Ali quietly so they wouldn't give themselves away."

"Good job! You're a smart kid!" Scott patted Jobi on the head. "You're growing up right before my eyes, son. Now get to bed, buddy. We're going horseback-riding in the morning."

"Sure thing, Rev. Scott; that sounds cool." Jobi kept his voice down, feeling pretty proud of himself. After hugging Gene and Susan, he made his way to his bedroom, smiling.

"Jackie," Gene whispered. "I told Mike he has two hours with you. I can't take another chance being caught in Susan's room."

"Alright, Gene, two hours and then you'll return. Susan, please don't worry about Gene being alone with me. I promise I won't attack him in his bed or elsewhere in our shared rooms." Jackie laughed softly and slipped inside the master bedroom to wait for Michael.

Gene and Susan walked quickly down the hall and disappeared behind her bedroom door, locking it securely. Susan excused herself, promising to return quickly as she whispered, "Darling, give me five minutes to use the toilet and brush my teeth."

"Five minutes? I'd say take your time, sweetheart, but our two hours will fly by." Gene pulled his shirt over his head and sat down on the side of the bed to remove his shoes when he heard Susan slap the countertop loudly.

"Shit! Thanks a lot, M.N.!" she stated in an aggravated voice causing Gene to walk over to the door and call softly,

"Is everything alright in there, Susan darling?"

"That depends!" Susan walked past him in her bra with a towel wrapped around her stomach. She pulled out some clean panties and ran back inside the Bathroom.

"Hey, what's going on, girl?" Gene walked in the Bathroom and found his young wife pulling her gown over her head. "Susan?"

"I have a visit from M.N.... Mother Nature!" Susan rolled her eyes up toward the ceiling as she rinsed out her stained underwear. "I'm certainly glad I came prepared for her little visit! I just forgot to count the weeks and it slipped up on me!"

"Shit, there's goes our romantic night under the sheets!" he laughed softly as he gave her a loving hug. "It's Mother Nature's way of keeping your old man off of you every night. We can just hug like this, kiss and talk. Just being next to you, Susan, makes me a happy man."

"You always say the right thing. I love you, Gene Scott." Susan returned his bear hug, then watched him open the lid to the toilet to relieve himself.

"I couldn't wait, darling...too much wine, water and coffee." Susan laughed as she climbed into bed.

"Pee away, sweetheart. At least you don't have to worry about unwanted surprises waiting for you."

"I wouldn't exactly say that, little darling." Gene walked out and climbed up to hug her. "You didn't go on birth control, did you, sweetheart?"

"No and that's funny, isn't it?" They propped up in bed and Susan snuggled in his strong embrace. "I got pregnant so soon after we got married."

"When it's time, my beautiful girl, we'll make another baby." Gene held her tight. "It's not from a lack of sex. I can't keep my big hands off of you."

"That's perfect with me, Rev. Scott, because I happen to enjoy your big hands touching me as much as my hands love to touch your sexy body." Susan closed her eyes, thinking about how lucky she was to have Gene's total love. "Rev. Scott, it's so good to be loved by you."

"Susan, my beautiful Susan, I thank God every single day for bringing you into my life and for letting me love you, a man old enough to be your real father." He squeezed her lovingly as his lips brushed against her hair. "There'd be no purpose for living if it weren't for you."

"Then our hearts beat as one, darling, because I wouldn't want to live without you." Susan looked up into his serious blue eyes, and his lips melted over hers in a warm fiery kiss.

He pulled away as he rolled his eyes up toward the ceiling and mumbled, "Damn, Scott, this is no time to get a hard-on."

Susan giggled as she laid her hand over on it and glanced up to offer her help.

"Would you like me to relieve this bad boy?"

Gene chuckled as he pulled her into his arms. "Shit, woman, you're so good to me; but if my girl has to wait, I'll wait. Trust me, Susan, when we can make love again, I won't be able to keep my hands off you."

"Great! Don't leave out one single part of me, Mr. Scott." Susan glanced at her bedside clock and noticed it read 12:50 a.m. "Oh, darn! Gene, our time's almost over."

"It's always hard to leave you, Susan." Gene leaned over to smell her beautiful hair; then closing his eyes, he kissed her head. He took her face in his hands and spoke seriously, "Susan, don't lie in here and worry about me in that bedroom with Jackie. I always put my pajamas on in my dressing room before I go into her presence and she sleeps in a gown. Our king-size beds are well-separated. I saw to that on the first night."

Gene kissed her lovingly before climbing out of bed to put his shirt and shoes back on, then took her hand.

"I trust you, Gene." Susan got up to walk him to the door.

"And don't worry about me in here by myself. I will double lock my door."

"That's my girl!" Gene bent over and kissed her good night. He slowly opened the door and saw Michael propped up against the wall. Gene looked down the dark hall before whispering to the sad face in front of him, "Mike, what the shit are you doing out here?"

"Waiting for you to finish having sex, damn it!" Michael looked flustered, causing Scott to smile broadly.

"What happened with your night of fun, buddy? Did Jackie get a headache?"

"Very funny, pal! No, she didn't get a headache; she got her monthly period!" Michael couldn't understand why Gene thought that was so funny. "Jackie forgot to inform me that her birth-control pills were on the sugar ones, meaning the little sex reaper came along to stop our play!"

Scott patted his friend's shoulder and smiled down at his wife who was listening to the conversation.

"Honey, you really don't have anything to worry about now. Old M.N. paid Jackie a visit too."

"Poor fellows." Susan laughed when Michael finally smiled, realizing Gene was in the same boat. "Mike, just remember, when you have to wait for it, it makes lovemaking that much better." She blew Scott a kiss and closed her door.

Chapter Thirteen

The next day after breakfast Gene and Susan, along with Jobi, Jackie and Michael, rode their horses to a high hill overlooking a big valley below. A large group of elephants were making their way to a small river. As the two women and Jobi began setting out a picnic lunch, Gene and Michael rode on up to the highest point.

Pulling out their field glasses, they scanned the horizon beyond the valley where another hill rose up. A large mountain villa came into view. Michael said, "Can you see it, Scott? That's got to be the Blackwell's place." Michael then moved his glasses toward the north side of the villa and spotted men going in and out of a cave. "I think I found one of the stolen gold mines."

"They're mining alright! Those big carts are full of rocks." Gene focused his glasses in on the pile of dark rocks. "It appears that cart's missing its sparkle." The preacher winked at his friend. "Those thieves can't be happy about that sorry load."

Michael shook his head in disgust. "The feds said that property was the first one Blackwell stole after threatening the owner and his family. That poor old man might as well have handed that creep his deed for nothing with what he paid him."

"When this is over, the rightful owners will get their property back." Scott looked back over at the villa and chuckled. "Blackwell's villa is modest compared to mine, but he's stolen a lot more mansions and I only have one. He's getting them for a steal."

Susan stood up after putting the food out and shielded her eyes to see her husband and Michael up on the ridge, still lost in their surveillance of Mr. Blackwell. She called up, "Hey, fellows, what are you looking at? Are there some pretty girls over there sunbathing in the nude?" she teased as Jobi stood up to hear their answer.

"Susan, you're the only one I want to see nude, beautiful." Gene noticed Jobi laugh at his remark so he mumbled, "Shit!" Michael slapped his back, laughing himself.

"We can't help our big mouths, Scott. Women have a way of bringing out the beast in us."

Gene chuckled as he returned to his surveillance of his crooked neighbor. "That mine must be loaded. Blackwell's men haven't stopped going in and out of that cave at a fast rate. That shithead Blackwell not only stole their homes and land, he's also taking their future wealth and then acts so cocky about it, flashing his wealth around."

"Well, I'm certain the bastard will give a big share to his favorite charity…his fat bank account!" Mike looked back at the villa, then laughed sarcastically. "Get a load of that, Scott! Looks like Toby has a couple of girlfriends up there. See them sitting around the pool having drinks."

Scott turned the glasses and zoomed in on Toby, sitting between two blondes, kissing and hugging.

"Well, well, it looks like good ole Toby's a ladies' man." He narrowed his eyes at the young flirt. "I hope the jerk gets a sunburn so he can't come over Monday!" Feeling Susan's soft hand on his arm, Gene looked down into her eyes. She reached up and took the field glasses away from her husband so she could see first-hand what had them so intrigued. She instantly spotted the flirty neighbor.

"Would you just look at that! Toby Blackwell has his hands all over those broads! Coming onto me like I'm special!" She handed the glasses back to Gene as she mumbled, "That big jerk!"

"Susan?" Gene took her hand, questions in his eyes. "You sound disappointed."

"Me? Disappointed in that thing?" Susan laughed out sarcastically. "Ha! I was feeling sorry for the little creep, thinking he was into me and I had to happily pop his conceited bubble!"

Gene laughed as he lifted Susan into the saddle and led the horse down the hill, Michael leading his horse behind them. After tying the horses with the others, they walked up and looked down at Jackie, who had lain down on a spread with her hand on her head. She cracked open her eyes and smiled weakly up at the three staring faces.

"Guys, stop looking at me as though I'm dead. I'll be fine in a little while after those pain pills kick in." Jackie took Michael's hand when he squatted down next to her, concern written on his handsome face. "These damn cramps have been giving me one doozy of a headache, but it's easing up now."

Susan looked down sympathetically, "I guess I'm one of the lucky ones, Jackie. I've never had cramps with my monthly." Susan saw Jobi coming from behind a bunch of bushes zipping up his pants. "Little brother, I hope you looked where you relieved yourself."

"Sure thing, sis!" He walked over, eyes filled with questions. "Sis, what is your 'monthly'?"

"Yeh, sis, tell the kid." Gene chuckled when Susan frowned over at him. "You might as well tell him, Susan. He has to know sooner or later, sweetheart."

"Know what?" Jobi looked from Susan to Gene, even more confused.

"Jobi, hasn't Dad told you anything about…you know…sex?" Susan tried to avoid Gene's big grin as he was enjoying her try to explain the facts of life to her teenage brother.

"Sure, sis. Dad told me where babies come from, and it's not a cabbage patch like my friend Leroy told me." Jobi got down next to his sister as she started getting out sandwiches. "Does having sex with Rev. Scott and Jackie having it with Michael give you cramps?"

Susan looked over at her friend for help. "Jackie?"

Jackie sat up and motioned Jobi over. "Jobi, you know when a man and a woman have sex, and I take it your father told you how it's done." Jackie couldn't help but smile watching the young man turning a bright shade of pink. "Jobi, do you know what the man and woman do?"

"When they have sex? A…yes, Dad did tell me those facts."

"Then you may or may not know, this act between a couple sometimes make a baby, so of course the girl gets pregnant. Her body has to supply the blood to the growing baby inside her. Are you with me so far, kid?"

"Sure, Jackie. The baby's growing inside her and it needs blood to live and grow. Right?" Jobi's interest peaked as he got to his knees.

"When the girl's not pregnant, her body has to get rid of the blood supply that builds up each month and make room for a fresh supply just in case she gets pregnant." Jackie frowned over at Michael who started laughing. "Would you care to finish this story, laughing Jack Flash?"

"No. No, sweetheart, you're doing fine." Mike bit his lip to keep from laughing as Gene chuckled over the funny situation. Susan reached up and pulled the big guy down beside her.

"Behave, buster, or you'll be telling Jobi the facts of life."

Gene smiled and patted her leg as he winked at Michael who was trying hard to keep a straight face. Turning toward Jackie, he gave her his winning smile as he spoke softly, "Continue with your very good explanation, Jackie. You're doing very well."

Jackie narrowed her eyes angrily at the handsome preacher, then sat up straighter to continue her discussion with the juvenile.

"The old blood must come out to make room for fresh blood, so once a month we lucky girls get a period which last four to five days, flushing out the old blood. That is what your sister meant by 'monthly'."

Jobi turned his head to one side as he looked down innocently at Jackie's pantie line and frowned in confusion. He blurted out, "I don't see it coming out!"

Michael couldn't control his laughter as Jackie reached

over and slapped his leg hard.

"Mike, don't you dare laugh! This isn't funny!"

"Jobi, stop staring at Jackie!" Susan pulled him around to face her. "You can't see anything because we wear protection in our underwear to catch the stupid blood!"

"Jobi?" Jackie turned him around to face her. "Susan's right!" She gave Michael and Gene a fake smile as she added, "That's the only time we girls can rest from these men climbing all over us, right, Susan?"

"Exactly! I think it's Mother Nature's way of punishing our men for wanting sex every single night!" Susan covered her giggles when Jobi turned to stare at Gene and Michael.

"Well, guys, I guess that explains why you can't wait to get your woman in bed!" Jobi laughed. "Not having it for four to five days! Boy, you fellows have it bad! I hope I can show a little restraint when I get married."

"Look, buddy, I'll restrain your butt if you don't cut out the cute remarks!" Gene rubbed his head playfully. "Just wait, kid, when you find the right girl, you'll be in the same sinking boat as me and old Mike here." He put his arms around Susan and smiled down into her blue eyes. "And if we don't behave ourselves, we might end up in the doghouse."

"Oh, I get it, they cut you off for a while if you upset them." Jobi reached over and patted his sister's leg. "You wouldn't do that to poor old Scott, would you, sis? You sure did want him in your pants for a long time before you tied the knot!"

Susan reached over and punched her brother in the arm as she narrowed her eyes. "Listen, little brother, I think this conversation's gone on long enough!" Feeling everyone watching her, she reached for the plates and started passing them around. "Let's eat! I'm starved!"

"Sounds good to me! I'm hungry enough to eat three of those sandwiches." Gene said a blessing, then helped pass the food around. "By the way, Jobi, my little Susan would never send me to the doghouse, right, sweetie?"

"Who could resist you, Gene Scott!" Susan reached over to

kiss him as she laughed. “Besides, there’s not enough room in that doghouse for you and poor Shags. You’re welcome under my sheets anytime!”

“Could we not talk about sex?” Michael ripped into a chicken leg and mumbled with his mouth full. “It’s bad enough having to wait for way too many days!”

Jackie patted her lover’s leg before drinking her tea, then looked from Michael to Gene.

“So, fellows, what was so interesting over on that hillside?”

“I saw Toby Blackwell entertaining two blonde swimming beauties, drinking and smooching!” Susan said with a chuckle as she wiped mayonnaise off her husband’s face. “What else did I miss, sweetheart?”

“You missed the north mountain where Blackwell’s miners were bringing out rough diamonds.” Scott reached for another sandwich. “There was no sign of your granddad, I’m afraid. Maybe we’ll catch something the next time.”

Susan laid down her half-eaten sandwich, feeling anxious about her missing grandfather.

“Oh, Gene, where can he be? Granddad’s got to be alright!”

Gene wiped off his face and hands before he pulled Susan over into his arms.

“Sweetheart, your granddad’s a very smart man, and he’s been in several rough situations before and came out fine. Remember the Bouta Barga tribe’s poison arrows—real savages, right, Jobi?”

“Sure, sis! Granddad’s a champ at getting out of sticky situations.” Jobi smiled brightly when Gene gave him a wink of approval for his response.

“Yes, I know, Jobi. Granddad was my first hero.” Susan laid her head over on her husband’s shoulder. “Then Rev. Scott came into my life and became my hero, then my husband and great lover.”

“There you go again!” Michael stood up and pulled Jackie to her feet. “Let’s go and check on the horses since you’re feeling better, hon.”

Susan watched as Michael and Jackie walked away all hugged up. She quickly started putting the left- over food away and stood up, handing Gene the picnic basket.

"Poor Michael, and I thought you had it hard, Gene. I need to go back to the house, sweetheart, and pay the bathroom a visit."

"Okay. Jobi, grab those blankets and carry them to the horses. Let's get this girl home." Holding Susan's hand, they made their way to the horses as Gene spoke softly to her, "Susan, I just don't show you how hard I have it when I can't make love to my sexy little wife." He squeezed her hand and helped her on her horse. "Saddle up, gang, it's time to go back."

"Good! I need a change." Jackie glanced over at the young teen who looked like he was about to question what she meant. "Don't ask, kid!" The others laughed as they rode slowly back to the house.

Chapter Fourteen

Sunday morning came and Scott sat silently by a lamp reading his old worn Bible. Jackie awoke and sat up quietly in bed to watch the handsome preacher deep in scripture. He closed it gently, removed his glasses and bowed his head in silent prayer. Before rising from his chair, Gene placed the cherished Bible in the table drawer, then stood up to stretch. He turned to see his roommate smiling.

"Gene Scott, how long have you been up and dressed?"

"Good morning, Jackie. I've always been an early riser." Gene flashed her a handsome smile as he walked over by her bed. "Are you feeling any better this morning?"

"I feel terrific, Gene. Thanks for asking." Jackie pulled the sheet up over her nightgown. "Sometimes getting to sleep early with no hanky-panky is good for you!"

Gene chuckled as he walked to the door. "I'm off to get my breakfast. I'll see you in the breakfast room."

Jackie checked the bedside clock…7 a.m. "I'll be down in thirty minutes." She waved as the handsome man closed the door, then climbed from the bed and said to herself, "Gene Scott, you're such a devoted husband. Susan's one lucky girl to have won your love." She smiled and danced to the shower.

Susan walked up behind her husband, put her arms around his neck and whispered close to his ear,

"How did my handsome dad sleep last night?"

"I would have slept better if I'd been with you, baby girl!" Gene pulled her around and, knowing they were alone, kissed her. Susan raised her head and looked around.

"Where's everyone this morning, Dad?"

"Max and Laura are busy in the kitchen fixing our breakfast. Henning's still in bed…lazy butler! The two young servers are brewing coffee and squeezing fresh orange juice." Gene reached for one of Susan's breasts, gave it a little squeeze, then chuckled. "I've got my own tender melon to squeeze!" He watched the kitchen door closely, ready to stop his play at the first sight of their servers. "Jackie's still getting ready and the whereabouts of Dr. 'Fields' is anybody's guess! I haven't seen him since he had dinner with us on our first night here."

"Yeh, come to think of it, I haven't seen the family doctor around anywhere either." Susan took her seat beside her husband. "Maybe he's staying in one of the guest houses around back."

"Sounds like the charming doctor. He's probably afraid to show his face and actually have to go to work." Scott squeezed Susan's hand under the table as the two young natives came from the kitchen carrying trays of bacon, sausage, eggs, potatoes, biscuits, coffee and juice. They carefully placed everything out on the buffet table, then bowed politely to Gene,

"Breakfast is set up, sir. Anything I can get either of you?" Rata didn't take his eyes off the pretty girl with the long black hair and blue eyes. Gene got up and stood in front of Susan as he reached for a warm plate and passed it back to her, then got his own plate before answering the young man,

"There's one thing you can get me, Rata. You could tell me where I might find Dr. Fields."

"Yes, sir, Dr. Fields stay to himself in guest cottage. He request breakfast be served there at 9 a.m. in morning. I think he sleep in, sir."

"Lazy as ever! Let's hope he can move that fat ass of his if we need him to do a medical job!" The preacher picked up the empty trays and handed one to each young man. "You may go now; we're good."

"Yes, sir, enjoy." Rata tried to see around the big man. "You too, missy. If there anything we can get you." Being unable to see the pretty girl, they turned and disappeared behind the kitchen door.

Gene turned to help Susan up and as they began filling their plates, he whispered,

"Don't lead those boys on, sweetheart. They might take that warm friendly smile of yours as a sign that you're interested in them. They both like you a bit too much. I've seen that look before."

"Oh brother! You can't be friendly anymore without someone thinking you are into them!" Susan carried the food to her place and went back for coffee and juice. "I guess I'll just sit like a nun and stare at my plate when those kids are in here."

Gene chuckled as he reached over and kissed her before sitting down, his plate running over. He stared down at the amount of food on his plate.

"By the looks of this plateful, I'm going to have to swim ten extra laps in the pool later this morning." Gene picked up his fork as his attention fell on Susan's half-filled plate. "Baby doll, you eat like a bird."

"I've got to watch this girly figure, Dad." Susan's smile brightened up the breakfast room as she reached up and pinched Gene's cheek. "My man likes me hot and sexy!"

"Damn right, beautiful!" Gene took a big bite of his crispy bacon as he winked at his wife, then smiled up at Jackie when she came in and picked up a plate to fill. Setting her half-filled plate down, she went back for coffee. Gene smiled down at the half-empty plate and shook his head. "Shit, another bird!"

"What's on the line-up today, Julien dear"—Jackie smiled down at Scott's full plate—"besides eating a large breakfast?"

"When it's safe to get in the water, I'm first going to splash away some of this big breakfast doing laps! Then the boys and I are riding back to that hill overlooking the valley to check on our dishonest neighbor. When I return, I'll be paying our shy doctor a little visit. Then my lovely daughter and I are going to take a hike and see what we can get into."

"Make the most of today and have fun because tomorrow the Blackwell family's paying us a long visit. Right, Dad?"

Susan reached under the table and patted his leg, bringing out his big smile.

"That's correct, smart girl, so we all need to keep our eyes open." Gene stood up and stretched. "My swimsuit is calling!" He bent over and cautiously kissed Susan on the cheek. "If you can get in the water, darling, you can join me."

"I can do that, Dad!" Susan smiled as she drank the rest of her juice and propped up on her elbows to wait for Jackie to finish before going upstairs to put on her swimsuit.

Gene and Susan were joined by Jobi in the pool. They played for almost an hour before Gene climbed out and smiled down at the brother and sister picking with each other.

"Kids, be careful out here. I've got to change and get Michael and James lined up to go with me to check on Blackwell. I should be back in a couple of hours, so change into some hiking clothes and boots. We can pay the doctor a quick visit and have a light lunch before our hike."

"I'll be ready, darling, and see that a light lunch is ready." She giggled and held up her arms for Gene to help her out of the water. "I take it by your eating light, you're joining the birds."

"After that whopper of a breakfast, bring out the birdseed!" He chuckled as he watched her towel off. "No more pool fun, sweetheart?"

"I've had enough pool for one day, Rev. Scott. Besides, it's no fun without you!" Gene hugged Susan and chuckled.

"That's good to hear, darling. I keep thinking someday you'll grow tired of me and want a new model."

"Gene Scott!" Susan slapped his backside. "Look, mister, I will never, and I mean NEVER grow tired of you…ever!"

"Just checking." Gene kissed her lips after checking to find the coast clear. "It's just good to hear you say it. As for my feelings for you, Susan Scott, I want you with me for all my tomorrows!"

James and Michael followed Scott up the steep hill and found the clearing for better viewing. All three pulled out their field glasses and adjusted them for the distance. There was no sign of life around the villa or the pool so the three observers turned their attention toward the mine. Even though it was Sunday, the miners were busy moving their big wheelbarrows in and out of the caves with rich dirt. Gene narrowed his eyes as he watched the men working like bees on the Lord's Sabbath.

"Looks like the heathen devil's working his men seven days a week! I wonder if the jackass pays double time for the weekend."

"Those dumb workers don't know one day from another, and any amount of money probably looks like a lot to them." Michael, along with Gene and James, watched as men scattered the sand through large sifters. After the sand fell through, the three watching could make out the different sizes of rocks left inside the sifter and noticed them sparkling in the bright sunlight. They watched as the dirty miners would hold up a shiny stone, and huge smiles would spread across their weather-beaten faces.

"Looks like they hit a rich vein, those stealing bastards!" Gene turned his attention back to the villa as Michael grunted in disgust.

"If there's one thing I hate, it's a rotten thief striking it rich on stolen damn property!"

"So how are we supposed to catch these dudes? I don't get the set-up man." James looked at Scott, whose attention was on the villa. "What do you see over there that's so interesting, man?" James focused his glasses on a red car that had pulled up in front of the villa and spotted a couple getting out. A young teenage boy climbed from the back seat and looked around. "Wonder who those people are?"

"Well, shit, James, you're full of questions!" Scott glanced over at him briefly in aggravation, then turned back to the strangers who'd just arrived at the Blackwells. "To answer your questions, first of all, I have no clue who's paying Mr. Crook a visit and second, I'm still trying to figure out how to catch this jackass. It has something to do with me being a big diamond buyer and when I bargain with him, everything will start to come together. When I know something constructive, Tabor, I'll let you know. Got that?"

"Sure thing, Scott, no sweat, man. I'm glad I'm not the only one here who doesn't know what the hell's going on." James noticed Michael was caught up in the new arrivals so he leaned over and asked him, "Has anyone come out to greet those people yet?" He focused his glasses back on the villa.

"Not yet," Michael grunted. "Maybe they'll cancel their visit tomorrow if they have unexpected guests. That would suit me fine if I didn't want to seal up this case and find Dr. Rogers."

Gene watched as Katherine and Toby came out to welcome the visitors. Mrs. Blackwell put her arms around the woman and hugged her as Toby shook hands with the man driving, then hugged the young man. Gene lowered his field glasses and frowned. "Now that was a strange sight. Did you boys see that pervert just hug that young fellow?"

"Maybe dear old Toby is one of those fellows who goes for guys or gals." James shook his long hair. "That's one weird family."

Michael said, "I say they're kinfolk who've come visiting and they're really close. Toby didn't look like he had any attraction for the same sex the other night with Susan." Suddenly realizing that was the wrong thing to say around Scott, he added, "And the way he was hugging those blondes by the pool, I'd say Toby prefers women hands-down."

"Saved your butt there, Mike." Gene chuckled when he noticed Michael sweating, then turned his attention back on his blond neighbor. "If that big flirt wants to keep the use of his hands, he'll keep the damn things off of my wife!" Scott jerked the glasses down and put them in his pocket as he started down the hill to where they left the horses, James and Michael running close behind him.

"Let's get back, fellows. There might be a message from our stealing neighbor!" Gene climbed up in the saddle and stared over at Mike, who started laughing. "Mike, care to share what's so damn funny?"

"Maybe the stealing neighbor won't come, but I don't think anything will keep his lusting wife at home, my friend." Michael reached over and punched Gene's strong arm. "Jackie informed me that Katherine Blackwell has the hots for you, man!"

"Good lord! What is it with all these women drooling over Gene?" James pulled his horse around. "I can see why Toby's gaga over Susan. She's young, sexy, with a great figure." He saw Gene narrow his eyes as he sized him up and balled his fist. James swallowed as he tried to defend himself, "Not me, man! I'm a happily-married dude with a sexy young chick of my own. But, Scott, I just don't grab it. Sure, you're good-looking, but so are we, me and Mike here. It must be that strong body women go for." James smiled weakly at his laughing friend. "I guess skinny me is a little bit jealous."

"Let's face it, James, old pal, when it comes to the fairer sex, ladies find Rev. Gene Scott irresistible."

"Alright, you two jokers, that'll be quite enough of this bullshit! Let's move these horses before I start knocking the bullshit out of you!" Without another word, Scott headed back to the stables.

Susan was waiting as promised, wearing her khaki shorts, white shirt and jungle boots. Gene smiled his approval, then noticed they were being observed by the downstairs maids, who pretended to be dusting the great hall. Susan had spotted them when she came down and was prepared to act out her part. Getting a cap off the fancy hat tree, Gene slipped it on his head as he asked,

"Are you ready to visit our good doctor, baby girl?"

"Sure, Dad. I just can't believe he's that shy not to come over once in a while." Susan took her husband's extended hand as they walked to the cottage overlooking the rose garden. Before Gene could knock on the cottage door, Susan spotted William Danfield sitting with his back turned, reading a book. After pointing him out, the couple slipped up behind him and Gene laid his hand on his shoulder, causing the doctor to jump.

"Danfield, you can't hide forever!" Hearing Scott's voice, he jumped up quickly as the book slipped from his trembling fingers. The "old" friend looked up sheepishly as he managed to speak,

"My God, Scott! Never slip up on a man like that! You just about gave me a heart attack!"

"Being such a great doctor who almost single-handedly brought peace on our first mission in Africa, I'd think you could fix yourself right up." Scott faked a laugh. "Would you even know if one of us needed you?"

"The young lads would inform me of any trouble." William could read Scott's mistrust as he stumbled with his words. "I was merely trying to stay out of your hair, hoping you wouldn't hurt your fool self and need my services."

"That's very considerate of you, Dr. Fields." Gene noticed the gardener had stepped inside the rose garden near them with one ear perked up while he trimmed the bushes. To alert Susan and William, he nodded his head, pointing the intruder out, then continued, "But you'll be available should any mishap happen to one of my family members, Fields?"

"Indeed, I will, sir." After being alerted, Danfield had seen the spy as well and acted out his part. "My services are at your disposal, Mr. Armstrong. Day or night, I'll be at my post." The doctor cast his eyes on Susan as they roamed down her body. "We meet again, my lovely S…sweet Jessica." He grimaced when Scott's strong grip bit into his shoulder, and the doctor could hear the anger in the reverend's tone as he spoke,

"I trust you like your accommodations, Dr. Fields? You must because you rarely leave them!" Gene moved in close to his ear and spoke between clinched teeth, "One of my servants tells me you have the habit of sleeping in and taking your breakfast alone here in your cozy cottage at 9 a.m. Is that pretty accurate, doctor?"

"I do enjoy reading in the wee hours of the night, sir; that is, if there are no jungle beasts lurking close by making eerie sounds. A doctor needs his sleep to do his job well." William forced a weak smile. "And to answer your question, yes, sir, I must admit I enjoy the peace and quiet inside my little cottage while I have my breakfast, as I do all my meals."

"And to think you're getting paid good money for this 'pie' job! And since you're on the clock, Fields, I suggest you get to bed by 8 p.m., get dressed by 6 a.m. and get your lazy ass to the big house to join us for breakfast at 7 a.m. sharp!"

"If that is your wish, sir." Danfield felt Scott release his shoulder and breathed out in relief. "I'll start first thing in the morning."

"Good! And, Fields, you may have your lunch and dinner wherever you like unless I ask you." Gene took Susan's hand. "One meal a day is all I can take with you. Tell the good doctor goodbye, Jessi."

"Goodbye, Dr. Fields. It's really good to see you again." Susan faked her smile and walked silently beside her husband until they reached the big front porch. "Gene, why did you ask Danfield to have breakfast with us if the man gets on your nerves?"

"The Blackwells are arriving tomorrow." Scott smiled slyly. "I'll be placing the flirty doctor on Katherine's right side. You know how he throws himself on married women, and maybe Hal's wife won't be staring at me the entire time."

"Can you believe that woman!" Susan's hands went to her hips in disgust, just thinking about it. "Openly flirting with my husband!" She suddenly noticed William Henry III standing in the column's shadow and spoke a little louder, hoping he hadn't heard her last statement. "I just can't stand some bimbo making advances to you right in front of Mom!" The last statement alerted Gene of a snooper nearby, and he nodded his head as she stomped her foot. "It just makes me so damn mad!

Openly flirting with my mom's husband!"

"Jessi sweetheart, women find your daddy irresistible for some oddball reason." Gene put his arm around Susan and smiled broadly. "I don't get it. Do you, sweet girl?"

"I can say how I feel about you. You're the best dad in the entire world." Susan stood on her tiptoes and kissed him. "As for you being irresistible, I couldn't say. To me, you're just plain dad." She opened the door and added nonchalantly, "On the other hand, your adorable wife finds you incredibly irresistible, you handsome devil."

Gene followed Susan in and after looking around the big empty hall, he chuckled and pulled her into his arms and smothered her with a kiss.

"Damn, you're a good actress! You, my beautiful darling, can come up with me while I get in my cute shorts." The loving couple raced each other up the wide steps, laughing.

Chapter Fifteen

The rest of the day flew by and the make-believe Armstrongs were walking up the staircase, ready to turn in when the F.B.I. agent stopped them. They noticed he wasn't alone. The upstairs maid followed slowly behind him.

"Excuse me, Mr. Armstrong, but Hal Blackwell is on the phone and asked if it would be a burden on you if he brought three extra people with him?"

"Why the hell not!" Scott laughed. "I'm rich! I can afford it, right? We have plenty of rooms to spare, each with a personal bath!"

"Very good, sir." The agent heard the maid stop at the top of the stairs. "I'll tell Mr. Blackwell we will be expecting six visitors tomorrow."

"That's great, Henning! Now I can go tuck my daughter in bed." Gene smiled down at the wide-eyed maid, whose mouth had dropped open. "I take it you can tuck yourself in, Mrs. Gaston?"

"Tuck myself…? A…yes, sir." The nosy maid pushed past the fake butler and raced to the servants' staircase at the end of the wide hall as the agent stared up at the grinning preacher.

"Rev. Scott, just what are you doing?"

"That's nothing for you to worry about, Henning. Mr. Blackwell's waiting. Don't make the gentleman hang on." Gene turned him around and gave him a small push. "He'll think I'm trying to come up with a reason to say no." He bent down close to his ear, "We need the jackass here so I can work him. Now go!" Gene laughed as the agent walked swiftly down the steps. Shaking his head, he took his wife's hand and they walked together to her room where he stayed with her for two hours before returning to the master suite.

Getting into bed quietly so he wouldn't wake Jackie, who lay on her side in the other king-size bed, Scott switched on a reading light so he could read until he grew sleepy. He was in deep sleep when he felt a hand running down his chest. Gene tried to open his eyes and, through a cloudy vision, he could see Jackie lying next to him. He could hear her soft British voice speaking softly, "Julien, my sexy husband, make love to me."

Gene tried to move to push her away, but something kept him from moving. Hearing the sound of weeping, he looked up and saw Susan looking down at him and Jackie. Michael appeared from nowhere and pulled Susan into his arms. Gene could only watch and listen as Michael started toward the door with Susan.

"Susan, I'll take your mind off all this! Let them have each other. You'll grow to love the way I'll make love to you." Then Gene saw them disappear and he sat straight up in his bed, sweat rolling down his chest as his heart pounded. He looked at the other bed and saw Jackie still on her side, fast asleep. Running his hands over his wet hair, the relieved preacher let out his breath.

"Damn! A terrible nightmare!" Gene rolled over and thought about Susan, hoping her dreams were about him. After a long while, Gene finally fell asleep while down the hall, Susan was tossing and turning, a bad dream filling her senses as she saw Toby Blackwell walking up beside her bed.

As if by magic, Toby began stripping her gown off with his eyes. She tried to scream for Gene, but all that came out was a muffled squeak. Just as Toby was about to touch her breasts, Gene walked in and started over to stop the molester. Before he reached him, Jackie and Katherine appeared, grabbed his arms and began talking in unison,

"Let her go, Julien! You can have us, you handsome stud! One at a time or both together!"

Susan sat straight up, breathing heavily. The dream had been so real, she knew she could never go back to sleep without her husband. She threw off her covers, slung her feet around to the floor and slipped into her slippers as she whispered to herself,

"Shit! It was a dream! I need Gene!" Susan went to the door and peeked out into the dimly lit hall and found it deserted. Glancing back at her clock, she knew why. It was only 2 a.m. and everyone else in the big house would be asleep in their rooms, so she walked rapidly down the hall to the master bedroom, praying on the way that the door would be unlocked. To her relief it opened and she walked in quietly. Seeing Gene asleep on his side, Susan climbed in beside him and slowly put her arm around him. Thinking it might be another dream, Gene turned and looked into his wife's beautiful blue eyes. He blinked his eyes twice to make sure it wasn't a dream.

"Susan, you're in my bed, sweetheart."

"Gene, I had a nightmare and I needed my husband. I need to fall asleep in your arms, darling." Susan was relieved when Gene pulled her into his strong arms and held her tightly.

"It must have been what we had for dinner, Susan, because I had my own nightmare thirty minutes ago." He recalled the dream. "Jackie was attacking me in my bed and I couldn't talk or move. You were watching us, crying your little heart out until Michael came in and swept you away to make love to you!"

"Toby was standing beside my bed and by some magic, he stripped off my clothes with his eyes. He was about to touch my breasts when you came in to save me, but Jackie and Katherine grabbed you for their own stud!"

"Damn! Poor baby." Gene moved his hand down over her breasts. "Toby better keep his hands off those breasts. Those beauties are all mine."

Susan laughed softly, "Can I stay, please?"

"Just try and leave, girl!" He pulled the covers up around them. "How much longer do we have to wait?"

"Poor baby, just a couple more days and I'll be ready for action." Susan snuggled in his arms. "I love you, Rev. Scott. Good night."

"I love you too, my wonderful woman." Gene kissed the top of her head. "Good night, Susan." The loving couple fell asleep in each other's arms.

Jackie opened her eyes and rolled over, expecting to find Scott out of bed and dressed, reading his Bible. She noticed the first rays of morning shining through the closed shades. Jackie sat up straight when she saw Gene still asleep and not alone. She climbed quietly from the big bed and wrapped her cozy robe around her, then looked down at the loving couple wrapped in one another's arms. She whispered in disbelief,

"Susan?" She gently shook Gene's arm to wake him. "Scott, wake up! It's almost daylight."

Gene opened his drowsy eyes and saw Jackie standing over him. He mumbled, "Am I dreaming again?"

"Gene, Susan's going to get caught in our room if you both don't wake up!" Jackie pointed down at Susan, still fast asleep on his chest."

"The poor kid's exhausted. We both are. We both woke up having nightmares." Gene gently shook his young wife. "Susan, wake up, sweetheart. It's almost morning."

"Gene?" Susan opened her eyes and saw Jackie. "Am I still dreaming?"

Jackie laughed as she shook her head. "I should be offended if you see me and still think you're having nightmares, but dreams can make you say and do crazy things like this! Susan, you're in Gene's bed and it's getting light outside. It's almost 7 a.m. and the kitchen staff will start to wonder where we are."

"Damn!" Gene threw the covers back and climbed from the big bed, pulling Susan up with him. "Jackie's right, Susan. Those nosy maids and cooks might decide to come looking for us and find you in our room."

"I have a plan, Scott. You get dressed while I walk Susan back to her room. I'll take care of those busybodies if they're up and about." Jackie smiled up at Scott's hair that was tossed down in his eyes, then walked out the door with Susan. Wanda

Gaston and Laura Rite stood smiling as they whispered in the hallway.

"Ladies, I hope you're both on your way downstairs for breakfast. There's one thing I hate from my hired help, ladies, and that's nosy people."

"Oh, gracious me, no, madam. We just happened to be on our way downstairs when we heard your door open." Laura Rite looked from Jackie to Susan. "You didn't have another nightmare, did you, child?"

"No, Miss Rite. Jessica came to our room this morning to borrow some female protection to wear in her swimsuit. She only brought pads."

"Oh!" the upstairs maid blushed. "I never thought of that."

"Don't sweat it, Wanda." Susan hugged Jackie. "Thanks, Mom! Now I can swim today. See you and Dad at breakfast." Susan waved over her head and went down the hallway to her room.

"Ladies, if you'll excuse me, I must get ready." Jackie opened the door and glanced back at the nosy women. "Now Julien has to wait for me and I know he must be famished by now." She stepped inside and closed the door, then jumped when she noticed Gene standing behind it. "I guess you heard."

"Everything." Gene laughed. "Armstrong married a very smart rich lady, Mrs. Armstrong."

"That's correct, Mr. Armstrong. Well, not so rich but very smart." Jackie patted his face and walked to her dressing room for a quick change, calling back, "You can go on down before they send up a search party. Can't keep them waiting."

"I'm going then," he called, then mumbled to himself, "And if Danfield says one thing about my being late, I'll crack an egg over his sorry head!"

Jackie, Gene and Jobi were waiting at the front door when the Blackwell family pulled in at 9 a.m. sharp. Hal got out of the driver's side as a middle-aged man, slightly younger than the diamond thief, climbed from the front passenger seat.

Katherine got out from the back, along with a woman resembling her and a young boy about Jobi's age. Hal shook Gene's outstretched hand.

"Julien, my friend, may I introduce my brother-in-law and the best diamond salesman on my payroll, Eric Robinson; his lovely wife and Katherine's younger sister, Emily; and their child Randy, who just turned fifteen last week."

Gene smiled at the shy kid. "Randy, you and my son Richi are the same age—what luck! I think it's been hard on Richi not having any kids his age to hang out with here. He has tons of friends back home in the States. Sport here is four years younger than his sister. They get along great and are very close, but I'm sure you youngsters will have much more in common."

"You're right, Mr. Armstrong." Eric Robinson hugged his shy child. "This kid's been bored ever since we left the States. Like your Jobi, my pal had to leave friends behind to travel with us and Randy has all summer until school starts back."

Jobi stepped up next to Randy and smiled brightly. "Hi, Randy! I'm Richi! Boy, am I glad you're here! There's tons of neat stuff we can do. There's swimming, horseback-riding, tennis, hiking, pitching ball or just hanging out! Are there any of those things you're interested in?"

"Yeh, Richi, all of them!" Randy smiled for the first time. "I'm on the baseball team at the academy I attend. Not bragging, but they chose me as the main pitcher for our team! I swim, play tennis, hike and I absolutely love to ride horses. What can we do first, Richi?"

"If it's alright with Dad, we can get Stretch to saddle up some horses for us and take in the trails Dad showed me. They're safe from any wild animals." Jobi looked up at Gene hopefully. "Please, Dad?"

"Just the lower trails I showed you, sport." Gene patted the young teen's head. "And you're right, those trails are pretty safe. Just don't wander beyond the fence. There's a jungle out there, buddy."

"Thanks, Dad! You rock!" Jobi started to leave with his

new friend when Scott took his shoulders.

"Hold your horses, sport! You and Randy are free to ride horses only if Stretch rides along with you. There may be a fenced-in border surrounding our property, son, but good fences don't always keep dangerous animals out. Stretch has a hunting rifle and he's not afraid to use it."

"No sweat, Dad. Randy will like Stretch. He's one cool cat!" Jobi smiled down at his new friend. "Maybe we can talk him and his wife Meg into another cookout and fix hot dogs over an open fire! You put your hot dog on the end of a sharp stick and hold it over the fire. It's a blast!"

"Sounds heavy, Richi! I'm in!" Randy waved at the grown-ups, "See you later, Mom, Dad, Uncle Hal and Aunt Katherine!"

Emily Robinson smiled as she watched the two new friends walk away, chatting as if they'd known each other for years.

"You've made my child very happy, Julien." Emily looked at the handsome preacher smiling down at her. "I must say my sister Katherine wasn't stretching the truth about you. You are one hunk of a man."

"Mrs. Armstrong, you're quite a dish yourself! A handsome couple indeed." Eric Robinson lifted Jackie's soft hand to his lips and kissed it gallantly. "And thank you, my dear, for allowing my family to spend a few days with you in this beautiful home."

"You are more than welcome. As my husband always says, 'The more, the merrier.'" Jackie motioned for the fake butler who was waiting just inside the grand entrance hall. "Mr. Henning, will you please show our guests to their rooms?" She smiled beautifully at the two couples. "You may leave your bags here. Rata and Makata will bring them up shortly."

"Thank you so much, Judith." Hal pulled a Forbes magazine from his briefcase and handed it to Jackie. "This is the latest ten-richest-list issue and I thought you may have missed getting a copy. If you have one already…"

"No, we haven't received a single issue since we left the States. Thank you, Hal." Jackie couldn't resist looking down another minute. She smiled at the cover, featuring a big picture of Gene Scott. "Darling, you got the cover this month."

"Little rich me?" Gene chuckled and pulled the magazine from her hands. "Damn if I didn't!" He saw himself dressed in a white silk shirt with bold letters under his picture reading, "Julien Armstrong, second richest man in the world!" So that's why they wanted that photo of me. Damn, you can't keep any secrets these days."

"Please keep that copy. I have more at the villa." Hal slapped Scott on the back and made a painful face as he managed to say, "There's a great article inside about you and your charming family."

"Speaking of family, where's that beautiful daughter of yours?" Eric looked around the hall and saw only housekeepers dusting the long hallway. "My nephew Toby's crazy about her. She's all he's talked about since our arrival."

"My little Jessica is very beautiful as you've said; but, be warned, I'm very possessive of her and who she sees." Gene chuckled.

"Julien loves his daughter very much. She's always been daddy's little girl, and he checks out any boy who acts interested in her." Jackie took Gene's arm, smiling radiantly, "Ladies, I thought we could play a game of croquet before lunch…mother and daughter against very pretty sisters. Does that interest you?"

"That sounds like a smashing idea, my dear." Katherine followed Henning up the stairs and called down, "We'll slip into something more appropriate and be down shortly." The sisters walked beside each other whispering about their handsome host and how they'd prefer playing a game with him.

As soon as their guests disappeared inside their rooms, Gene grabbed Jackie by the hand and pulled her inside the library to have a look at the Forbes magazine article about the fake Armstrong family. The bigger picture inside showed Gene, Jackie, Susan and Jobi, standing out on the big front porch, surrounded by columns.

The other photos included Gene and Susan in the pool with the words stating, "Father and daughter having fun." Another photo showed Jackie and Jobi riding horses. Jackie read out loud about their wonderful made-up life. "The feds make it look and sound so real."

"They do their homework." Gene couldn't take his eyes off his wife in the pool, wearing her little red bikini. "Where's that girl?" he said, mostly to himself. Susan had heard him when she slipped up behind him and looped her arms around his neck.

"Your girl's right here, Dad!"

Gene patted her smooth hands and pulled her around on his lap. "Come here, darling. Wow! Little short shorts with a matching halter top. Tempting!"

Susan giggled and glanced down at the magazine in his spare hand.

"We got in Forbes magazine? When and where did they take those pictures?"

"The feds are very sneaky, sweetheart. The porch photo is when we were saying goodbye to the Blackwells, the pool shot is the morning we went swimming after M.N. came calling and the photo of Jackie and Jobi is when we were coming back from our picnic." Gene ran his hand up her leg and smiled into her eyes. "Boy, you feel good, darling. Speaking of M.N., how much longer will she be around?"

"One more day, handsome, and I'm all yours!" Susan stopped talking when the library door opened and Henning walked in.

"A little big to be sitting in Daddy's lap, aren't you, dear?" The serious fed brought out a chuckle from Scott as he pulled Susan tighter.

"What do you want, Henning?"

"I took the liberty of asking the Blackwells if Toby would be joining us, since you did not notice the young man's absence."

"Oh, I noticed, Henning. I just didn't care." Gene hugged

Susan, then looked back up at the frowning agent. "Well, don't keep us in suspense, Henning. What did they say?"

"Toby Blackwell will be arriving sometime later today. It appears the young man had guests of his own to see off." The secret agent rolled his eyes in aggravation. "You really need to let up on that young man. He may tell Jessica things that could help crack this case."

"Listen, I won't sit back and watch that jackass flirt and put his filthy hands all over my wife!" Scott lifted Susan gently up from his lap and stood up, towering over the agent. "That's not going to happen, damn it!" Gene stopped, sensing the presence of someone, then caught movement at the door as Hal and Eric peeked inside.

"Hal, Eric, are you fellows ready to go to my office for a little business?" Gene Scott's smile was contagious, and both men broke into their own big grins. "I say we get this business over with so we can start having fun for the remainder of your visit."

"That sounds good, Julien." Hal Blackwell looked down at Susan as he continued to speak to the tall preacher, "You're my kind of man, my friend. Business before pleasure." His hand reached for Susan's. "And you, my dear Jessica, do these old eyes proud. It's a pleasure to see you again."

"Thank you, sir, that's most kind. It's good to see you as well." Susan stepped up close to her handsome husband. "Mr. Henning tells us your son Toby will be joining us later this evening."

"Yes, my dear. Toby will be arriving around dinner time. Believe me, sweet Jessica, nothing will keep my son from coming." Hal turned to his brother-in-law and motioned toward the shapely young woman. "Jessica, I'd like you to meet Toby's uncle and my terrific brother-in-law, Eric Robinson."

"It's a pleasure to meet you, Mr. Robinson." Susan extended her hand and watched as the stranger lifted her hand to kiss.

"It's very nice to meet you, Jessica. Toby's description of

you was perfect. A vision of beauty! A goddess!"

"Thank you for your lovely comments, sir, but I fear they're overstated." Susan reached for Gene's hand and he squeezed it softly as he smiled down into her beautiful face.

"My very beautiful daughter has received many such compliments in her short lifetime, and her inward beauty keeps her sweet and humble." Gene hugged her as he smiled at Katherine and her sister when they walked in dressed for croquet. "Ladies, I see you're ready to take on my lovely wife and daughter."

"Oh yes, Julien. We're ready to play and win." Katherine batted her false eyelashes at Gene. "Not to brag, darling, but croquet is a game we both excel at. Right, Emily?"

"Katherine dear, I must warn you and Emily; I always play to win!" Susan pulled Jackie up from her chair. "Come along, Mom. Let's show these women what we've got!"

They all laughed as the four women walked out on the west lawn, where the gardener had the game set up. Gene Scott watched with pride as his smart little wife led the women to the starting rings. He motioned for the men to follow him down the hall to his office.

"This way, gentleman." Scott waited for the fake butler to open the office door before tapping him on his shoulder. "Henning, we don't want to be disturbed while we're in our meeting. Understand?"

"Yes, sir! I will keep the staff preoccupied at the south end of the house. Now, if you will excuse me, I shall take my leave." The fake butler walked down the hall and disappeared around the corner where he slipped inside a locked room and dialed a secret number. The federal agent on the other end sipped on his coffee as he said,

"McLeod here! Go ahead, Henning."

"Sir, Scott is inside his office with the suspects at this very moment doing business. Now we can find out if he's as good as our men reported."

"About time! Now keep that bunch of workers busy while

we listen to how the big man handles crooks!" Stanley McLeod hung up the receiver and motioned for his men to listen closely.

Chapter Sixteen

Scott pulled out an expensive box of cigars and held them across the large mahogany desk.

"Gentlemen, would you care for a smoke?" Taking one himself, Gene lit it and took a big puff, filling the room with smoke and aroma. Both other men took a cigar also and lit them smiling.

"Julien, very good choice! Cuban, the very best!" Gene waited for both men to inhale their expensive smokes before speaking.

"Now, tell me a little bit about how this diamond deal will go through. I buy only the very best choice stones, gentlemen."

"And we can guarantee that's exactly what you'll buy from us, Julien." Eric Robinson flipped his ashes in a large gold ashtray dominating the middle of the desk. "We offer our diamonds three ways: fresh from the mines, raw and uncut; stones that have been cleaned and ready to cut; or for fine gentlemen like yourself, Julien, diamonds that are cut to perfection."

"Perhaps if I showed you a small example of what I desire in a diamond, it may help you with the choices you have." Gene stood up and walked over to a wall safe, then dialed in the code. He pulled out a royal-blue box filled with beautiful diamonds, some real and some perfect imitation stones. He opened the box and turned it around so they could view the selection. With a smooth hand, Gene pulled out the largest real diamond and handed it to Eric.

"This is just a small drop in the bucket of my holdings, my friends. I can't see traveling with a lot of priceless stones when my plan is to find a seller like you." Gene chuckled, knowing that his holdings back home were really a big mortgage on their large farmhouse, property and two beautiful twins. "I keep my largest collection back home in my big vault."

"Julien, I haven't seen a better collection anywhere." Eric passed the large diamond to his brother-in-law to examine. "Magnificent—wouldn't you agree, Hal?"

"This is exquisite, my friend!" Hal handed the large diamond back to Scott as his eyes scanned the blue box, placed under a bright light to help bring out the sparkling diamonds, faked or real. Gene quickly replaced the real diamond and closed the lid as he listened to the diamond thief bragging, "This helps us know what you are after, Julien. I can assure you, we won't disappoint you as the crook who sold you one fake diamond did."

Scott looked up and chuckled. "You spotted it! Great! I just needed to know if you could tell real diamonds from fakes, gentlemen." Scott replaced the blue box inside the safe to keep them from spotting more fakes as he continued, "The thing you need to know, gentlemen, is that I'm highly educated when it comes to diamonds, so I trust you'll never push a fake on me."

The listening feds stared at one another as one rookie spoke up, "I just knew the gig was up when that Blackwell spotted that fake diamond, but Scott came back just on the spot."

"You can trust us, my friend," Hal said.

"Yes, Hal, I believe I can." Scott walked back to the desk and took his cigar from the ashtray and took a puff before continuing, "I'm sure your prices will be in line with my other distributors, gentlemen."

"I think you'll be pleased, Julien. We have our price list right here, broken down in ounces, carats and pounds." Eric pulled the price list out and handed it to the preacher.

Gene looked over the prices as he thought to himself, *Rev. Gene Scott could not afford one ounce of this but...Julien Armstrong can.* He laid the paper down and put out his hand. "Hal, Eric, I'm ready to do business. These prices are very reasonable." Gene about choked on his smoke as he forced himself to continue, "Now that we agree on the selling price, gentlemen, could you tell me about your mining business and how many mines you own?"

Stanley McLeod felt sweat run down his face as he listened to Scott. He mumbled, “Damn it, Scott, don’t push them!”

“Scott sounds mighty sure of himself!” Herbert Vance swallowed nervously. “What if they grow suspicious and check him out?”

“Get quiet, both of you! It just might work! Scott’s no fool!” Bennet Smith moved nervously in his seat as he leaned in to hear better.

“We own seven mines at the moment, but we’re working on purchasing what would be our biggest and best mine.” Hal sat up. “Our resources tell us it’s the best vein of rich diamonds Africa can offer. I must get that land!”

“So you travel around, find mountains with diamonds on private property and buy the land from an individual owner?” Scott leaned back in his chair. “You’d think the poor shmuck would mine the mountain himself and get rich.”

“Julien, you’re priceless.” Hal Blackwell patted the table as he laughed. “The owners know nothing about the diamonds being in their hills and we certainly don’t tell them. We offer to buy the land for a development or a business.”

“I assume you pay the idiot a good price for such a land grab.” Gene Scott did not change his position as he folded his hands behind his head and smiled.

“We think it’s a fair price.” Eric laughed

“This last owner, I take it, doesn’t want to sell his land.” Scott’s voice remained calm and relaxed.

“We have ways to persuade him, my friend.” Hal crossed his legs and took a puff of his short cigar. “I *WILL* get that land, one way or the other.”

“Hal, Hal, my friend, tell me you wouldn’t stoop to murder to get what you want.” Gene chuckled as Hal Blackwell’s eyes grew large.

“Murder? I can assure you, Julien, I personally would never snuff out some old fool’s life.”

“That’s good to hear, my friend.” Scott’s smiled was contagious, bringing smiles to both Hal and Eric. “I don’t think

I could do business with a murderer. This old geezer who refuses to sell his land—does he have any family or is he all by himself?"

"He has a daughter. The best part is the old fart has shacked up with a young African woman from the Bouta Barga tribe. I'll say one thing for the old man; he still has what it takes to make a woman happy."

"Damn! It'd be a shame to kill off that old man!" Scott laughed loudly. "He still has a spark of life in him. You say he wants to hold onto that *worthless* piece of land?"

"Julien, Julien, you're a breath of fresh air!" Eric Robinson stretched out his stiff legs. "Most of our clients are all business, but you're a pleasure to be around."

"Likewise and if you can't get through to the old goat, give me a try. I've never met anyone I can't persuade to see my point of view." Scott stood up and stretched his arms over his head. "Damn if I'm not getting hungry for lunch!"

"That sounds terrific, friend! My breakfast seems to be a past memory as well." Hal stood up laughing. "And I may just take you up on your offer about talking to that stubborn jackass."

"Anytime, anywhere, friend. Just speak the word." Gene walked over and opened the door. "Let's go see if our women have finished their game." He led the way to the sliding glass doors.

Bennet Smith looked around at his companions, who all sat shaking their heads in disbelief. "Shit, that Scott is good! He just about cracked this case with one meeting!"

"It did get a little hairy for a while." McLeod ran his fingers through his thick red hair. "I just knew he was about to blow it." He looked over at his quiet friend, who sat staring at the speaker phone. "Herbert, are you speechless?"

"That was the darnedest thing I've ever heard! Scott almost had me convinced he was Julien Armstrong!" Vance stood up and wiped off his sweating brow. "No wonder headquarters insisted on Rev. Scott! You'd never guess that man was a Bible-toting minister!"

"And God willing, he might even be able to save Dr. Rogers." Stanley McLeod put his head in his hands.

The four women walked through the double glass doors. Susan and Jackie were laughing, while Katherine and Emily were looking at one another, shaking their heads in disbelief. The sisters spotted their handsome host, and Katherine walked up, smiling.

"Julien, your wife and daughter are too great a match for us. Your Jessica made perfect hits every time!"

"Maybe you're just out of practice," Gene teased as he winked at Susan. "I guess you found out my pretty wife and my little girl always play to win, even when they're brave enough to challenge me."

"Don't most women play to win, my friend?" Hal laughed as his eyes fell on Susan. "Tell me, Jessica, how long have you been playing croquet?"

"Oh, just today, Mr. Blackwell, but I catch on fast when it comes to games, right, Dad?" Susan laid her head over on Gene's chest and his arms went around her.

"A quick learner, that's for sure." Gene took both Susan's and Jackie's hand and looked over at his guests smiling. "Is everyone ready to eat lunch?"

"That rousing game did make me hungry." Susan glanced up into her husband's blue eyes and his smile grew mischievous.

"I can think of a few other rousing games!" Gene added.

Jackie laughed softly as she looked at the small group, sensing their growing discomfort over Gene's statement, while looking down at his "daughter".

"Julien Armstrong, you're such a tease! Always picking with Jessica!" Jackie's beautiful smile and calming words made them relax. "Pay him no mind. He can be a handful." She took a firm grip on Scott's hand as she added, "Megan and

Edgar have set up a beautiful luncheon for us outside. Shall we go out to the rose garden?"

"That sounds marvelous, as long as there are no flies or mosquitoes invited." Hal took his wife's arm as he looked down toward the stables. "Where do you suppose those kids are?"

"I can assure all of you Mr. Ward will take good care of them. He's excellent with children." The group stopped when they arrived at the rose garden to find the table set and torches lit to ward off any unwanted insects. "Mr. Ward knows to take Richi and Randy onto the small sunporch at noon to have their lunch. Cook has set them up in there."

"Name cards?" Emily smiled at the formal setting. "I prefer them. There's no question where to sit."

Jackie returned her smile, knowing the place cards were Gene's idea. He wanted to be sure Susan was seated beside him so he could watch her. Taking her chair beside Scott, she gathered her napkin in her lap as she spoke,

"I hope you enjoy home cooking: fried chicken, potato salad, pimento cheese sandwiches and refreshing iced tea, perfect for this heat."

"I love the simple things in life." Katherine's eyes were glued on Gene before gazing over at the huge fan. "Like this big fan, placed here to help cool us off." She sighed. "Our cook's always preparing gourmet meals. This is a pleasant change, just like the owner of this southern plantation house."

"My wife doesn't hide her feelings, Judith. Katherine finds your husband exciting," Hal said.

"Julien's a very, very exciting man, Hal. I've learned to live with the fact that women find him irresistible." Jackie glanced over at Susan who was giving Katherine the evil eye. "Unlike our Jessica there. She's very protective when it comes to her father and his affection. Aren't you, dear?"

"Yes, I am, Mother! Women are always throwing themselves at my dad!" Susan picked up her chicken leg and ripped her teeth into it and managed to add, "He loves me! And he loves Mom and Richi! His family comes first with him!"

"Yes, you do, darling." Gene pulled her head over and kissed it. "Let's not go imagining things though. I don't think Katherine has plans to attack me right here in front of my friend Hal."

"Of course, I have no intention of going after your father, my dear." Katherine Blackwell had turned red from the young woman's objections. "I know Julien's a happily married man and I'm very happily married to Hal. I just admire a good figure of a man, like some people admire a beautiful painting."

"My sister was never known for holding her tongue, Jessica. She's always been very outspoken." Emily wiped her mouth as she smiled over at her sister. "If she thinks it, she says it. I do believe this is the first time she's been called out because of a remark."

"Alright, Katherine, at least you're honest." Susan forced a smile. "I forgive you." Susan felt Gene pat her knee gently, a sign that he approved her words. "What are you planning after lunch, Dad? I take it your business is completed."

"Our business meeting went well, so now it's time for adventure." Gene winked at his wife. "If everyone feels like me, after this big lunch, I say a nap is in order. Then we can change for horseback riding. Any takers?"

All the guests agreed it was a great plan as Hal said, "Couldn't sound any better!"

"Great! Judith and I will meet you in the grand hall around 2 p.m." Scott stood up and stretched. "A short nap, then we're off to the races!" Everyone laughed, then departed to their rooms. Gene pulled Susan aside before she went down the hall to her room.

"Honey, I'll come to your room after everyone else is settled in. There's something I need to tell you and I think it's good news."

"Granddad?" Susan's heart skipped a beat when he nodded an excited positive. "Do hurry, sweetheart!" She raced down the hall and slipped behind her bedroom door.

Gene waited until the coast was clear. He turned to see Jackie had stretched out on her bed and was sound asleep. He slipped quietly out and walked quickly to Susan's room. She asked breathlessly when he stepped inside,

"Tell me, darling, everything you know!"

"Susan, your granddad's alive. Blackwell has him hidden somewhere. If they trust me as much as I think they do, they'll take me to him." Gene pulled her into his warm embrace as happy tears ran down her cheeks. Then Susan looked up into his beautiful blue eyes, her mind full of questions,

"Why are they taking you, Gene? Did you ask them about Granddad? Maybe they plan to lay a trap for you—hide you away with Granddad!" She grew agitated. "What if they're playing along just to trap you?"

"Susan, you should know by now I'm a pretty good judge of character and these land-stealing bastards are pretty easy to read. I have them convinced Big Julien can talk that old man into seeing things my way." Gene looked at her seriously. "Besides, you know your old man can take care of himself, darling."

"Oh, Gene! I'd just die if something happened to you!" Susan clung to him. "And what about the feds—how will they know if Blackwell takes you?"

"The feds know pretty much everything that goes on around here, Susan. My office is bugged and the agents heard everything we said." Gene chuckled. "The guest bedrooms are bugged and I wear a special hidden mic when I'm around Blackwell. Also bugged are the roof tops, the bars, the stables, the guest houses, the pool and the tennis court, rose garden, kitchen, dining room and pretty much every room in this big plantation house. We are never alone!"

Susan looked around the room nervously as she whispered, "Not our bedroom, Gene? Please tell me the F.B.I. agents haven't heard us make love!"

Gene chuckled as he pulled her into his arms. "No, my beautiful sexy wife, I'd kill them first! Our time for turning the federal department on is over. I set my limits and our time together won't be entertainment to excite a bunch of grown men." He parted his lips over hers in a passionate kiss as he mumbled in her ear, "Tomorrow night we make love, right, darling?"

Susan looped her slender arms around his strong neck. "Tomorrow night, Rev. Scott, I will be waiting for you, wearing nothing but a smile and one hot body!"

"God, Susan, you're turning me on!" Gene Scott could feel himself getting aroused. "I'd better get back and get dressed for horseback-riding. Will you be riding with us, sweetheart?"

"I'd just be the seventh wheel, Gene. Besides, I promised Jobi I'd meet his friend Randy at the pool." Susan reached up and kissed his waiting lips. "Don't let flirty Katherine ride beside you." She pulled out her red bikini and laid it on the bed.

"The little red bikini?" Gene pulled her into his arms. "Let's hope Toby doesn't arrive early while I'm away and catch you in the pool." Gene's lips melted over hers for one long kiss. "If for any reason the little weasel does show up, don't let him touch you, sweetheart." He ran his fingers over her breasts. "These beauties are mine!"

"Yes, they are, Rev. Scott!" Susan laughed. "I'm a big girl. I can take care of a wolf."

"Good! I'm counting on you, sweetheart." Gene winked at her as he slipped out the door.

Chapter Seventeen

The couples rode their horses down the prepared trails until Gene stopped his lead horse and looked up the mountain trail that overlooked the valley and the place where they'd seen the Blackwell's villa. Pretending the trail was new to him, Gene turned around in his saddle to speak to the ones behind him, "I haven't tried this trail yet, but my ranch foreman tells me your villa can be seen somewhere up there across the valley."

"Would it be in that direction, Hal?" Katherine called from the back, where she was riding with the ladies. Hal looked up the hill and scratched his head.

"Could be, I suppose. I get turned around in the jungle. Everything looks the same. There are hills across from the villa. Let's ride up and check it out; if there's a villa on the far hill, I'll know if it's ours."

"Everyone ready to explore a new hill?" Gene turned his black stallion and started up the hill, calling back to the three women, "Tom Ward's been up here, ladies, and he'd have warned us if it weren't safe, so you can relax."

Jackie smiled to herself, knowing it was the same path they'd taken the day of their picnic. As they reached the top, the women decided not to venture up further to the highest point, so the three men left their horses below with the other horses and climbed up the steep path to the clearing. Looking across the valley, Eric pointed out the villa on the far hill.

"Look, Hal, that's yours alright, pool on the right and tennis court on the far left."

Gene noticed what he didn't see…any sign of Toby Blackwell. He glanced over at Hal Blackwell who had squinted his eyes, trying to focus in on the distant house.

"Is it your place, Hal?" Gene knew it was but he acted dumb.

You really need field glasses to see it clearly, but there's no mistaking it. That's our house alright. Small world."

"Damn! Business partners and next-door neighbors!" Scott slapped his back, nearly knocking him over. "You're right, it's a small world after all!" They looked a while longer and then rejoined the ladies.

Susan smiled at Jobi when she saw him and his new friend splashing each other in the pool. She sat down on the side of the pool and put her feet in the water.

"Looks like you two are hitting it off."

"Sis!" Jobi swam over, Randy close behind. "Randy, this is my sister, Jessi."

"Hi, Randy. I think you saved my brother from going crazy around all the adults. He may be fifteen but he's still a kid!" Susan flashed her beautiful smile. "How about you, Randy—having fun?"

"Yes, ma'am, Richi's the greatest!" Randy beamed. "We like doing the same things and he's really cool."

"Come on, sis, we're about to dive off the diving board. I told Randy what a great diver you are, winning an award and everything." Jobi climbed up the steps out of the pool and walked up the tall ladder. Looking down he saw Susan and Randy chatting. "Hey, sis, come on! Whatcha' waiting for?"

"Coming, Jobi!" As Randy climbed out of the water, Susan noticed he had on an old-timey swimsuit like boys wore in the twenties. She followed behind him, wondering where he found one in such perfect condition. "Randy, where did you find that vintage swimsuit? That's really heavy."

"You recognized my old suit! That's really cool, Jessi." Randy stepped to the side of the ladder and motioned Susan forward. "You may go first, Jessi. I'm glad you like my swimsuit. You'll see me wearing lots of old clothes and caps. I really dig old dudes."

"That's really artistic of you and quite refreshing in a young person." Susan walked to the end of the diving board and started to jump when she noticed movement on the side of the pool.

"Wow, Jessica, you look enticing!" Toby stood smiling in his swim trunks. "The downstairs maid told me I could find you here."

"Did she?" Susan knew Randy was waiting to dive, and she could tell her brother was growing inpatient wanting her to jump.

"Come on, sis, Randy's waiting!"

"I'm coming! I'm coming!" Susan closed her eyes and dove into the water. When she came up to the surface, she stared into Toby Blackwell's green eyes.

"Beautiful dive, Jessi." He smiled, "Aren't you glad to see me?"

"Sure, Toby. I'm sorry if I seemed surprised. We were expecting you later, that's all." Susan started swimming, Toby right behind her. When she reached the steps, she climbed out, grabbed her towel and wrapped it around her. She looked out at her brother and his friend playing, trying to avoid Toby's stare. "I'm watching these kids while our folks are on a horseback ride. They should be back any moment."

"Oh? Your daddy's not here?" Toby's eyes scanned her body. "Need any suntan lotion rubbed on you, sweetheart? I'm really good at putting it on in just the right places."

"I bet you are." Susan kept her attention on the kids, splashing around. "Your cousin's really been good for my brother."

"Randy's a neat kid, but I can be good for you too, Jessi, if you give me a chance." Toby took her hand and turned her around to face him. "They're fifteen, Jessi; they don't need constant care. All I'm asking is a chance to show you just how good we could be together."

"Toby, I told you about my boyfriend, and I really am in love with him." Susan pulled her hand free and wrapped her towel tighter. "I'm sure a good-looking guy like you has plenty of women hanging around."

"I have my share of women, Jessi, more than I need." Toby

didn't take his eyes off of her. "But they're not the ones I want, Jessi. I want you!"

"Why, Toby? You hardly know me." Susan looked up toward the house for any sign of Gene, but no one was in sight. "You only saw me one time. You can't be serious."

"Call it love at first sight. I really want you, Jessi, more than I've ever wanted anyone." Toby put his arm around her. "Just give me some hope here, Jessi."

"Toby, I don't really know you." Susan tried to laugh, but her voice shook. "You really don't know me."

Toby was getting upset as he grabbed Susan. "I KNOW ALL I NEED TO KNOW AND I KNOW I LOVE YOU!" he said loudly. Jobi looked over at the scene and realized his sister was in trouble. He swam quickly over and climbed out. When he reached them, he knocked Toby's arm off his sister.

"Leave my sister alone! She already has a boyfriend, Toby, and he's very jealous!" Jobi could tell Susan was frightened, so he continued to talk, "Her boyfriend's really strong, Toby, and we think he's coming anytime, man!"

"Cousin Toby, maybe you'd better forget Miss Jessi if she already has a boyfriend." Randy had joined the excited group. "Besides, you just met her."

"What does a kid know?" Toby frowned. "I'm not afraid of this so-called boyfriend."

"Oh, he's real, Toby, and he's not far away!" Jobi prayed Rev. Scott would show up and put a stop to this. "Can't you just be friends with my sister like me and Randy?"

"Sure, kid. I can start out as her friend." Toby looked into Susan's scared eyes. "But sooner or later, I *will* have you." He pulled her into his arms making the towel come loose and fall to the pavement. "How about one little kiss, sweetheart?"

"How about you getting your damn hands off my woman!" Gene Scott picked up Toby and threw him in the pool. Susan ran into Gene's arms and he held her tight as he stared down at the brazen young man. "Maybe that'll cool you off, asshole!"

"Julien, what's going on here?" Hal walked up and saw his

son in the pool staring angrily at the big man. "Toby, are you fooling around again, son?"

"Man, you're sick, really sick! Your woman? You'd think Jessi's your lover instead of your daughter!"

"What I choose to call my daughter is none of your damn business!" Gene's eyes shot fire. "Nobody gropes my daughter! Did she invite you to touch her?"

"No sir, she did not!" Randy looked disappointed in his cousin who had girls willing to welcome his advances. "Jessi told Toby she has a boyfriend. Richi told him how strong her boyfriend is." Randy looked at Scott. "Gosh, Mr. Armstrong, you're really strong too."

Gene looked down at the odd-looking bathing suit and smiled at the wide-eyed kid.

"Yes, I am, Randy, and I did warn Toby to keep his hands off of her."

"Julien, I don't know what to say." Hal Blackwell stared at his son, still giving Gene the evil eye.

"May I suggest you have a long talk with your son and straighten his little ass up! Your family has access to almost everything on my plantation, but damn it, my daughter's off limits!" Gene picked up Susan's towel and wrapped it around her shoulders, then pulled her toward the house, calling over his shoulder, "Richard, get your butt in the shower and get dressed for dinner. This conversation is over!"

After Scott and Susan were behind her door, he took her into his arms and hugged her as he whispered, "Take care of wolves, can you?"

Susan clung to him, feeling safe at last. "I thought Toby was coming later. He slipped up on me."

"Well, that's it! I'm calling Pogo. He's the only one I can trust with you." Gene looked into her luminous blue eyes. "We need a boyfriend for Jessi."

"How long will that take?" Susan took a deep breath. "It took us days to get here."

"I was Rev. Scott then. I'm richer-than-shit Julien Armstrong now." Gene chuckled, "I'll bring him here on my private jet if the feds want me to continue with this scam."

"In the meantime, what about Toby? He'll be here for three more days and expect me to entertain him all day tomorrow." Susan sat down on the edge of her bed. "What can I do?"

"I won't let you out of my sight, darling. Trust me, I'll be keeping watch over you!" Scott ran his hand over her hair. "Where I am, you'll be right beside me, Susan."

Susan stood up and threw her arms around his neck. She knew she'd be safe in Gene's arms.

Gene Scott walked into his shared room and pulled off his boots. He reached for the phone and dialed his home number.

After five rings, he mumbled, "Pogo, pick up that phone!" After the seventh ring, Gene heard the familiar voice of his young friend, "Scott residence."

"Pogo?" Gene relaxed in the big chair. "I was beginning to think you'd gone off, buddy."

Pogo laughed, "Scott! I was out back. What's up?"

"I need you, Pogo—I need you to come to Africa!" Gene waited for a response.

"Yeh, sure, Scott! You know I'll come if I can help you, man!" Pogo fell into the kitchen chair. "How can I help you?"

"I need someone I can trust with Susan to play her boyfriend." Gene stood up and started pacing the floor. "You're the only one I can trust, pal."

"That's true, you know you can always trust me, Scott. I'm not ready to die," Pogo teased. "Some dude flirting with your woman?"

"The son of the target I'm after!" Scott watched Jackie walk out of her dressing room wearing a long black dress, smiling over at him as she sat down and started brushing her dark hair. Gene returned the smile and continued with his conversation, "Pogo, I know this is asking a lot, but can you leave in a few hours? There'll be a private jet picking you up at TarSa Airport."

"A…sure, Scott. Will someone call me with the time?" Pogo picked up a picture of Gloria and closed his eyes.

"Yes, they'll call you as soon as they know their schedule. Now listen to the feds, Pogo. They'll fill you in on who you are and everything there is to know about your character, including the relationship between Jessica—that's Susan—and you." Gene turned his back to Jackie so she couldn't hear his next remark, "Pogo, I trust you, buddy. Don't let me down."

"Damn, Scott, you know I'd never do anything to hurt you!" Pogo looked at the photo of Gene and Susan hanging over the fireplace mantle. "I love you, man. You can trust me."

"That's my Pogo! Thanks, buddy." Gene felt relieved. "God bless you with safe travels, and, Pogo, I love you too, buddy." Gene hung up after saying goodbye and rested his hand behind his head.

"Julien Armstrong, you'd best get a shower and dress for dinner. You wouldn't want Toby to beat you to the table, would you?" Jackie gave a soft laugh when the preacher jumped out of his chair. "Wear your black silk pants and shirt tonight and we'll be the most glamorous *married* couple in the room."

"Jackie, we'd be the best-looking couple in that room with overalls on." Gene slumped his shoulders, feeling depressed. The thought of Toby being anywhere near Susan was on his mind.

Jackie walked over and straightened him up as she said, "Gene, get happy! Tomorrow night you can make love to your wife. Soon that young man will be just a bad memory, but you'll have Susan's love forever!"

"That's right, Mrs. Armstrong! Susan loves her old man!" Gene winked and walked swiftly to his dressing room.

Chapter Eighteen

Pogo picked back up the phone and dialed the Weber Mansion. The butler answered on the second ring, "Weber residence. Who are you calling?"

"Johnson, may I speak to Gloria? Tell her Dave is calling." Pogo thumped the desk with his fingers while he waited.

"One moment, sir. Miss Weber must have heard the ring. She is coming this way." Pogo smiled when he heard her footsteps coming quickly, then the butler's smooth serious voice, "Miss Weber, Dave is on the phone. Would you care to speak"—Gloria grabbed the telephone from his hand—"I take that as a 'yes.' Please excuse me."

"Thank you, Johnson, you may be excused." Gloria watched the stiff butler walk slowly away. Then she lifted the receiver to her ear as she said softly, "Dave? You're calling me early. Is everything alright?"

"Gloria, can you come over now?" Pogo closed his eyes, knowing it wouldn't be easy telling the woman he loved he had to leave for Africa in a few hours. "Scott called. He needs me in Africa. I'm leaving anytime."

"I'll be there!" Gloria's heart began beating with agony. "I love you!" She hung up the phone and dashed out the door.

Pogo was waiting when Gloria drove up. She jumped from the car and ran into Pogo's waiting arms. He hugged her tightly, the thought of leaving her tearing at his heart.

"Gloria, my darling, I couldn't tell him 'no.' He needs me."

"Of course, you have to go, Pogo." Tears filled her green eyes. "Now I know how Susan felt when Daddy sent Gene away."

"A federal agent called me with instructions to be at the airport in two hours." Pogo pulled the beautiful redhead inside the house and shut the door. "He told me just to pack my personal things since they'd have clothes for me. I'll be a college man, training to be a doctor and I'm rich!" Pogo laughed at the idea, knowing he was as poor as a church mouse. "I guess it's a good thing I can act."

"Oh, Pogo, you'll do great!" Gloria held him tightly. "I'll miss you every single second, my darling." She pulled away, suddenly realizing when he returned, their alone time in the farmhouse would be over. "Oh, Pogo, darling, when you come back, Gene and Susan won't be far behind you. When…when will I see you?"

"Don't worry, sweetheart, you'll be the first person I see when I get back, not to mention the fact that Gene and Susan will be taking an ocean liner home…a gift from Dr. Rogers." Pogo pulled Gloria back into his arms. "After that, we'll find somewhere we can be alone. But for now, I'm packed and ready to go. All I need right now is you, Gloria. I need to make love to my girl."

"My dearest Pogo, I need to make love to my man just as much. It will be something to hold onto until you come back to me." Taking his hand, Gloria followed the man she loved for a passionate hour of beautiful unforgettable sex.

Pogo and Gloria lay wrapped in each other's arms, breathing heavily after their intense lovemaking. He caressed her face lovingly in his hands.

"I need to lock away your beautiful face in my mind and heart. How can I leave you, Gloria? I can't get enough of you. I love you so much!"

"It's going to be hard for me too, Pogo." Gloria ran her soft hand down his tanned chest. "I could stay right here in your arms forever. God, Pogo, I love you!" Gloria reached up and kissed him, dreading the moment he must leave. She looked up into his eyes with a sweet serious calm and said, "Gene and Susan need you, darling. They wouldn't have called otherwise."

"I know, Gloria. I know I have to go. Thank you for

understanding and caring about their welfare. They're the only family I have." Pogo sat up and ran his fingers through his thick brown locks. "I owe that man everything! Scott saved me and cared for me when I had no one." He glanced out the window in thought as he added, "And he loves me."

"And you love him. I know that, my darling." Gloria pulled him up. "Get a shower; then I'll drive you to the airport. I know you'll come back to me! I know you love me!" She hugged him, tears filling her eyes. "Pogo, it's because I love you so that I'm going to let you go without begging, without a childish tantrum that I used to use in the past to get my way. I'll be here when you get back, darling, waiting. I promise!"

"I'm really glad you came into my life, Gloria Ann Weber!" With tears in his eyes, Pogo kissed her, then walked to the shower.

After a light breakfast the following morning, the Armstrongs and Blackwells decided to spend some time at the pool. Gene sat at the foot of Susan's bed while she pulled her bikini bottom over her shapely hips. He smiled at her cute behind, then stood up.

"Let me help you with that top, darling." He took the blue top and threw it over his shoulder as his hands moved gently over her young round breasts. The handsome preacher kissed her neck and whispered in her ear, "I'm looking forward to tonight, Susan." Gene's breathing grew heavy with desire. "God, you feel good, little woman. Shit, I wish that bunch of sunbathers weren't waiting on us!"

As he pressed up against her, Susan could feel Gene's growing arousal from all the caressing and the lack of sex for five days. She closed her eyes feeling her own passion swelling.

"Rev. Scott, if you don't stop fooling around, I won't let you out of this room!"

Gene squeezed his eyes shut, knowing he had to back away before he grew too hot to stop.

"Damn! It would be hard to explain why we're an hour late!"

Susan reached for her bikini top. I need to put this top on now, Gene. You can stay as long as you like tonight, sweetheart."

Gene pulled the bikini top out of her hand and mumbled, "Turn around. I've got this." He tied the string securely in the back, then looked down at his trunks and grunted, "Why does this thing stay up so long?"

"To satisfy me, darling!" Susan reached up and kissed him. "Are you ready for some daddy and daughter fun?"

"Airplane? You betcha!" Gene took her hand and headed down the stairs.

Everyone watched as Gene and Susan walked up the ladder to the diving board. Susan followed Gene off the diving board and when they surfaced, he lifted her up over his head, his muscles drawing attention from the ladies. After he threw her, Susan landed a safe distance from him as Toby watched beside his father.

"That's one weird man! He acts like he has the hots for his daughter!"

"Toby, son"—Hal slapped his son's knee playfully—"Julien just loves his little girl, that's all."

"I love her too, damn it!" Toby frowned when he noticed Gene's hand slide over Susan's breast as he lifted her again. "I *will* have Jessica, one way or the other!"

Hal Blackwell took a firm hold of his son's arm as he spoke quietly, "Look, Toby, Julien Armstrong is a very important client, worth millions. We cannot afford to make him mad! Just forget about that girl!"

"Hell no, old man! Screw your business!" Toby's eyes blazed. "I'll get that woman when the time is right!"

After Gene and Susan climbed out, he rubbed some suntan lotion on her back; then she did the same for him. The ladies watched in envy, but Toby watched them with suspicion. At twelve sharp, Ali walked up to Gene's lounge chair.

"Sir, the lunch has been set out at the large pool table when you're ready. And, Mr. Armstrong, Tom would like a word with you after you've finished eating."

"Of course! Tell Stretch I'll be down later and thank you, Megan." Scott helped Susan up, then Jackie. "Everyone, lunch is ready." Gene led the way to the shaded round table.

They had just started to eat when Pogo walked up, dressed in white slacks and a sky-blue polo shirt. The federal agents had filled him in on everyone's roles in the undercover group. Susan jumped up with excitement and looped her arms around his neck.

"Brian! You came early, darling! We were expecting you next week! What a wonderful surprise!"

"Jessi, you look beautiful!" Pogo returned her hug, knowing his friend wanted their relationship to look authentic. "Boy, have I missed you, sweetheart." He turned and smiled down at Scott. "Julien, sir. It's so good to see you and Judith again. This summer course seemed to take forever, but now I'm free for the rest of the season."

"That will make our Jessi happy, my boy!" Gene got up and walked over to the young couple, who looked like they were madly in love. He put his arms around their shoulders and laughed out. "My friends, isn't this a beautiful couple?"

Toby stared up at Pogo with envy as he spoke softly, "I see you're real. I was beginning to think Mr. Armstrong and Jessica made you up to keep me away."

"Let me guess—you're the fellow who's been after my girl." Pogo smiled down at the bewildered face and put his hand out. Toby reluctantly reached up and took it in a firm handshake. "I can't blame you, man, my Jessi's a perfect prize."

Susan looked down shyly, pretending to be embarrassed. "Brian, sweetheart, I'm sure Toby has many pretty girls wanting his attention."

"There are a few, Jessi"—Toby forced a smile for her—"but none as beautiful as you."

"Yes, my daughter's both smart and beautiful." Gene motioned for Ali, who was carrying a spare chair. "Thanks, Meg. Richi, scoot over closer to Randy so Brian can sit next to his girl." After the couple was seated, Gene continued, "Let me introduce this young man to all of you. Brian Hampton is studying to be a doctor so he can take over for Dr. Fields, who's retiring next year." Still standing, Gene patted Pogo on the back and chuckled, "And if Brian plays his cards right, I just might let him marry my little girl."

"Oh, Dad!" Susan laughed, "Brian is wonderful, and we do plan to get married as soon as he's finished his medical degree. Right, darling?"

"Try and stop me!" Pogo glanced at Scott and found him smiling. "That is, as long as I stay on the good side of her daddy."

"We both love you, dear." Jackie smiled over at Pogo, who returned it. "And I'm certain Jessi's wedding will be the talk of all the papers back home."

Hal bent over and whispered in Toby's ear, "Son, Jessica is spoken for, so give up this foolish idea of you and Jessica."

"My plans are made, Father. Boyfriend or no boyfriend, Jessica Armstrong will be mine!" Toby whispered back, never taking his eyes off the prize.

"We'll discuss this later, Toby." Hal looked disappointed in his hard-headed son.

"Talk all you like, Father. My mind's made up and you won't change it!" Toby reached over to get his food being set in front of him. "She's what I want! I always get what I want!"

Everyone enjoyed the meal and the small talk, all but Toby, who was hatching a plan to get Susan. After the meal was over, Gene Scott stood up and stretched, then smiled at Pogo.

"Brian, go get your swim trunks on, son, and keep your girl happy at the pool. Ladies, you may lounge around the pool a few more hours if you like. Hal, how would you, Eric and Toby like to join me for a doubles tennis match?"

"That sounds great. I've had enough swimming, and

sunbathing's not my thing." Hal put his arm around his son. "Toby, we'll let you pick partners if that's alright with Julien."

Gene laughed, "Sure, but I bet good old Toby wants to kick my ass! It's a sure bet the boy will play against me, right, son?"

"Got that right, Armstrong!" Toby faked a smile. "I pick Uncle Eric. He used to play a lot in college and I'm a champ myself!" His eyes held Gene's coldly. "I'll love beating the crap out of you, sir!"

"Cocky little son-of-a-bitch, aren't you, boy!" Scott smiled, "Well, kid, I play to win at everything! So watch your sweet ass!" Gene turned to see Jobi and Randy staring at him. "I take it you kids want to go ride horses, right?"

"That's right, Dad, although your tennis match sounds like a great spectator event." Jobi knew by the preacher's expression he'd better not push his luck. "The fact is, Dad, we've played with the adults long enough, so riding horses really sounds like a cool idea!"

"Alright, kids, go to your rooms and change, then meet me at the bottom of the steps. I'm heading down to the stables." Gene waited for the teenagers to run toward the house, then turned to the gentlemen waiting. "Fellows, you may go ahead and get ready for tennis, and Henning will show you to the courts while I go have a word with my ranch foreman. I'll be along soon to whip butt!"

Chapter Nineteen

Gene Scott was waiting at the bottom of the steps, dressed for tennis, when Jobi and Randy came bounding down the steps. Gene chuckled.

"I bet you two don't get ready that fast for church or school." He patted the teens' backs and escorted them to the stables where James was giving his two hands their orders. The three new arrivals stopped to listen, unseen by the rude workman or James.

"Listen, Ward, I say it'll do no good to put up a new fence on the north side! The one there is perfectly fine!" Nick Barrow narrowed his angry eyes.

"And I say we do need to, Barrow! Those cross planks are about to rot out!" James argued back as Gene walked up.

"Stretch, what the shit's going on?" Gene sized up Hal Blackwell's undercover goons. "Don't like taking orders, Barrow?"

"No, sir, not when the orders are stupid! Those planks are fine. They're good for another year or so if you ask me!" The rude man spat tobacco juice at Scott's feet, causing the preacher to poke him in his belly.

"First, Barrow, watch where you spit out that shit! Second, no one asked you for your opinion!"

"Mr. Armstrong, these men always think they know more than I do. They're always second-guessing my judgments. All it'd take is one light push and those boards would break in two." James shook his head in defeat.

"Calm down, Stretch! Let me handle them!" Scott moved over in front of the two stable hands and got in their faces, "Listen, fellows, let me make myself clear. If I fire anyone around here, it won't be Stretch! Get it? So I suggest if you don't like taking orders from my man, just pack your shit and get your ass off my property." He gave a little chuckle as he gently patted them on their cheeks. "But, hey, if you want to keep your job, I suggest you get your lazy butts down in the north pasture and fix the damn fence!"

"Yes, sir," they both said in unison as they backed away from the big man and hurried to the wagon, filled with new boards and nails, then drove away in a cloud of dust.

Gene laughed, then looked down at James, more relaxed. "Was there anything else you needed to tell me, Stretch?" The handsome preacher slapped James lightly on his arm, causing him to lose his balance and almost fall.

"Yes, sir, there's one more thing you should know." James spotted the two teenagers standing behind Gene and asked, "I take it you fellows want to ride horses? Go on and pick out two and bring them in the stable so I can put their saddles on." After the young people raced off to find their favorite mounts, James stepped up close to Scott, just in case someone might be hiding nearby and listening. "I rode back up the hill this morning to check things out, seeing as how the Blackwells are here and the workers have been left alone. I saw several people walking around in front of the villa, then someone came from the house, carrying a tray of food and disappeared inside a rock."

"Secret door!" Gene noticed the kids coming toward them with two mares. "That could be where they have Dr. Rogers! Go with Jobi and Randy, say you need to ride up on the hill to check on your ranch hands and make sure they're working. I'll inform Jobi to stay on the main trails with his friend."

"Great! That way if those two spies are watching me, they'll think I'm just escorting a couple of kids!" James smiled at his tall friend. "And, Scott, thanks for taking up for me back there with Barrow. It felt good."

"Sure thing, Stretch!" Gene laughed as he waved for Jobi while James helped Randy with the saddle and told him about his plans to break away from them long enough to check Blackwell's place from the hill. Patting Jobi on his head, Gene added, "And don't go wandering off in the jungle, buddy. I don't have time to make any rescues."

"No sweat, Rev. Scott," Jobi whispered back to his favorite preacher. "Just go beat that loudmouth, Toby, in tennis! I have faith in you and know you'll win, old daredevil Gene!" Jobi laughed and ran off to join his new friend.

Gene walked onto the court and was greeted by Hal and Eric, but Toby had hate in his cold green eyes for the pretend owner of the Armstrong's plantation. Choosing to ignore the angry young man, Gene picked up a racket and twirled it around.

"Is everyone ready?" Scott asked and watched Toby jump over the net so he could face his opponents.

Twisting his head cockily, Toby stated, "I'm ready for you, Armstrong!"

"Good! I like someone who's trying to knock my socks off!" Scott chuckled as he took in his audience. "It's too bad I'm going to knock your damn jockeys off first!"

"Don't count on winning this one, sir." Toby slammed the ball across the net, making a point.

"You caught me off-guard that time, sonny boy, so consider that a lucky point!" Scott turned and smiled at his partner. "Sorry, Hal, but we're about to beat the shit out of your smart-mouth bragging son!" Gene turned so fast that Toby didn't see the ball until it flew past him and made a safe landing.

After three sets, Gene and Hal were patting each other on the back for winning every game. Scott looked at Toby when the rude sore loser slung down his racket, cussing.

"Sorry, kid! Never try to outsmart Julien Armstrong! I always get my man. It'd be wise to remember that!" Gene slapped Hal on his back, catching him before he toppled over into the net. "Way to go, partner! It feels good to win, wouldn't you agree?"

"Yes, it does! I finally whipped my son and I must admit that it feels great!" Hal motioned for his brother-in-law to come over beside them. "Julien, Eric and I've been talking about your offer and we'd love for you to speak to the old goat, Dr. Rogers. You just have a way with words, my friend, and if anyone can convince that hard-headed old man to sell, it's you."

"Hal's right, Julien." Eric Robinson watched his nephew walk away, mumbling to himself. "If the offer still stands, we think you might get that old geezer to listen to reason."

Gene turned his back to them as he put away his racket and smiled triumphantly before turning back around to face them. He looked thoughtful at the two men waiting, then smiled.

"You both really have a lot of confidence in me. You know, I really would like to meet the horny old bastard! He might give me a few pointers on how to keep the sexual drive at such an old age." Gene Scott chuckled with mischief. "I really do enjoy sex. Women feel so damn good!"

"Julien, you're a man after my own heart!" Hal laughed with him. "I can't get enough of them broads!"

As if right on cue, the three men saw the ladies walking toward them. Katherine stopped right in front of the handsome preacher to admire his shorts and legs.

"Who won the games, gentlemen? I put my money on Julien and his partner. I think you'd be good at everything."

"As a matter of fact, Katherine dear, Armstrong and Blackwell senior did win…all three sets." Hal took his wife's arm and smiled at her. "As a matter of fact, your son wasn't happy he lost to us older men."

Emily looked admiringly at Gene and smiled, "Oh dear, poor Toby. First he lost the girl, now the tennis match; but as they say, the best man won."

"The best 'men,' Emily darling." Jackie walked over and hugged Gene, feeling safe with Susan not around. "Julien's good at everything he does! Especially at being a wonderful husband!"

"I think it's time for my shower before dinner." Katherine looked on with envy as she took her sister's hand. "Coming,

Emily?" As they walked to the house, Katherine whispered, "Judith's a lucky lady!"

Chapter Twenty

James stopped his horse when he reached the hill trail. "Kids, I'm going up on that hill to check on my boys, so just stay on the trail. I'll catch you later."

"Sure thing, Stretch." Jobi moved his horse forward as he called back to his friend, "I really like Stretch, but we haven't been able to talk much lately, being around adults all day."

Randy pulled the chestnut mare up beside Jobi. "Yeh, it's better this way! I really like you, Richi. I think you're the best friend I've ever had."

"No fooling! I just bet you have lots of friends, Randy. You're neat!" Jobi smiled proudly, then looked thoughtful as he added, "But it's funny, I feel the same way, Randy. You're my best friend too."

"That's why I think I can tell you my secret, Richi. I trust you." Randy's eyes got big with suspense. "Do you promise never to tell a soul…ever?"

"Sure, Randy, you can trust me…honest." Jobi sat up in his saddle, anxious to hear the secret that made his friend so mysterious.

"I'm afraid, Richi! I'm terrified my parents are doing something wrong!" He looked down, feeling embarrassed. "They don't tell me anything, only that Uncle Hal gave Daddy a wonderful job making lots of money."

"How long has your father been working for your uncle?" Jobi felt sorry for his friend when Randy looked up sadly.

"Only two years, but it seems like a lifetime. Daddy used to work for a good company in America and we had a home, nothing big but it was warm and full of love. I went to my neighborhood school and every Sunday the three of us attended Faith Baptist Church." A tear ran down his cheek. "I was so happy then. Mama was happy because she had a flower garden and a part-time job in the local flower shop while I was in school. Richi, we were a real family and were happy with our life."

"That's why your folks put you in an academy so they could travel, selling diamonds for your uncle." Jobi couldn't understand the strange feelings he was having for Randy and it bothered him a lot.

"I think my uncle Hal is bad, and my cousin Toby will stop at nothing to get what he wants!" Randy reached across and took Jobi's hand. "Richi, if Mama and Daddy go to jail, I'll have no one!"

Jobi felt even funnier when his friend took his hand, and he swallowed back his anxiety. "What about your grandparents, Randy?"

"All four of my grandparents are dead! I'm scared, Richi!"

"Randy, you're my friend! You'll always have me!" Jobi touched his friend's shoulder in a reassuring manner. "I won't let you be alone! My parents will help you if I ask them!" Jobi climbed down off his horse, getting an urgent call to relieve himself. He quickly tied the horse to a tree limb before saying, "Wow! I really have to pee! I forgot to go before we left the house and I drank that big Coke! How about you, Randy?"

"I feel the need to go as well, Richi." Randy got down and secured the mare, then looked up nervously. "But before I go to those bushes, I think there's another secret I should tell you." Randy reached up and removed his hat, revealing a long red ponytail as it fell down.

"You're…you're a girl?" Jobi's eyes grew wide. "That explains why I've been having these feelings."

"Feelings like you really like someone in a special way? Lots of fluttering butterflies in your stomach?" Randy blushed. "I have those same feelings, dear friend." She pulled a plastic bag from her pocket and took out a few tissues before looking up shyly. "I can't pee like you do."

Jobi felt his face flush as he offered to let her go first as he moved around in agony. "I'll watch for you. I'd say take your time, but I don't think I can hold it much longer." He turned toward the horses as she slipped behind some bushes.

After relieving himself, Jobi came out, walked over to the horses and untied them.

"How come your parents named you Randy?"

"They thought they were having a boy and wanted to name me after my Grandfather Randy Turner, Mama's daddy. My middle name is Renee after my grandmother." The cute redhead smiled lovingly at Jobi who took a step closer to her.

"Can…can I kiss you, Randy Renee Robinson?" Jobi was serious as he gently touched her face, glad she was a girl.

"I thought you'd never ask me." She puckered up her lips as she closed her eyes. Bending down slowly, Jobi brushed over her lips with his, causing her to smile, love showing on her young face. "First time, Richi? Let me try." Randy looped her arms around his neck and kissed him tenderly.

Jobi wandered over to his horse in a daze until he felt something happening in his shorts. He reached down to feel when she had her back turned, then swallowed as he thought, *Shit! I have a hard-on. I hope James doesn't notice. I'd get ribbed for sure.* Jobi carefully climbed back up on the horse as he watched Randy put her ponytail back under her hat, then turned to smile at him.

Jobi reached over and took her hand, thinking trust must come both ways in real friendship. He knew in his heart that he could trust her to keep his secret.

"Randy, I have a secret too. If I tell you my secret, you have to promise you'll never tell a soul, not anyone, and that includes your parents, especially your Uncle Hal, Aunt Katherine and your cousin Toby!" Jobi squeezed her hand lovingly. "If you tell anyone, Randy, people I love very much could be in danger. I'm putting my faith in you, Randy Renee!"

"Richi, I promise to keep your secret for as long as I live! Scout's honor!" Her face was sincere as she waited for more.

"My name's not Richard Armstrong; my name's Jobi Andrews." He waited for the girl's reaction.

"Jobi?" her hand trembled. "Then…Jessica isn't your sister? Are you adopted?"

"No, I'm not adopted but Jessi is my sister, only her real name's Susan Scott. She's married." Jobi continued with his revelation, feeling surer of his friend's trust. "Julien Armstrong isn't my father. He's my brother-in-law—Rev. Gene Scott."

"Are you saying he's your sister's husband?" Randy couldn't keep herself from laughing as she said, "No wonder he defended her with his life! How romantic!" she gushed. "And he's a preacher! Dang!"

"A very good preacher and an even better crime-fighter. Rev. Scott is a bad-ass missionary and he doesn't take any bullshit off of anybody!" Jobi bragged.

"So you're saying Rev. Scott and all of your undercover group are here to catch Uncle Hal?" Randy started shaking uncontrollably. "That means…Mama and Daddy could go to jail!"

"Randy, Rev. Scott's a compassionate man under that tough exterior. He'll help you and I'm sure he'll do all he can to help your parents when the feds realize your uncle's the leader of the land steal."

"Uncle Hal has been stealing land from innocent people just to get their diamond mines?" Randy went white. "I knew Uncle Hal could be conniving, but a thief? Dang!"

"Your uncle has my grandfather locked up somewhere. He was kidnapped because he wouldn't sell his ranch to your uncle for pennies! There are twin mountains on his land which must be loaded with diamonds." Jobi looked into the young girl's face, hoping he hadn't spoken out of trust and gotten everyone working on the case in trouble. "Randy, you can't say a single word about this."

"Jobi, I won't tell anyone! I promise!" Randy Renee choked out the words as tears ran down her pretty young face. "I don't want my family to go to jail, but if they've been helping Uncle Hal steal land, then they must be stopped! It's not just man's laws they're breaking; they're breaking God's laws, too!"

Chapter Twenty-One

Everyone came into the dining room for their last meal with their company. Gene and Susan knew what lay ahead after everyone retired for the night. Smiling at his guests, the preacher ran his hand up her leg under the table. She closed her eyes and smiled. Someone called for a toast and Susan heard Scott mumble "shit" under his breath as he pulled his hand away to pick up his glass. Susan picked up her glass with her left hand and placed her right hand down between his legs. Gene jerked up and almost dropped his glass.

"Damn!" he laughed when everyone looked at his sudden reaction. Hal lifted his glass back up as he continued with his toast,

"To Julien and his lovely family, gracious host, good business partner, not to mention a great tennis partner as well and hopefully a long-time friend."

"Thank you, Hal. I think this visit has helped us get acquainted and learn more about each other." Gene took a quick sip, set his glass down and grabbed his wife's hand. Susan smiled up at him as she pulled her hand away.

While waiting for the second course, Gene was making small talk with his guests when he casually placed his hand behind Susan's neck and started rubbing it up and down. To return his affection, Susan started rubbing the inside of his leg. Two seats away, Jobi reached under the table and took Randy's hand, which did not go unnoticed.

Pogo stared at the two boys and blinked, not sure what had just happened. Hearing whispers and the names Jessica and Julien, he turned to see Gene and Susan, obviously unaware that everyone at the table had stopped to observe their actions. To save the night, Pogo reached around Susan's neck and knocked his big friend's hand off. He flinched from Scott's angry look so he forced out his words,

"Hey, Julien, let me rub that cramp out of Jessi's neck so you can eat your salad."

Pogo glanced at Jackie, who mouthed, "Thank you." Then Jackie reached over and patted Gene's cheek.

"Jessi always gets a stiff neck when she stays in the pool too long. Her daddy's always been the one to rub it out and now that Jessi has a doctor for a boyfriend, he's trying to take over the rubbing."

After realizing why Pogo had knocked his hand away, Gene smiled at the interested party.

"What can I say? She's my little girl." He winked at Pogo, making him relax. "I know Brian will be the one rubbing my Jessi's neck after they are married." He looked down lovingly at Susan. "I'm going to miss being there for you, sweetheart."

Susan laid her hand on Gene's shoulder, then smiled at the company. "Dad has me spoiled. He's the best daddy ever, and he knows how to get that cramp out quickly."

"I've had a lot of practice, kiddo"—Gene held up his strong hand and chuckled—"and the hands to work with!" Finally, everyone relaxed and started laughing, then returned to eating their dinner.

After dessert was finished, Gene glanced at Susan and winked as he pushed his chair back and patted his stomach.

"Boy, I don't know about the rest of you, but this has been one busy day. So if it's alright, this big guy will be turning in early. Jump into my pajamas, read till I'm sleepy, then it's good night, sleep tight and don't let the bad bedbugs bite!" Gene's hand ran up Susan's leg as Susan ran her foot up his leg and covered it with a fake yawn.

"I'm pretty sleepy myself, Dad. Too much sun and fun with Brian in the pool." Susan smiled at Pogo. "Hope you don't mind, Brian. I'm just going to go up and slip into my pajamas and turn the lights out."

Another fake yawn escaped her mouth as Gene closed his eyes, knowing soon he'd have her in his arms.

Toby stood up, breaking the moment. "I'll be leaving now too! I know when I've been defeated!" Toby reached his hand across the table to Pogo. "You're a lucky man, Brian. If you ever change your mind, call me!" Pogo shook Toby's hand, then put his arm around Susan.

"Nothing will drive me away from Jessi. I love this woman!"

Toby stared at Susan, taking in her entire body as his voice came out steady and relaxed.

"Jessi, we would've been good together!" He laid his napkin on the table, never taking his eyes away from her. "I'm packed. You don't need to see me out! I'm going back to the villa." Toby turned sharply and stared at Gene as his words came out, dripping with hate. "Thank you, Mr. Armstrong, for your hospitality!" he said as he turned and walked out the door.

Gene's serious eyes stared after him until he was out of sight. Then he took Jackie's hand and forced a smile at his guests.

"If you'll excuse my family, we're going up. You may stay down here as long as you like, and we'll see you in the morning." Gene watched as Hal helped his wife up.

"We need to get to bed early ourselves. Good night to you all."

Gene turned to Jobi who still sat talking to his friend, unaware that everyone else had gotten up from the table.

"Son, go on up to bed!" Gene smiled at Jobi's friend. "You too, kid! Your parents have already gone up. Good night, Randy."

"Good night, Mr. Armstrong. I had a great time." She turned toward the door and ran up the stairs, the thoughts of leaving her friend tearing the young girl in two. After saying a quick good night, Jobi raced up the steps after her.

Pogo followed Gene, Susan, Jackie and Michael to their bedrooms and started pacing the floor. He couldn't get the scene of Jobi and Randy holding hands out of his mind. Gene returned from the bathroom and put his arm around Susan. Noticing his young friend pacing the floor, the preacher chuckled,

"What's up with you, pal? You act like you've been eating jumping beans!"

"Didn't you tell me Randy's a boy?"

"That's right! Randy is Eric and Emily's son." Gene gazed down Susan's top and a smile formed on his lips. "What are you getting at, Pogo?"

"That's what I was afraid of." Pogo started pacing again. This time he had everyone's attention. Scott stared at his friend.

"Pogo, what the shit are you not telling us?"

Having everyone's attention, Pogo swallowed, then said, "I saw Jobi and Randy holding hands under the table!"

"You what?" Susan rushed over and grabbed Pogo's arm. "Are you trying to tell me my brother is…"

Gene took Susan's hand and pulled her around. "Susan, calm down. Michael, get Jobi in here now!" He looked tenderly at his wife. "Let's not jump to conclusions, sweetheart. Let's hear what Jobi has to say."

Michael came in the door with Jobi close behind. He looked around the room at all the questioning eyes. Susan walked straight over to him and gripped his shoulders tightly before asking,

"Jobi, what's wrong with you? Are you trying to give me a heart attack?"

Looking confused by her statement, Jobi backed up and defended himself.

"Hey, sis, what are you talking about?" Jobi looked over at Scott. "Rev. Scott, what's up?"

"You might want to tell us, buddy." Gene pushed the young teen lightly on the bed, then sat down next to him. "Why were you holding Randy's hand under the table?"

"Oh! You saw us." The young man's face turned red as he looked at the faces around the room. "It's not what you think, guys. Randy is a…a…"

"A what, Jobi? A gay?" Susan felt helpless over the situation.

"Gosh no, sis!" Jobi laughed at the very idea. "Randy's a girl!"

And the room's reaction was, "A what!"

"That's right…a girl! A very sweet and pretty girl with long red hair." Jobi looked around at all their relieved faces. "She's afraid for her parents now that she knows what they've done. Randy Renee's a good Christian girl, Rev. Scott, so she wants them stopped before they hurt anybody else!"

Gene Scott looked into the boy's loving eyes and placed his arm around his shoulder.

"You told her, didn't you, Jobi?"

"She trusted me with her secrets, Rev. Scott. I had to trust her, didn't I?" Jobi looked hurt, feeling everyone he loved was questioning his actions. "Sir, Randy really is my friend."

"Jobi, you've got a good heart, son." Gene could read real trust and faith in the young teen's eyes. "You really trust Randy with your secret?"

"Rev. Scott, I can't explain it, but I have a special feeling for Randy Renee and yes, sir, I trust her with all my heart." Jobi looked up at Scott with sincere eyes.

Remembering his own unexplained feelings for Susan on the ship, Gene gave Jobi a warm fatherly hug, then spoke softly, "Alright, buddy, I trust your judgment. Run on to bed and don't worry about this."

"Thank you, Rev. Scott! Thank you for believing in me!" Giving the preacher he admired one more hug, Jobi went out the door, happy the secret was out.

Michael looked down at his big friend, not as sure of the girl's innocence as Jobi and Gene were. He had to voice his opinion,

"So you think this Randy kid is on the up-and-up? She could be a very good little actress. After all, she did pretend to be a boy. She had me convinced."

"Mike, sometimes we have to go on faith. Jobi's a smart young man and I trust his judgment. If you feel uncomfortable about her knowing our identities, keep your eyes on her, but I say the kid's telling the truth." Scott stood up and took Susan to the door and peeked out. "The coast is clear!" He looked back at Pogo, then Michael and Jackie. "You two love birds have two hours to do whatever you do. I'm taking my woman to bed now before someone else throws another curve ball. Pogo, get to bed!" Gene pulled Susan out the door and they went quickly down the hall to her bedroom. Once inside, doors securely locked, he pulled his wife into his arms.

"Tomorrow, sweetheart, my new *friends*"—he rolled his eyes up with sarcasm—"are taking me to talk to your granddad. I think we're about to break this case wide open."

Susan threw her arms around her husband's neck and smiled brightly. "Oh, Gene, that's wonderful! So Hal and Eric really trust you! You are the best!"

"The best at…everything?" Gene pulled her dress over her head.

"Especially this!" Susan undid the buttons on his shirt and pulled it off.

"How about this?" Gene unsnapped her bra and slid it off.

"You do that exceptionally well, Rev. Scott." She unzipped his pants and pushed them down. He kicked them to one side as his eyes held hers. "Looks like we're left with only our undies, handsome!"

"Not for long, beautiful." Smiling, Gene reached down and pulled her dainty bikini panties down. She stepped out of them and kicked them over onto his pants. Slowly, Susan pulled down his boxers and smiled at his complete manhood.

"My, my, Rev. Scott! That's some sexy soldier standing at full attention!"

"You got that right, little darling, and he's ready for some action!" Gene pulled Susan closer in his arms as he kissed her passionately. His kisses fell down her neck as he lifted her off the floor and caressed her nipple with his lips before laying her down on the big bed, kissing her every step of the way. He studied her beauty for a moment, then spoke softly, "Susan, my beautiful Susan! God, how I love you!" Lying across her, Gene filled her with his complete manhood and as promised, his soldier had plenty of action until the cannon fired off in an array of colorful fireworks.

They held tightly to one another as their hearts beat as one. Breathlessly, Gene whispered in her ear, "Susan, my darling Susan, you are so good for me."

"And you, my dearest Gene, always make me feel so sexy and beautiful." Susan ran her fingers up his muscular chest. "You're the very best thing that's ever happened to me."

Gene squeezed her gently as he took a deep breath. "My love, you are sexy, beautiful and smart! That's why this guy can't get enough of your love."

"Maybe it's because we're sleeping in separate rooms that make the days drag by, but those were the longest five days we've ever had to wait." Susan snuggled in Scott's warm embrace and Gene laughed softly.

"Torture, that's what it was, little darling. I guess at home the kids keep us so busy, the days fly by." He looked thoughtful, then forced a weak smile as he confessed, "Well, maybe a little less torture. It's always hard on me."

"Poor baby." Susan reached up and kissed him. "We have a few more weeks before Mother Nature's next visit."

"Good! I'll wear your butt out!" Gene hugged her as he glanced over at the clock. "Speaking of our kids, I bet the little rascals are growing like weeds."

"Oh, Gene, I miss them so much." Susan laid her head over on his shoulder. "Do you think they'll remember us?"

"Susan, darling," Gene chuckled. "Our young'uns will never forget their mama and daddy." Gene sat up and looked at the clock again, then dropped his head against the pillow and mumbled, "Shit! Where did our two hours go?"

"My soldier was busy firing his weapon." They both laughed, then she said seriously, "Gene, you will be careful tomorrow? I want you to save Granddad, but, darling, if anything happened to you, I'd die!"

"Susan," Gene took her face in his hands. "Trust me,

darling! I won't take any stupid chances. I'll be extra careful. You know me, Susan; you know what I'm capable of." He pulled her up and kissed her tenderly. "Damn, it's hard to leave you!"

"Then stay, darling, stay with me tonight." Susan hugged him tightly, not wanting him to go.

"God, woman, it's tempting!" Gene kissed her with tender passion. "It won't be long, darling. This nightmare's almost over, and then we can go home to our bed."

"*Our* bed!" Susan's smile was radiant at the happy thought. "*Our* home! *Our* family! *Our* life so we can just be ourselves!"

Scott pulled up his pants and threw his shirt on. "Love you, darling." He smiled at Susan as she buttoned up his shirt. "Be sure to lock your door and put the dead-bolt on. I still don't trust Toby Blackwell!" Gene walked over and checked the windows to be sure they were locked, then walked to the door. "We'll see the Blackwell family off in the morning, then wind this case down."

Chapter Twenty-Two

Gene Scott stood on the porch steps with Jackie and Jobi as the Blackwells and the Robinsons loaded their cars. Hal closed the trunk and walked back to the porch to shake Gene's hand. "Julien, I'd like to thank you and Judith for our wonderful visit. Perhaps your family can come and stay with us soon." The diamond thief smiled over at Jobi and Randy, who were sharing quiet words with each other. "I think it's going to be hard for those two to be separated after they've become such good friends."

"I agree, Hal. I believe those kids have grown real close." Gene made his way down the steps and walked his crooked neighbor to his car. "If my meeting with the old geezer's still on, I think we decided on 2 p.m. today? I'll have my man drive me over if you'll give me directions."

"That won't be necessary, Julien. I'll send my man to pick you up." Hal moved up close and spoke in Gene's ear, "Due to high security around my compound, you must come alone this time. Not even your bodyguard can assist you." Hal stood back and smiled broadly as he patted the tall handsome man on the back. "But then you'll be among friends, right?"

"Sure, no problem." Speaking with confidence, Gene motioned for the two young friends who were caught up in their conversation. "Randy, I think your family's waiting on you."

Hal climbed in his car, cranked up the motor and waited as Randy shook the preacher's hand and looked up with tear-stained eyes. Gene Scott gently laid his hand on her head and smiled warmly. "Hang in there, kid; everything's going to be fine."

"Thank you, sir, I pray it will." Her words came out weak, and the passionate preacher knelt down and gazed into her sad eyes.

"Randy, prayer's a powerful thing, and God hears all the words you say to him and he'll help give you the strength you need."

"You're a good man"—she leaned up to whisper in his ear—"Rev. Scott." She ran and got into the back seat and stared out the window at her new friend as they drove away.

Jobi walked up beside Gene and watched the car drive out of sight. He sighed, "We've just gotta help her, Rev. Scott! We just gotta!"

"We will, buddy. Now stop worrying." Gene turned toward the house when he heard Pogo calling his name, panic in his voice. Gene raced up the steps to where Pogo was doubled over, trying to catch his breath. "Calm down, pal, and tell me what's wrong!"

"It's Susan, Gene! I can't get her to open her door!" Pogo followed Gene as he made his way quickly into the house and up the steps, Jobi and Jackie following closely behind.

When they reached her door, Gene pounded loudly, calling her name, "Susan! Susan! Sweetheart, open this door." No sound came from within the bedroom. Trying the knob, the door was still securely locked so the strong preacher motioned for everyone to move away as he stepped back, then charged, ramming into the door with his shoulder and knocking it open. He looked around in desperation as he called out, "Susan!" Gene's heart began to sink when he spotted the open window. He ran over and looked down where a ladder had been set up and was hidden in the boxwoods under the window.

"Damn that Toby Blackwell! I'll kill the son-of-a-bitch!"

"Scott, wasn't that window locked?" Pogo noticed the lock was still in place, but the frame was pulled out. "Looks like he broke in after you left her! Susan had to have been asleep."

Without another word, Gene ran out the door past the nosy maids and down the steps, where he ran head-on into Stan McLeod and Herbert Vance.

"Whoa there, friend, we need to talk."

"Like hell! Get out of my way!" Gene started to push his

way through when two more beefy agents stepped in front of the door to block him. "Listen, fellows, I don't want to hurt you; but if you don't get the shit out of my way, I'll plaster you to the damn wall!"

"Scott, what the hell is wrong with you?" Stanley McLeod remained cool, despite the big man's threat.

"I thought you goons were watching this damn house!" Scott yelled. "You have men staked out in every crack, yet you managed to let that little jerk kidnap my woman! Now get out of my way! I've got to find Susan! You're wasting my time and that jackass has a head start!"

"Scott, let my men search for your wife." McLeod held up his hand to avoid being struck by Scott's balled-up fist. "Listen, Scott, you're about to crack this case wide open, save Dr. Rogers and put an end to this ring of diamond thieves!" He motioned to his men. "Get every available man we've got and find Mrs. Scott! Get Wiggins on the case right away! Toby Blackwell couldn't have taken her far. The jungle's a dangerous place to travel in the dark." His voice was intense as he waved them away. "Now go! Get on it!"

"Yes, sir! We'll find the girl and bring her back!" The beefy red-headed agent took off with his orders.

"Look, McLeod, Susan's my wife, damn it! I'll save her!" Scott's attention was drawn to his upper arm where Herbert Vance had grabbed it tightly. "Let go, Vance, if you want to keep your damn hand!"

"Scott, please listen to us. We've got the best men possible looking for your wife. Wiggins can sniff out a kidnapper. He'll find her! We need you!" Vance pleaded and placed his fingers close together, indicating a small distance. "Scott, we're this close to catching Blackwell and his diamond ring! Up until now, you've accomplished everything we were unable to do!" Vance could read the raw emotions on Scott's face and see the genuine tears welling up in his eyes. "Scott, for God's sake, put a little trust in us! We did in you!"

"Susan's my whole life! If something were to happen to

her, I just wouldn't want to live!" Gene's deep love for Susan broke the barrier of his strong resolve, and he couldn't control his tears any longer. "Susan's my everything! Without her, there's nothing!"

Pogo had been standing behind his big friend, listening to their arguments. He felt his heart breaking for his best friend, seeing him so emotional. Pogo stepped up in defense.

"Listen, you morons, if Scott helps you, you'd better pray that you find his wife safe and sound!" He stared at them angrily. "Because if something happens to Susan, Scott will go with her, and I'll lose my best friend in the entire world!" Pogo's eyes blazed as he added, "Then…I'll kill you, you…"

"Pogo, pal, relax." Gene Scott composed himself and gently patted his friend's back before looking down at the waiting agents. "I'll keep this damn meeting with Blackwell, but you'd better keep your end of the deal or you'll regret the day you met Gene Scott!"

Chapter Twenty-Three

Susan forced her eyes open. She could make out a dimly lit room with a distinct musty odor and a hint of an old familiar smell. It was, she recalled, some type of man's aftershave. Turning her head slightly to one side, she focused her blurry eyes on something against the wall. She thought, *Is that a chair or a small table perhaps?* Then as her sight became clearer, she could see it better. It was a man chained to the wall. Susan's heart began beating faster with fear when she heard a familiar voice calling her name,

"Susan, dear child, can you hear me, sweetheart? It's Granddad." William Rogers had seen Toby Blackwell carry his granddaughter's limp body into the cellar and lay her on an old blanket that was draped across the table in the middle of the room where he'd been held prisoner. Dr. Rogers had witnessed the brazen young man run his hands over Susan's body and stop to cup her breasts. The anger had raged in the good doctor as he fought the chains that held him securely to the wall. William Rogers remembered how the young man had laughed at him and made his rude remark,

"Getting excited, old man? Well, this one's mine. Your young hottie's waiting for you back at your ranch and if you cooperate with us, you just might screw her again!" Toby Blackwell had leaned over and kissed Susan on the lips as he whispered close to her ear, "Rest now, my beautiful Jessi. I'll return later, my darling." He'd walked out and closed the door with a click, the familiar sound of the key turning. Susan interrupted her grandfather's thoughts as she said softly,

"Granddad? How did I get here and where's Gene?" Susan sat up and grabbed her throbbing head, which was splitting with pain because she'd been drugged by the desperate young man.

"Susan, baby, that Blackwell boy carried you in here last night. He must have kidnapped you after Gene fell asleep." Rogers shook off the bad feeling that the crazy kid might have hurt Scott while he slept. "I can't understand why Scott didn't wake up when that crazy devil took you from your bed."

"Granddad, Gene wasn't with me. He had been earlier, but we're working undercover and I'm supposed to be his daughter, so he had to go back to the master bedroom." Susan managed to move her legs around so she could slide off the high table. Then she made her way over to her grandfather, knelt down and touched his weather-beaten face. "Granddad, Gene couldn't risk getting caught in my bedroom with all the spies roaming around the plantation house the feds put us up in."

"So the feds brought Scott in to rescue their butts!" Dr. Rogers gave a hardy chuckle, despite the trouble he and his granddaughter were facing. He knew first-hand that Gene and Susan didn't like to be separated from one another. "I bet having separate bedrooms has been real hard on you two lovebirds."

"Oh, Granddad," Susan laughed as she hugged him. Then a dreadful thought struck her and her words slipped out, "Oh shit! I bet Gene's found me missing by now and is going out of his mind looking for me!" She looked frantically around, then back at the prisoner. "Granddad, where are the keys to this lock?"

"Blackwell carries them on his keychain, and the other set must belong to Toby." The old man sneered, "I haven't signed those papers yet and God help me, I NEVER will!"

"Granddad, I just remembered Gene's supposed to come here today with Hal Blackwell to talk to you and pretend to convince you to sell your land to this land shark." Susan's eyes grew wide with the reality of the situation. "Gosh! Now that I'm missing, his first thought will be to rescue me! He might not even come!" She touched her grandfather's arm nervously. "If by some miracle Gene does come, he can rescue both of us!

Granddad, you must slip him a note so he'll know I'm here, just in case Toby moves me someplace else!" Susan jumped to her feet, her eyes scanning the dark cellar.

Rogers watched his granddaughter look around for something to write on and finally understood her plan. "Susan, that's a great idea, child. Now, to find something to write on and with." His mind started thinking of what Susan could write on as she searched a shelf filled with wine bottles.

She mumbled, "Nothing here! Where's my bag when I need it? Granddad, have you ever seen Blackwell or Robinson use any paper in here for anything except that stupid contract they keep sticking in your face?"

"The contract! That's it! Susan, go over there to that desk!" Dr. Rogers pointed to a small dark desk sitting in the far corner. "The last time Blackwell was here with the contract, he got mad and I remember him laying it down angrily on that desk. That was a few days ago!"

Susan raced over to the desk, afraid Toby would be coming back soon. Looking around, she saw the contract down on the dirty floor. Reaching down, she grabbed up the paper as her other hand slung open the desk drawer and she smiled at the single pencil laying inside.

"Thank you, Lord!" She looked at the two sheets and saw typing on both pages. She turned to her granddad. "Now what? There's typing on both pages!"

"Susan, the second page isn't completely filled in. Almost half the bottom's empty! Tear off the bottom and write your note there, but hurry, honey, before one of the Blackwells return!"

Quickly folding the paper back and forth to create a crease, Susan carefully tore the paper, while keeping her eyes on the door and praying every step of the way. "So far, so good, Lord!"

"Gene darling, Toby Blackwell kidnapped me and brought me here last night after drugging me. The jerk never realized he'd put me in this cellar with my own granddad. I pray you chose to come here to help Granddad. In so doing, you can rescue me as well. My love, I don't know when Toby will return, nor do I know if he plans to leave me here or take me someplace else on the property. Granddad will know where he saw me last and let you know if and when you have a chance to ask him. I love you, Gene! You're my hero! I know your first instinct was to drop everything and come for me. You're my life too, my darling, and I won't let that jerk touch me. Just hurry, sweetheart! Your Susan." She folded the note and placed it in Dr. Roger's hand.

"All you have to do is give this note to Gene, Granddad. He'll do the rest." Susan kissed his thin cheek. "Kata's safe with her people. She's a very sweet young woman, and I'm glad you two found each other."

"Thanks, baby, I knew you'd understand, you know, the age difference." Tears came to his once-bright eyes. "After your grandmother Louise died, things were lonely until I met Kata and she filled that empty place in my heart and bed. I just hope and pray Scott doesn't hate us for it."

Crying, Susan took his weather-beaten hand and kissed it. "Granddad, Gene Scott could never hate you. You had Mother and Mother had me!" She started to hug him when she heard a lock click in the door, causing her to stand up quickly.

Toby Blackwell opened the door and walked in, then stepped over to where she stood and jerked her around to face him. "My, Jessi! Getting acquainted with the prisoner? Just what have you been up to, beautiful?"

"If you must know, I've been trying to find out who this poor old man is you've chained like an animal! You creep!" Susan spit in his sneering face as she started to storm out. "I hate you, Toby Blackwell!"

Narrowing his eyes, Toby yanked out a handkerchief and wiped off his face. He grabbed her wrist and looked down angrily. "Aren't we brave for someone who's been won fair and square?"

"Won? You bastard, you stole me out of my bed!" Susan

raised her voice in defiance. “Only a few moments before, I’d been lying in the arms of my lover, making passionate love!”

“Brian Hampton?” Toby frowned. “Tell me, Jessi, does your bulldog of a father know about you and Brian having sex under his nose?”

“Not Brian, you idiot! Couldn’t you tell who my lover is? My father, Julien Armstrong!” Susan shouted, knowing this would probably set the crazy young man over the top, but she could only see herself with the love of her life in bed, act or no act. “He’s my lover! He’s the only man I want or need, you low- down jackass! Stepfathers aren’t exactly blood kin, are they?”

“Stepfather? Father, stepfather—they’re both the same to me! That man might have raised you, but he has no claim to your body, Jessi!” The angry young man grabbed her arms tightly. “Good Lord, Jessi! That is sick, real sick! No wonder the wife-cheating bastard didn’t want me to touch you! No wonder he couldn’t keep his damn hands off you!”

“Frankly, I couldn’t care less what you think! I feel the same way he does! So just let me go! He’ll kill you, Toby. My father will stop at nothing when someone messes with his girl!”

“We shall see, Jessica Armstrong!” Toby Blackwell dragged her, kicking and fighting, into the next room as he looked back at Dr. Rogers who’d been taking in the terrible scene. “You? Old man? Keep your damn mouth shut if you want to keep living! This room is soundproof, so don’t bother trying to listen!” Slamming the door shut, Toby pulled Susan to a post and tied her there securely. After sticking a cloth in her mouth, he moved his face in close to hers,

“Now, you listen, Jessica, I’m going up to the house and get a chilled wine bucket, grab two glasses and a bottle of wine from the wine cellar! Then we’re going to get to know one another very intimately.” Toby touched her face. “I’ll make you forget your old man!” Toby walked from the room, locked the door behind him and placed the only key inside his pocket.

Chapter Twenty-Four

The room was spinning in Gene's head. All he could think about was Susan. He could hear McLeod's voice as he gave him orders,

"Scott, you'll go with Blackwell's man alone. Michael, you and our men will follow at a safe distance. We'll have a mic well-hidden on you, Scott, so just speak in a normal voice and it 'll pick up everything. Got it?"

"Any news about my wife?" Gene Scott stood up and slapped the table. "Damn it, McLeod, if you screw this up, I swear I'll go crazy!"

"Scott, we're on top of it! My men are hot on the little creep's trail, trust me!" The agent looked down and swallowed, not really knowing how his men were faring. "It's almost 2 p.m. These men are usually right on time. We've got to split, but rest assured, Scott, we'll be ready to rush in when we think it's time."

"Only if Scott doesn't get in trouble!" Michael stepped up to face the agent in charge. "If I smell any danger about to happen, McLeod, I'm going in, ready or not!"

Gene patted Michael on the shoulder and looked over at his young friend.

"Pogo, I want you to stay here with Jobi. He needs you, buddy."

"Scott, the way I see it, you need me more. Jackie and Ali can keep an eye on Jobi!" Pogo put his arms around his big friend. "Please, Scott, let me do this!"

"Then go in and tell Jackie, Ali and James to watch the kid. I don't want him following us! Things could get messy!" Scott smiled at his long-time friend. "Thanks, pal!"

Pogo smiled, feeling relieved, then ran up the steps to tell the two girlfriends and James to watch Susan's brother.

At 2 p.m. sharp a long black limousine pulled up to the pillared mansion. Gene walked out and climbed into the back seat. The serious driver rolled his eyes up to the review mirror to see the big man he'd just picked up. Scott forced a smile at the stern face staring back.

"I'm ready if you are, buddy." Gene sat back. "Roll these damn wheels, driver!" A smile came to the hard face as he relaxed and drove from the plantation house and headed down a narrow dirt road. Twenty minutes later, the long black car pulled up in front of the stone villa. Gene climbed out and looked around as the car left him standing on the walkway. Before he could make it up to the front door, Katherine Blackwell opened the door and stepped outside smiling.

"Julien, welcome to Villa Blackwell. Hal will be right out, darling." She stepped closer, admiring the handsome figure standing in front of her. "Could I get you something—wine, gin, bourbon or me perhaps?" she giggled as Gene laughed lazily.

"My dear Mrs. Blackwell, are you flirting with me? What will Judith and Hal think?"

"They wouldn't have to know, would they?" Katherine touched his arm. "Would they, Julien?"

"But, Katherine, we would know." Gene smiled as Hal walked out and watched his wife's hand slip off Gene's arm.

"Julien, it's good to see you, my friend." Hal pulled his wife by his side and chuckled. "Is Katherine hitting on you, Julien?" He turned his wife around to face him. "Dear, please go inside before you embarrass yourself!" Hal watched her go inside, then motioned his hand toward the big rock nearest the villa and walked along beside Scott.

"Women! You can't live with them and you can't live without them!" Hal pulled a key from his pocket and placed it in a small silver lock. "This is our wine cellar and where we'll keep Dr. Rogers while he makes up his mind."

Stepping inside the dimly lit room, Scott saw Susan's grandfather chained to the far wall, staring at him. He thought as he stepped closer, *Please don't act like you know me, William.* Gene looked down at the tired ragged man who'd been so strong when he'd helped him build that hospital three years earlier. Gene chuckled as he looked down at his old friend.

"So this is the old man who can still make whoopy with the women?"

"Julien, may I introduce Dr. William Rogers, the fine gentleman I need to buy land from." Blackwell turned when he heard his brother-in-law walk inside the cellar.

"Sorry I'm late, Hal. I've been having a word with my nephew." Eric didn't notice how rigid Gene became at the mention of Toby. "Has Rogers changed his mind?"

"I've just brought Julien in to meet the good doctor, Eric." Hal looked over at the desk in the corner. "If I could just show you the contract, Julien. I think I left it over there."

"And it might as well stay there, Blackwell! I'll never sign that contract!" Rogers wanted to keep the dangerous man from opening the folded contract and finding the second page torn off at the bottom. "One lousy contract! I'll never sign that piece of garbage!"

"Suppose Mr. Blackwell draws up another contract and offers you what your land is worth? Will you sign that?" Noticing Hal moving nervously about the offer, Gene leaned in close to the thief and whispered, "Hal, one big diamond would cover your loss and you'd have a shit pot full of diamonds."

"You're right!" Hal's eyes lit up at the prospect. "I'll do it, Rogers! Will you sign that contract?"

"NEVER!" Rogers shouted. "I'm not interested in selling my land at any price! I love my home!"

"Damn, you're one stubborn old man!" Gene chuckled as he stepped closer. "Shit! How does this sound? The new contract states Blackwell can lease your land to work the diamond mine. He pays you rent, plus, let's say, thirty percent of the profits and after he's mined it out, he moves on out and the land still belongs to you!"

Blackwell walked up next to Scott and whispered, “Thirty percent? Couldn’t I just pay rent for the mountains?”

“Hal, my friend, don’t be so greedy!” Gene gently slapped his face playfully, causing him to cough. “Look, Hal, you’ll still make a shit pot full of money and get those two mountains you’ve been after without killing anyone!” Gene’s face turned serious as he added, “Then you can keep me as a buyer.”

“Hal, this offer seems fair to me.” Eric Robinson bent down close to his brother-in-law and spoke softly, “You’ve never killed anyone over this, have you, Hal?”

“Eric, Eric!” Hal laughed. “Me? Personally, no, I’ve never lifted a finger against anyone. Besides, Eric, getting the land is my concern, not yours. Your job is in sales and you’re the best in that field.”

Gene walked over and looked Dr. Rogers in the eyes. “What do you say, old fart? Is it a deal? I think you’d be a fool not to take it!”

“Alright! I’ll do it! I’ll sign that contract…after I read it first!” Susan’s grandfather hoped Gene would move closer so he could hand him the note she’d written to him.

Gene turned and patted the diamond thief on his back. “You’ve got your deal, Hal!”

“Great! Then let’s go to the villa and I’ll have my secretary type it up before he changes his feeble mind.” Hal looked up at Gene in admiration. “You did the impossible, friend! Come along with us, Julien.”

“May I ask the old geezer one more question?” Gene walked over next to Susan’s grandfather and knelt down. Rogers carefully slipped Susan’s precious note into Gene’s hand and winked. The preacher lovingly squeezed the doctor’s hand before speaking. He knew Hal and Eric were waiting and watching him. “What’s your secret, old man, for being able to have sex at your age? It’s something I might need to know one day.”

“You? I doubt that, son.” William looked into Gene’s blue eyes as he simply said, “It’s love, my friend. A special love that brings you back to life and makes you feel young again."

Gene winked, then smiled at the man he admired before rising to his feet, knowing he had to act for the two men taking in their words. He looked down at Rogers and laughed loudly as he said,

"You're full of shit, old man! It's probably some Bouta Barga juice, drugged with whoopy weeds!" When the door shut behind Scott and his laughing companions, William Rogers said a soft, "Thank you, Lord!"

"Julien, wait out here. There's a bench just inside the rose garden. This won't take long." Hal and Eric slipped inside the front door as Gene Scott walked to the garden bench and sat down. Looking around to make sure he was alone, he pulled out the note. His heart lifted when he saw Susan's handwriting and began reading. He closed his eyes, relieved to know she was close by, then re-read the words as tears formed in his eyes. Gene placed the note inside his pocket and turned toward the villa.

"Damn you, Toby Blackwell! Where's my wife?" Gene sensed movement on his right side and spotted Toby unlocking the silver lock and disappearing into the cellar. *Could Susan be in there? Is she that close to me?* He stood up quietly and followed Toby into the cellar, but looking around inside, the only person he saw was Dr. Rogers.

Chapter Twenty-Five

Toby Blackwell poured two glasses of red wine and smiled seductively at Susan. He lifted his glass in triumph, "Now, my beautiful sexy Jessica, I'll finally make love to you and there's no one to stop me!" He removed her gag and lifted the glass to her lips. "Drink this, darling, it'll make you feel good."

"Why, Toby? Did you put a sex drug in my glass?" Susan turned her head as he was about to pour the rich red wine into her mouth. "Get away from me, you…you pig!"

Laughing, Toby pulled her head back around and kissed her hard, causing her to yell, "Stop!" She tried with all her might to pull her head away, but Toby held it firmly in his hands.

"No one can hear your cries for me to stop, Jessica. You might as well give in because it won't do you any good to fight me. Just relax and you might enjoy it. I'm really a very good lover, sweetheart."

Smiling, Toby turned the glass up and swallowed the contents. "Jessica, I'm going to make love to you whether you choose to enjoy it or not. I know I certainly will. It's something I've been dreaming about, Jessica. You and me, naked and all over one another."

Susan shut her eyes, trying to think of a way out of this nightmare. Then a thought came to her. If she pretended she might change her mind, maybe she could stall for enough time so Gene could come to her rescue. She'd hang onto that hope that a miracle would happen and Gene would come here. She forced a smile at her abductor as she said softly,

"Toby, if you'd untie me and give me some of that wine you seem to enjoy, I might change my mind. It's hard to feel loved when you're tied up and also can't feel and touch."

"Do you mean that, Jessica? If I untie you, you'll behave yourself and do as I ask?" Toby poured the empty glass full again before untying the rope and asking, "You're really going to try, Jessica?"

"Yes, Toby. Believe it or not, I'm beginning to get turned on here."

Toby smiled triumphantly as he untied the ropes that held Susan captive.

"That's more like it, Jessica." He picked up the full glass and handed it to Susan. "Start drinking, so you can catch up with me! I promise you'll enjoy a younger lover over an old one any time, beautiful!"

"I'll be the judge of that." Susan took a small sip. "It's true that I've never slept with a younger man, not even Brian, but Julien knows how to satisfy me and he never disappoints."

Susan jumped when Toby grabbed her arms angrily, causing her to drop her glass.

"Stop talking about that freak father of yours! You belong to me now, Jessica Armstrong! You're mine and I won't share you with anyone, especially Julien Armstrong!" Toby ripped her gown down, revealing her breasts and Susan screamed.

As all of the excitement was happening in the soundproof room, Gene raced over to the doctor, his attention on every corner of the big room.

"She's not in here, Scott! The Blackwell boy has her in a soundproof room." William Rogers nodded with his head. "Over there, behind the black door! You can't hear her if she's calling you! Go help her!"

Without letting another second pass, Gene raced over to the black door and checked the knob. Finding it locked, the strong preacher stepped back, then charged the door, knocking it off its hinges. He slung his arm around and sent Toby Blackwell sailing across the concrete floor. Before the young man knew what had hit him, Scott took three giant steps toward him and set his foot on his chest. Gene stared at him for a minute, then reached down and lifted him off the floor in one swift movement. The frightened kidnapper's feet dangled in the air as he tried without success to free himself from Scott's strong grip. Pulling his face up even with his own, Gene Scott yelled,

"Take my girl out of her bed, will you, you son-of-a-bitch!" Too angry to control his emotions, the preacher slammed his fist into Toby's face, knocking him completely out cold. "Little wimp!" Dropping him on the floor, Gene ran over to his wife, who was sobbing, both from fear of being raped by the crazy young man and the relief of being saved by her true love. Susan threw her arms around her handsome rescuer and said with complete joy,

"Gene! Gene, darling, you came! You came!"

"Susan, my sweet darling Susan!" Gene hugged her tightly, the emotions of relief bringing tears to his eyes. He'd been going crazy with worry and now his Susan was safe in his loving arms and he didn't want to let her go. "I love you so much, Susan! My darling, I was beside myself with worry!"

Hal ran into the room after finding the cellar door unlocked and the wine room's door broken completely off its hinges. Frantically looking around, the diamond thief saw his son lying unconscious in the corner of the room. Then he turned his attention to the man he'd grown to love as a friend, holding tightly to who he thought was his daughter.

"My God! Julien, what's going on here? Did Toby…? He didn't! He couldn't!"

"Damn it! The little bastard could and did kidnap my girl!" Gene quickly removed his shirt to cover Susan's exposed breasts. "The little weasel was about to rape her when I decked him out! I should've killed the wimpy little jackass!" Taking Susan by the hand, Gene pushed his way past the startled man.

Eric Robinson came through the room and peeked inside the soundproof room. He shook his head when he spotted the spoiled young man out cold. He mumbled, "I knew that stupid boy was up to something!" He turned to see Susan clinging to Gene and with true sentiment, he walked over in front of them, speaking softly, "I'm really sorry, Miss Jessica."

About that time, Michael rushed in followed by four F.B.I.

agents. One grabbed Eric while the other three rushed in after Hal and Toby, still lying unconscious on the damp floor. Herbert Vance stared down at the swollen face briefly, then marched out to face Gene Scott.

"Scott, what happened to that young man in there?"

"It would appear my fist knocked the shit out of the little bastard! Got a problem with that, Vance?" The preacher hugged his wife protectively. "That damn kidnapper took my woman, tried to rape her and ripped her gown nearly off! If I'd killed the sniffling coward, he would've asked for it!"

"Scott?" McLeod had been unchaining William Rogers as he listened to the exchange of words between Scott and his partner. "We'd never have cracked this case if it hadn't been for you, but I hope we don't have to deal with a murder right here at the end."

Gene narrowed his eyes at the federal agent, sounding off with authority, "Tell me, McLeod, what happened to your men's search for Susan? They had no clue where she was, did they?" Scott held tightly to his wife as he raised his voice, "You lied to me, McLeod! Pretending those bozos were hot on the kidnapper's trail! It would appear I am the only one solving things around here, you jerk!"

"My men…well, a…" Stanley McLeod breathed a sigh of relief when his partner walked out of the soundproof room escorting Toby Blackwell, who was holding his head. "Looks like you got lucky, Scott."

"Which is more than you're going to do, McLeod, if you don't start answering my damn question!" Gene's eyes shot fire. "I kept my side of the bargain, McLeod! Your word doesn't mean shit!"

"Well, Scott, everything worked out for the best anyway. We got our men and you got your woman!" The agent motioned for his men to take the arrested men outside and read their rights to them.

Michael had been listening as he held up the weak doctor. "McLeod, everything worked out, thanks to Gene Scott!"

Gene's blue-eyed friend pushed passed the federal agent as he helped Susan's granddad out into the bright sunlight. Seeing the older man shield his eyes, Michael stepped in front of him to shield him from the sunshine. "Are you alright, Dr. Rogers?"

"Yes, young man, I am now. My granddaughter's safe in the arms of her husband. All's well with the world." William Rogers smiled at Toby Blackwell who'd been listening. The troubled young man stared at Gene and Susan as they walked outside, still hugging.

"Husband?" His gaze met Susan's. "Your husband?" He looked up angrily at Gene. "Jessica's your wife?"

"Damn right, you punk!" Scott almost shouted, still mad over the worry this young man had caused.

Hal Blackwell had been listening and watching as fear invaded his body. He couldn't believe this man he'd considered a real friend could actually be working with the United States government. As he looked at Gene, his words came out weak and shaken, "Your name's not Julien Armstrong?"

Then he looked down at Susan, wondering how he could've fallen into this man's trap. He'd seemed so convincing and up until now, he'd always been able to spot a spy. "And you, young lady, you're not Jessica?"

"My husband's name is Rev. Gene Scott and he busted your butt, Mr. Blackwell! The old man you chained in that cellar is my dear grandfather and my name is really Susan Scott!" Susan looked over at the shaken young man, who was staring at the couple with venomous hate in his eyes. "I tried to warn you, Toby Blackwell, that Gene would knock the shit out of you, but you were too stubborn to listen to my good advice!"

Eric Robinson couldn't believe his bad luck that might cost him the family he loved. Tears in his worried eyes, he looked over at the strong man holding tightly to the woman he obviously loved more than life. With his voice trembling, he managed to say, "You're a preacher?"

Eric turned when he heard his daughter call, "Daddy" as she ran over into his arms. "Randy, Daddy's so sorry, baby."

The shaken man choked back tears. “I’m truly sorry! I’ve messed up everything!”

“Daddy, why? We were happy when we lived in Atlanta! We had all we needed there! We had each other!” Tears ran down the young girl’s face as she looked into her father’s sad eyes. “What’s going to happen to you, Daddy? Will you go to jail forever? Will I ever see you again?” Seeing her mother walk up, Randy ran into her arms. “Mama, what’s going to happen to me if you and Daddy go to jail?”

“Jail?” Emily Robinson looked up at her husband whom she’d always trusted to make the right decisions for their family. She hugged her little girl as she tried to explain, “Randy, your daddy and I thought your Uncle Hal and Aunt Katherine were in an honest diamond business.” Emily looked confused when the feds handcuffed her husband and started reading him his rights. She spoke softly, as much to herself as to her daughter, “At least, I never knew they were breaking the law.”

“Mama, you really didn’t know?” Randy looked up at her mother for assurance. “Please, Mama, tell me the truth. I need to know.”

“Randy, baby…” Emily looked at her husband for answers. “Eric, would you please tell us what’s going on here and why you’re being arrested?”

“Emily, darling, Hal and Katherine made everything sound so great.” Eric’s voice shook as he looked at his sad wife for understanding. “I guess I got caught up in all the excitement, Emily, and before I knew it, I was in too deep to get out.”

“Eric, why? Was it the money?” Emily Robinson turned her head to hide her tears as Stanley McLeod stepped up and said,

“It would appear that Mrs. Robinson and her daughter Randy are the only two who didn’t know what was going on around here.”

McLeod then watched his man bring Katherine Blackwell from the house. He stopped them and said to her, “Mrs.

Blackwell, you're under arrest for aiding and abetting your husband in land fraud and possible murder charges." He turned to the officer holding her. "Read Mrs. Blackwell her rights, Bates; then take them in."

Katherine stared over at her husband in disbelief. "Hal, what happened? Who are these men and how did they catch us?"

"I'll tell you what happened, dear," Hal said sarcastically. "Julien Armstrong! He's what happened! That damn traitor was working undercover for the feds!"

"Julien?" Katherine felt sick as she looked over at the handsome man she'd been flirting with.

"Katherine, his name's Gene Scott!" Susan held onto his strong arm. "And I'm Susan Scott, Gene's wife!"

"His wife? You?" Katherine's knees buckled and the F.B.I. agent held her up. She stared at the handsome preacher for a moment before saying, "I don't understand. Your daughter is your wife?"

"Mother, shut up!" Toby stared at the couple with hate on his face. They'd tricked him and his parents. He gritted his teeth as he said, "I hate you, Scott, hate you! You're going to regret this, I promise!"

"Tough shit, kid!" Holding tightly to his wife's hand, Scott walked over to Randy and Emily. He touched Randy gently and she looked up at him with tears in her eyes. "Randy, you and your mother can come back with us. We'll send for your things later, but for now we need to head back. I'm sure Jobi's worried about his sister and you."

Randy let go of her mother's hand to hug the gentle giant. "Thank you, Rev. Scott. Can you put in a good word for Daddy? I don't think he knew what Uncle Hal was up to until he came here to work for him as a diamond salesman. I know Daddy would never have taken this job had he known up-front Uncle Hal was dishonest."

"Randy's right, Rev. Scott. Eric's a wonderful father and a very good husband. At his old job, which he loved, he always strived to be the best salesman he could be for the company he worked for. He always received the salesman of the year award. We did have a wonderful life in Atlanta. Money was never an issue." Emily watched the officer load her sister into the squad car, and she reached for her daughter's hand. "I trusted my sister when she called us, so excited about this great job opportunity. I should have known Katherine and Hal were capable of breaking the law to get what they wanted. They always loved making money and couldn't get rich enough."

"Mrs. Robinson, I'll do whatever I can to help Eric get a lighter sentence. I, for one, believe you." Gene patted the nervous woman on her arm as he watched Michael walk over smiling.

"Everyone's been loaded up, Scott. The four of you can ride back with me."

Gene Scott looked around, then peered over Michael's shoulder. "Mike, where's Pogo? He said he was coming! I haven't seen him!"

"Pogo was coming, Scott, but when you sent him to speak to Jackie, Ali and James about watching the kid, Ali came running inside, upset and out of breath. James had sent her to get help because those two ranch hands were getting out of control and making threatening remarks." Michael helped Emily and her daughter into the back seat, then turned to the preacher. "It was at that point Vance ordered Pogo to go help James after reassuring him the feds had enough backup to handle the job at the villa." Michael smiled down at Susan as he opened the passenger door for her, then continued, "Pogo raced off to help James. Jackie and Ali filled us in before we left to come here. That left Henning and Sorvino to watch the staff. We knew we couldn't depend on Danfield for help, so he wasn't informed about what was going down."

"Mike, let's get this baby rolling!" Gene climbed in and shut the door, then Michael sped off to the plantation. Gene looked from the window as the villa faded from view, then over at the driver. "Pogo and James might need our help, Mike!

Harvie Flint's not so mean, but that Tuffy Barrow is as mean as a snake, just like the fed said."

Susan looked up in the rearview mirror at the car behind them, but the dust made it difficult to see the occupants inside. She turned to her husband, whose mind was on his young friend at the stables.

"Gene, what about Granddad? Is he riding with Vance and McLeod?"

"The agents wanted to ask William a few questions, sweetheart, so they could tie up the loose edges." Gene kissed the top of her head. "They'll bring him to the plantation; then we'll take him back home to the Lazy Lizard."

Susan relaxed in Gene's strong arms, feeling safe and loved, as Michael drove to the plantation house.

Chapter Twenty-Six

Pogo slipped up on the scene. Tuffy Barrow had backed James into a corner inside the stable and was edging his way closer, smiling grimly.

"Listen, you skinny fence post, I'm sick and tired of you bossing me around! No stick-in-the-mud American is going to give Tuffy Barrow orders and tell me what I can and cannot do! Is that clear, boss man?"

"Look, Nick, Mr. Armstrong told you to take my orders or he was going to fire you! Is that what you want?" James might have been a thin man, but James Tabor was as tough as nails when some jerk was pushing him around so he held his ground. "You may be bigger than me, Barrow—that's for damn sure—but I'm not going to stand around and be threatened by a low-life drifter!"

"Oh, it's not a threat, Yankee! It's a promise! One cold fact, you bean pole!" The big bully laughed loudly as he grabbed James and lifted him off the ground and then looked over at his friend Harvie Flint.

"Let go of that man, mister, if you know what's good for you!" Carrying a shovel, Pogo marched up behind the overweight jerk. "I don't mind telling you fellows that I know I'm not able to take both of you on or maybe not even one of you, so I'll not hesitate to knock the shit out of you with this shovel!"

Growing angrier, Tuffy Barrow dropped James, then turned on Pogo, who stood holding the shovel in the air, ready to strike the overbearing bully.

"You little squirt! I'll wrap that damn shovel around your pretty boy neck! Why, you…" Before he could finish his threat, James picked up a fence post and hit Barrow on his fat head. He crumbled to the ground, out cold.

Pogo turned to Harvie Flint, who stood staring down at his mean still partner. He jumped when Pogo tapped him on the back.

"Do you give in peacefully, pal, or do you wish to join your friend on the ground?"

"I don't have a fight with you!" He glanced nervously at James, who had joined them. "You either, Mr. Ward. It was all Tuffy's idea to stand up to you, sir. We're just supposed to do our jobs."

"Which job, Flint? Who do you really work for? You might as well come clean. We know you're both spies." Pogo noticed James' sudden panicked expression and realized he didn't know the case was winding down. James laughed nervously as he pulled Pogo around to face him.

"Mr. Hampton, what are you talking about? Have you been reading crime novels again?"

"I never read crime novels, friend. Just relax, James, the gig is up!" Pogo kept his eyes on the ranch hand. "James, you'd better tie up that big fellow before he wakes up meaner than a wounded bear, and you, Mr. Flint, might as well start talking. Hal Blackwell and his crime family have been arrested by now, so go easy on yourself. It's over."

The undercover spy's eyes grew big in total surprise as he managed to mutter, "Blackwell…arrested! Damn, who caught us?" His face dropped. "Everything was going so smoothly! The boss was about to get the diamond mine he wanted and the richest client around."

"Perhaps you've heard of Rev. Gene Scott and his fearless group! They always crack their case and good prevails!" Pogo smiled proudly, happy to be a part of the Scott team and their brilliant leader.

"Rev. Gene Scott? As a matter of fact, I heard his name mentioned in one of our meetings." Harvie Flint swallowed, recalling the stories he'd heard about this man's achievements! "The boss always said he hoped that Bible-thumper didn't come near us. Who…who was Scott pretending to be?"

As if on cue, Gene Scott walked up smiling, happy to see the boys had things under control.

"Well, fellows, looks like you managed to take care of this situation on your own!" He looked down at Barrow laying on the ground, still out cold. "We could get this loafer for sleeping on the job!" Gene chuckled as Pogo and James joined in. All but Harvie Flint, who couldn't take his eyes off the tall man gazing down at his friend.

"Are you Rev. Scott?"

"The one and only!" Gene watched Tuffy Barrow straighten out his feet and open his cold eyes. A sharp splitting pain quickly furrowed his brow. McLeod and Vance walked up behind the preacher and watched him as he squatted down, hands on his knees and a broad smile stretched across his face.

"I've been wanting to do this for a long time. Tuffy Barrow, you're fired! Get your crapping ass off my land!"

The federal agents tried to contain their composure and refrain from laughing as they pulled the oversized bully off the ground.

"Looks like you've met your match, Barrow! I don't think Rev. Scott wants you hanging around!" Vance turned to Harvie Flint, who stood quietly listening. "Are you coming peacefully or do we drag you off in handcuffs like your partner here?"

"I'm coming!" Stopping in front of Scott, Flint shook his head. "You boys are good! Real good!" Feeling Vance push him forward, the fallen spy moved toward the big house.

Gene watched the men walk out of sight, then playfully slapped Pogo on the back, causing him to stumble forward.

"Good work, boys, we're going home!"

"Home?" Pogo smiled to himself as Gloria's face came into his mind. He hung behind as Gene and James walked ahead, talking about the case. Pogo's thoughts were on one thing; soon he'd be going home to his sexy Bath.

Chapter Twenty-Seven

The house staff had been rounded up and taken away when Dr. Danfield walked up looking confused as he watched the federal agents separating the spies from the innocent parties and undercover workers. He rubbed his hand through his ruffled hair where he'd been napping and mumbled,

"What's going on? Did I miss something?"

"Don't you always, Danfield?" Gene looked disgusted. "Just go pack your shit; we're headed home!"

"Home?" The doctor looked up, perplexed. "Is everything over? Why was I kept out of the loop? I might have been some assistance, Scott!"

"To be honest, doctor, we simply forgot you were here!" Gene turned and walked inside the large entrance hall. Susan had been waiting for him and walked over to hug him.

"Rev. Scott, we're going home and see our beautiful babies, then go up to our bed to sleep together."

"And plenty of other things in 'our' bed, beautiful!" Gene Scott laughed as he squeezed his wife gently, then lifted his eyebrows in mischief. "We still have three weeks before the love reaper strikes again."

Jobi walked up, holding Randy's hand as he smiled at the loving couple. "That was real cool, Rev. Scott. Don't hold anything back!"

"Look, kid, take that cute young lady out for a walk before I don't hold back kicking your ass!" Scott rubbed the youth's head lightly, then turned to see who'd entered the hall. William Rogers had stepped inside, followed by Vance, McLeod and someone who was a stranger to Gene and Susan.

"William, you're looking a lot better since you got out of that prison." Not waiting for a reply, Gene Scott turned to the stranger in their midst. "If you don't mind my asking, who are you?"

"The name is Smith, Bennet Smith. I'm the top agent over this investigation and you're the famous Rev. Scott I've been hearing so much about." He shook hands with the handsome preacher as he continued to give him praise. "My boys give you high marks, Reverend. They're no softies, no, sir! I have a smart group of men working under me." The top-ranked agent leaned up against the wall, smiling. "I listened to all the taped remarks between you and Blackwell. Excellent work, Scott! Simply brilliant!" Smith then stepped up beside Gene and placed a hand on his shoulder. "Are you sure you don't want to work for us, Scott? You'd be paid well and I know you and your group would make the perfect addition to our investigation work. What do you say?"

"Thank you for your kind words, Mr. Smith. I speak for all my wonderful team when I say we appreciate the job offer." Gene smiled as he hugged Susan. "First and foremost, I'm a devoted husband to this young lady. Second, I am a happy father of two adorable twins who have gone long enough without their mama and daddy. Besides, Bennet, I already work for the most important boss there is or ever was. He outranks you in every possible way, and I know my Heavenly Father is ready for me to get my butt back behind the pulpit and start winning souls again!"

"Our loss, my friend, but I get your point. I'm positive the Almighty God will never run out of things for you to do for Him." Bennet Smith smiled down at the beautiful young woman wrapped in the preacher's arms. "I can see the love between you and your husband, Mrs. Scott. It's special, very special and you'll never lose it. Your husband's a lucky man to have found you."

"I am a very lucky man!" Scott squeezed his wife closer to him, hoping this conversation was about to wind down so they could leave. "I'm very much aware just how blessed I am!"

"Mrs. Scott, you are lucky as well to have married Rev. Scott." Bennet Smith knew the couple were growing impatient and wanted to start back to Dr. Roger's home.

"I'm the luckiest girl on earth, sir, and also very tired!" Susan laid her head over on Gene's chest.

"I know you're anxious to get home, so I'd like to thank you, Dr. Rogers, for your co-operation and apologize for the long, drawn-out ordeal. I'll say my farewells now and Godspeed." With that, the head agent stepped out the door as McLeod shook Scott's hand firmly.

"It's been an honor working with you, Scott. Perhaps we can call on you again if the need arises."

"Perhaps our paths will cross in the future, McLeod, but it would have to be a chosen mission from my Lord." Scott smiled, harboring no hard feelings for their botched job rescuing his wife from Toby Blackwell. "May God go with you and Vance and keep you out of harm's way."

The two men nodded and walked out of the house.

After loading their big car with everyone's luggage, Gene and Susan said goodbye to their four friends from TarSa, who were headed for the nearest airport where Michael had left his private jet. Emily, Randy, Jobi and Pogo squeezed into the back seat. Gene smiled at the crowded back seat.

"Boy, it's a good thing this baby's big!" He opened the door for Susan and helped her in. "Scoot over into the middle, darling." Then Gene walked around to the driver's side as the doctor climbed in next to his granddaughter. He winked at her when she moved as close to her husband as possible.

"Have you got enough room, Granddad? I can move over closer." Susan patted Gene's leg. "The closer the better, right, darling?"

"You can sit on my lap if you want to, sweetheart." Gene's eyes twinkled with mischief. "I'll just put my hands on your chest and you can steer." All the passengers laughed at Gene's remark as Susan slapped his leg.

"Gene Scott, behave!" she blushed. "Just roll these wheels, buster!"

A few hours later, Gene Scott drove under the "Lazy

Lizard" sign and straight to Roger's home. They all climbed out and followed the owner into his house. He walked around looking for his live-in lover, but she wasn't there.

"Kata must still be with her people, awaiting my return." William Rogers checked his watch before pulling down a hunting rifle from his gun rack. "There's still enough daylight left. I'm going after her."

"Do you plan to stay with the tribe tonight, William? It'll be dark before you get back and I didn't just save you so you can get your ass eaten off by some wild animal! You can get into Kata's pants tomorrow!"

"Scott, have you ever had to wait to make love to your woman? Three days, maybe four or five?" William spoke close to Gene's ear. "It's been weeks, Scott! I need my woman now!"

"Shit, William, when I first met Susan, I had to wait until after we got married to have sex! Those long months I came over here to help you build that children's hospital were pure torture! More recently, I had to go five days without making love to Susan, due to Mother Nature's visit! I know what it's like to wait, trust me." Scott hit Roger's arm playfully. "But listen, William, it's not going to help your situation if you go out there and get killed. Besides, you'll survive the waiting, my friend. I should know! Somehow we survive and having the reward of having her in yours arms again will make up for the torture!"

"Alright, you're right, Scott." William Rogers replaced the gun and touched Gene's arm. "I'll leave first thing at daybreak and you can come with me."

"Me? Why would you need me, William?" Scott watched Susan place two frozen pizzas in the oven and set the timer. He looked around the kitchen for any sign of Pogo, but he wasn't there.

"I thought you might like to meet the Bouta Barga tribe, Scott." The doctor walked over and kissed his granddaughter's cheek. "Learning how to cook, sweet girl?"

"She bakes a damn good frozen pizza, and her sandwiches

are some of the best around." Scott opened the refrigerator, took out two cold beers, handed one to Rogers, then opened the other one and took a big sip. "Damn, that tastes good!"

"Better than me, stud?" Susan smiled at her husband as she got down some plates and napkins.

"Nothing's better than you, little darling!" Scott winked at her, then smiled over at William Rogers. "Why would I want to meet that tribe, William? Aren't they the devils with the poison arrows?"

"The same!" The doctor laughed. "But they won't hurt you, Scott. They're Kata's people. I was hoping you could convince the chief to let Kata marry me."

"Kata did mention her family wouldn't agree to your marriage, and I did tell her I'd make them understand." The preacher stood up to get two more beers when the timer went off. "I'll go with you in the morning and see if I can persuade those poison-arrow-carrying natives that they have no other course but to permit you and Kata to get married." Gene walked past Susan on his way to the table and patted her butt. "Susan, where's Pogo hiding? Why isn't he in here helping you fix supper?"

"Pogo said he had a phone call to make." Susan made a face at her husband. "Besides, Gene Scott, I can fix pizza without any help!"

Pogo had closed himself inside Dr. Rogers' office so he could call Gloria. Keeping one eye on the door, he thumped the desk anxiously as he waited for Johnson to get Gloria. His heart melted at the sound of her voice.

"Pogo, darling." Gloria spoke softly, knowing her parents were in the house. "It's truly wonderful to finally get your call. I've missed you terribly, sweetheart!"

"Gloria, my wonderful, beautiful lover." Pogo glanced up at the closed door, afraid Scott would come search for him. "I've missed you too, my darling redhead!"

"Pogo, when will you be coming home, darling? I'm dying

here without you!" Gloria closed her eyes to picture her Pogo's handsome face.

"Soon, sweetheart, very soon!" Once again, he looked anxiously at the door. "We cracked the case, or should I say Scott cracked the case with our help. At this moment we are at the home of Dr. Rogers, Susan's grandfather. I figure after we stay here a day or so, I'll be catching a flight home to you!"

"Call me when you arrive home, darling." Gloria took a deep breath, excited that she'd soon be in Pogo's arms again. "Promise?"

"Let anyone try and stop me, my love." Pogo heard the door squeaking as Scott peeked inside the office and waved. Pogo nodded his head at him as he tried to think what to say now to Gloria, who was waiting on the other end. "I've got to go now, Bath. I think Susan has the pizzas ready."

"Scott's there, isn't he, sweetheart?" She smiled as she tried to picture the awkward situation.

"You bet! That's absolutely right!" Pogo smiled, knowing he had Gene wondering just who this Beth was. "I'll call you when I get home after I get caught up with the housework and yard work at the Scotts' house! I'm sure the grass will need mowing and the garden will be sporting lots of new weeds!"

"I love you, Pogo, and I know you love me. I also know how Gene likes to rib you when it comes to girls." Gloria laughed as she added, "You do love me?"

"Yes, Bath! You know how much!" Pogo took a deep breath as he added, "See you soon."

"I'll count the hours, Pogo darling." Gloria kissed the receiver before adding, "See you soon!"

Pogo nervously laid the receiver down and stood up stretching.

Gene stepped over smiling broadly.

"Pogo, you young rascal. You really do like this girl Beth, don't you, buddy?"

"Bath's a very special girl." Pogo walked past Scott and started down the hall to the kitchen, trying to avoid his questions. Pogo glanced over his shoulder. "Let's eat, man! That pizza smells great!"

"Hey, Pogo, are you changing the subject?" Gene was close behind his friend as he went in the kitchen and started helping Susan slice the pizzas. "Hey, pal, tell me about Beth."

"There's nothing to tell, Scott, except she's very pretty, extremely smart and sweet." Pogo avoided looking directly at his big friend because Gene had a knack for reading his mind. "Bath and I've had a couple of fun dates, nothing steady yet. I like her and she likes me. We have a lot in common and that makes hanging out with her loads of fun!"

"Is she the Beth from church? That cute little redhead?" Gene looked down when Susan slapped his arm. "Hey, girl, watch that."

"Gene Scott, leave Pogo alone!" Susan handed him a cold beer, then set two Cokes down for Randy and Jobi. "He'll tell us when he gets ready."

Gene narrowed his eyes at her. "Susan Scott, your curiosity is just as strong as mine, so stop acting so cool about Pogo's big secret!" Gene took his seat and opened his beer.

Susan gave her husband a beautiful smile and looked to make sure everyone had a drink before taking her seat, a full glass of merlot in her hand. After taking a generous sip, she patted Gene's face.

"Sweetheart, we just have to be patient with Pogo. Your first real love can be exciting, remember? I'm certain Pogo will tell us everything after he's driven us both nuts trying to figure out just who she is."

"You're so precious, Mrs. Scott!" Gene reached over her to get a big slice of pizza, brushing her lips with his as he relaxed back in his chair. He looked up at Pogo, who still stood holding his cold beer. "Sit down, Mr. Mysterious, so I can give the blessing."

Pogo relaxed as he bowed his head after sitting down next to Emily. Scott smiled and closed his eyes.

"Sweet Lord, Heavenly Father, we give you thanks for this

pizza and the beautiful cook who prepared it." Jobi snickered and Rev. Scott playfully slapped his leg as he continued, "Guide us tomorrow with the right words for the Bouta Barga tribe and keep us safe from the poison arrows. Amen!"

Jobi took a big bite of his pizza to hold in his laughter as Randy reached for a slice and smiled at her close friend.

"I really like Rev. Scott, Jobi. He's real cool!"

"Scott's the best!" Jobi took another slice and laid one on Randy's plate, then licked his lips. "My sister makes a great pizza!"

"Yep, that's my girl, the pizza queen! Susan's got the frozen pizzas down pat! Don't you, darling?" Gene teased as Susan frowned up at him.

"One more cute remark from you, Rev. Scott, about my cooking and you'll be sleeping in your pajamas tonight!"

Chuckling, Gene reached over and ran his hand up Susan's leg, then leaned in close to her ear and whispered, "Looks like I'd better keep my big mouth shut!"

After Susan took her last sip of wine, Gene reached for the bottle and refilled her glass with a twinkle in his blue eyes. Trying to keep a straight face, Susan casually looked his way.

"Why, Rev. Scott, are you trying to get me tipsy?"

"Me?" He looked at her innocently. "What? Have my way with you?"

Susan couldn't control her laughter any longer as the others around the table began laughing too. She reached over and kissed his smiling lips, then turned to her grandfather,

"So, Granddad, do we all go tomorrow to visit the dangerous tribe with arrows? You know Jobi and I are Gene's shadows."

"Anyone who doesn't mind walking through the jungle is welcome." William Rogers looked around the table. "We'll be leaving at first light though. That might help you decide."

"So who's with me and William besides my two shadows?" Gene winked at Susan.

"Unless you need me, Scott, I thought I'd get up before

daylight and fix the brave jungle troopers a hearty breakfast. It'll help get you going, not to mention keeping you all alert in case any poison arrows happen to come your way!" Pogo washed down his last bite of crust with his beer. "After you march off into the jungle, I'll hang back and clean up William and Kata's kitchen."

"That sounds like a great idea, pal! It's always good to start the day off with a big breakfast, especially when your day requires a lot of walking in a hot jungle." Gene winked at his friend. "When you've finished cleaning up this kitchen, you should have plenty of time to call sweet mysterious Beth again when Susan and I aren't here to listen in on your mushy conversation."

"Very funny, Scott!" Pogo stacked up the paper plates and smiled down at Emily Robinson. "What about you, Emily, are you up to a jungle hike?"

"I think I'll remain here. I'm not much when it comes to the jungle." She shivered at the thought of walking through a thick overgrown path and the unexpected animals that might pounce out of the thicket. "Randy can stay here with me and stay out of your hair."

Randy's big eyes looked up at her mother, then dropped down sadly, hating to miss the chance to go with Jobi and Rev. Scott. Gene Scott could read the disappointment on the young teen's face. He reached over and gently raised up her chin.

"Mrs. Robinson, she'll be no trouble if she wants to tag along."

"Please, Mama, can I? I won't cause Rev. Scott any trouble!" Randy looked up pleadingly. "Could I go, Mama, please? It sounds so exciting!"

"If Rev. Scott's absolutely sure and says you can go, then you may go with them." It made Emily happy to see her daughter's big smile.

"Then it's settled! Randy's young eyes might see something we've missed. She'll make a great contribution to our team." Gene stood up and stretched. "Alright, gang, those who are going with us need to get to bed early. We must be up and dressed for breakfast by 5 a.m."

Pogo laughed. "Sure, Scott! You're going up to bed and go to sleep! I'm sure the rest of us will be sound asleep before you close your eyes!"

"Pogo, just get this mess cleaned up and get yourself to bed." Gene helped carry the few glass pieces to the sink. "You'll be fixing breakfast at 4 a.m., so stop with the jokes and get moving!" Gene took Susan's hand and pulled her up the steps mumbling to himself.

Susan smiled to herself as she walked straight to the bathroom, calling back,

"I'll get my teeth brushed, then put my pajamas on and hop into bed to get to sleep." Susan could see Gene staring at her through the mirror. "I obey and follow all rules ordered from our fearless leader."

"Get your sweet butt out here, young lady!" Gene pulled her into his arms. "My rules are made to be broken where you're concerned, my sexy little siren."

He parted his lips over hers as she draped her arms around his neck. His hand jerked her top over her head as she removed his shirt and ran her hand down his manly chest. Then came the bra, so his hands could caress her breasts. Their breathing grew heavier as their kisses became more intense.

Susan quickly unzipped his pants and pushed them to the floor, then kicked them across the room. With lightning speed, Gene Scott had his young wife naked, then stepped out of his boxers and tossed them on top of the mirror. Lifting her up with ease, Gene carried Susan to the bed and tossed her down.

Rev. Scott stood for a moment admiring his sexy wife, then climbed down over her to resume the kissing. The kisses fell down her neck, then slowly over her breasts as his hand moved between her thighs to arouse her even more. His heart was pounding with love and desire as he whispered, "Susan, my Susan, how I love you!"

"Gene, my heart is completely filled with love for you!"

Susan's hands moved all over his body, the need for Gene growing stronger. "Gene, make love to me, darling. I need to feel you, move with you and reach the heavens and stars!"

"Then get ready for blast-off, darling!" Gene filled Susan with his complete manhood, and they reached far beyond the stars when their passion was finally released. Only after Gene got his breathing back to normal did he roll over, pulling Susan with him in his arms.

Gene kissed her tenderly, then whispered, "Damn, that was good!" He sat up and looked around at the messy room, their clothes tossed everywhere. He chuckled softly, "It looks like someone was in a hurry around here."

"Maybe we shouldn't wear so many clothes and just leave the underwear off underneath." Susan laughed as she rolled to the other side of the bed and sat up.

"Or if we were somewhere all by ourselves, we could just skip wearing clothes altogether! Walk around in our birthday suits!" Gene got up laughing as they walked to the bathroom. "But since we live in a world filled with people, I guess we'll have to just enjoy pulling one another's clothes off."

"It is rather enjoyable, Rev. Scott, isn't it?" Susan started brushing her teeth.

Gene put his toothbrush back inside its carrier, then moved over behind his wife and put his arms around her flat tight stomach, as he kissed the back of her neck.

"I enjoy every minute of every day with you, Susan!" Gene gathered her hand in his and they walked to the bed. He pulled her around and looked into her beautiful blue eyes. "Of course, my favorite part of our day is at night after we say good night to everyone else we love, then close our bedroom door and make love." His hand caressed her face lovingly as he softly said, "I love you, my darling Susan."

"And I love you, my dearest Gene." Susan's fingers danced in his wet curls as his smile creased his cheeks. "I love your smile, the sexy curls on your neck and the way you make love to me. I love everything about you and I have from the moment

I saw you standing across the deck of that ship!"

With one last kiss, the loving couple climbed into bed, set the clock, cut out the light and said good night in each other's arms. Daylight would be arriving in a few short hours.

Chapter Twenty-Eight

The next morning the group got up early, ate breakfast and started down the path that led into the jungle. Gene Scott and Dr. Rogers each sported a hunting rifle over their shoulder while Susan, Jobi and Randy carried water, a first-aid kit and some snacks for the long hike to the village several miles upriver.

William Rogers had taken the lead, since he'd traveled many times to Kata's village. Randy and Jobi followed close behind him while Susan, then Gene made up the rear flank.

The Scotts scanned the surrounding trees, covered with thick hanging vines reaching to the ground. The thicket on either side of the narrow path looked dark and threatening. Despite their surroundings, things seemed to be quiet and peaceful with no immediate danger around. The preacher's gaze fell on Susan's tan legs and he smiled to himself as he mumbled,

"I've got myself one hot, sexy, young woman!"

"Gene, did you say something?" Susan's attention was drawn to a chattering monkey playing overhead in the trees. She wiped the sweat from her forehead with a big red bandana as she glanced behind her, waiting for his reply.

"Me…say something? No, pretty woman, I'm just thinking out loud." Gene chuckled softly when she turned back around and looked at him.

"Good thoughts, I hope? No planning strategy for the unexpected danger lying ahead?" Susan looked around nervously, so Gene reached up and patted her on the rear.

"Now, honey, stop worrying. I won't let anything happen to you, darling. Aren't you more afraid of getting mosquito bites in those cute little shorts?"

"Not in the least, Jungle Jim! Granddad gave me some

cream Kata makes to keep the biting pests away." Susan laughed as she called up ahead, "Right, Granddad?"

"You bet, sweet girl!" Dr. Rogers called over his head. "The village people have been making that recipe for years and it makes those irritating little bugs run the other way!"

"Why wasn't I told about this wonder cream?" Gene wiped sweat off his forehead. "I could have worn some cute shorts."

"You? Wear shorts in the jungle? The one who preached to me, Jackie and Ali the wrongs of wearing shorts in the jungle?"

Susan smiled at Jobi when he looked back, laughing. "I'm surprised you didn't give me the third degree this morning for putting them on."

"I guess I was too busy admiring my wife's pretty legs. Shoot me!" Gene kicked at a rock he tripped over. "I'll stick to my long pants and long shirt sleeves. That wonder cream won't help keep the poison vines or snakes from crawling up your legs!"

"Suit yourself, Jungle Jim. I'll stick to staying cool and pray my brave hunter will keep the snakes away and I'll just avoid those creeping vines from crawling up my legs." Susan stumbled over a vine, but Gene caught her before she fell. She reached back and touched his hand. "Thanks, sweetheart, my hero!"

"Keep walking, it's hot out here!" Gene called up to Rogers. "William, how much further to the village?"

"I'd say about two hours of walking." He laughed and pointed to a clearing up ahead. "We can take a break soon. There's a small clearing with a canopy of big trees to shade us."

When the group reached the spot, Susan, Jobi and Randy flopped down on a log and started pulling out snacks and water. Gene sat down next to Susan and patted her leg. She reached inside her pouch and pulled out a clean wipe and handed it to her husband.

"Clean your hands, handsome, before you start eating that snack. I don't know what Kata put in that cream, but it's got to be something strong. I haven't been bitten all day."

"Shit!" Gene wiped his hands clean, then ripped into the snack wrapper. "As soon as we get back, I'm putting you in the shower and wash that strong cream off!"

"Can't wait!" Susan took a bite of her oatmeal cookie.

The group finished their break and hit the trail again. After two more hot dusty hours, Dr. Rogers waved his hand, a signal to stop. They had arrived at the Bouta Barga village. Suddenly the stillness was ringing with shouts as ten warrior natives jumped out of the woods and surrounded the small group. Dr. Rogers remained calm as he spoke out loudly,

"Wonka! Take me to your chief, Wonka!"

"Moo-cha! Moo-cha!" The tallest man motioned them to follow him. When they reached the opening where grass huts were placed in a circle, the leader held out his hand for them to stop. "Stay, Englishman!" He walked over to the biggest hut made with sticks covered with moss, then went inside.

Dr. Rogers looked over at Gene, holding fast to the three young people who watched nervously.

"Scott, Wonka is the chief. He can speak fairly good English. I think Kata's father taught him the language when he stayed with them a while."

"Thanks, William. That's good to know, since I can't speak the Bouta Barga language. If I need to change these heathen savages, they've got to understand what I'm saying or I'll be wasting my time!" Gene pulled the three scared young people closer when a shaggy grey-haired native walked out of a hut, dressed in leopard skins and a lion's mane wrapped over his head. William Rogers smiled at his friend.

"Wonka! My good friend! I have come for Kata, to take her home."

"My good friend Prapa, we glad to see you alive!" The old chief smiled, revealing a missing front tooth. "Kata much afraid for you! She be happy now! Wonka, send for Kata!" The chief clapped his hands, and a young black boy ran up and bowed repeatedly in front of the old man.

"Fo-Fo, go get Kata! Bring here!" As the boy ran toward the end hut, the chief sized up the big man holding tight to the three smaller people. "Prapa, who big friend holding to three small ones?"

"Wonka, this is Gene Scott, a man of God." Rogers reached for Susan's hand. "This is Susan, my granddaughter, child's child!"

"Oh, yes, child's child!" The old chief checked out the pretty girl. "Much pretty, child's child."

"This boy is named Jobi, my child's child." Rogers playfully ruffled his grandson's hair.

"Jobi! Good name, strong boy!" The chief looked down at the shy girl and smiled broadly. "This one with hair color of flames, is she child's child?"

"No, my friend. Randy is a friend, like you are a friend!" William Rogers broke into a big smile when Kata ran up and threw her arms around him. "Kata, my Kata! Are you glad to see me?"

"Oh yes, Prapa! You safe! You home!" Tears ran down her bronze cheeks as she smiled over at the preacher. "Scott! He find you! He save you!"

"Yes Kata, Scott saved me and the bad people were sent away, never to return!" Dr. Rogers hugged the woman he loved.

The happy chief smiled over at the joyful reunion, then stepped up close to Gene and patted his arm.

"Mumm, much strong! You save Prapa, man of God! You good friend, yes?"

"Very good friend, chief Wonka, and that is why Kata and William, Prapa, need to get married. They are living together in sin against God. They need your approval. Can they have it, great chief?"

The chief stomped his foot and snapped, "NO! Wonka say Kata no marry Prapa! He English! He outsider!"

"They get married, Wonka, or Kata stays here!" Gene Scott walked over to a stack of large rocks adorned with green vines and jungle flowers. "Wonka, what is this?"

"No can touch, man of God! That Ra-Ruta, our sacred god!" The old chief bowed his head in reverence. "He mighty, He strong! God of wind and rain!"

"Sacred? Mighty?" Gene Scott laughed. "Wonka, that is a lot of crap! Wonka, Wonka! That is a pile of rocks, hard, cold, dead rocks!" He pointed to the sky. "There is only one God! He created everything on this earth! That includes the wind and the rain!"

Gene started walking around, pointing out various objects. "God made these trees, the ground you are standing on, the stupid rocks, the mountains, the sky, everything your eyes can see, taste or smell!" The preacher stared at the wide-eyed chief. "Wonka, God made you, me, Prapa, Kata and everything that lives on this earth!" Scott made his way back over to the pile of rocks and slapped them.

"Wonka, our God is not happy with you! He wants you to break down this false god. Use the rocks to build you a stronger hut; that's what they're good for. Just tear it down or you and your people will burn forever!"

"Burn? Fire?" the old chief stuttered. "Why…why Wonka and tribe burn in fire?"

"You and your people bow down to a fake god!" Gene raised his voice and the birds nesting in the trees scattered around in the air, frightened from the sudden noise. "Wonka, you and your people need to believe in the real God! The one and only God, who lives forever."

"Man of God, tell Wonka and my people about your God!" His voice came out shaky. "Tell how we no burn in fire." His old eyes looked around. "Where God? Wonka want to see."

"You cannot see God, Chief Wonka. He lives in your heart. God sent His son to earth over 2000 years ago to save us from the fire."

"Sound good, friend Scott. Then show Wonka Son! Chief want to see God Son!" The old man pleadingly took Gene's arm; then the wind began to blow, *a gift from God Himself,*

Gene thought, as he smiled. The old chief laughed as the wind cooled him off from the heat of the day. "Good, God wind? This right, Scott?"

"Yes, my friend! God has sent us a cooling wind, but you cannot see the wind, Wonka. But you can feel it and you know it's real." Scott took Wonka's shoulders. "It is the same thing with our God. You cannot see Him, but you can feel Him and you know He is real! My friend, Jesus, God's son, God's child, came to earth for a short time. He lived among His people and taught them how they should live and they told us through the written word. Jesus died on a cross for all of us, including you and your people, so we could be saved from the fire."

"Tell me, friend Scott, what God look like?" Wonka grew serious.

"His son, Jesus, told the people what God looks like. If you could have seen Jesus, you would be looking at the face of God. Jesus lived a perfect life on this earth, Wonka. He healed the sick, the blind could see, the cripple could walk and the dead man would live again. Jesus taught us to forgive and to love one another."

"Love? Like Kata and Prapa?" The old man looked their way, truth dawning on him at last.

"That's right, Chief Wonka! Jesus said when two people love one another, they become husband and wife—married, they become one." Gene walked over to Susan and took her hand. "I love this woman! She loves me! We are married, Wonka. We are one. God is happy with us."

The chief smiled and walked over to Kata and William. "You two get married! You come one! Make God happy!" Wonka smiled over at Gene. "Make Scott happy!"

Dr. Rogers touched his arm in respect. "Wonka, my dear friend, I thank you! I love Kata and I will always give her a home full of love." He put his arm around the young native woman. "Scott will marry us, make us one."

"Good! You say Scott man of God!" The old chief could not contain his emotions as he hugged Gene tightly. "Scott, my friend, thank you for saving my people from fire! We learn about this God! This Son, Jesus! You teach us, yes?"

"Chief Wonka, I promise you will learn all about God and His Son. When I return to Prapa's home, I will call my church and have them get in touch with the missionary committee and have them send just the right person for you and your people. Someone who can speak your language so everyone in the village can learn about God and His Son." Gene checked his watch. "They will send another man of God, Wonka. This one has got to get back home as soon as we have a wedding." Gene winked at Kata, then looked over at the pile of rocks. "Now, Wonka, you can start by tearing down that old rock pile! That will also make God happy!" He smiled, took Susan's hand and headed out of camp.

Mission accomplished!

Chapter Twenty-Nine

Back at the Lazy Lizard, William Rogers made arrangements for a simple wedding for him and his bride. He had purchased the marriage license in advance, along with the wedding bands in hopes Scott could convince the chief to let Kata marry him. Now the day had finally arrived, and Gene and William were waiting at the arch in Rogers' rose garden.

Jobi put a record on, playing a moving instrumental love song as Susan came through the sliding glass doors carrying a single red rose. She had volunteered to be Kata's bridesmaid while Pogo offered to escort the beautiful bride to the arch where the happy groom was waiting.

Gene's attention was only on Susan, who looked radiant in one of Kata's tribal dresses. He smiled as he thought, *I would marry that girl again and again! My beautiful Susan.*

Susan stopped in front of her granddad and kissed him. The happy groom winked at his grand- daughter, then took Kata's hand from Pogo, who turned to go stand with the other three spectators.

Smiling from ear to ear, Rev. Gene Scott started the ceremony,

"Dearly beloved, we are gathered here this fine warm evening to join in marriage William Prapa and Kata. To live together as husband and wife as long as they both live. To love one another, first and foremost, to cherish and care for one another in sickness and in health. For better or worse, for richer or poorer, unless you mine those two mountains and get rich on diamonds…" Gene waited for everyone to stop laughing, then continued, "Forsaking all others, till death do you part. Prapa, do you wish to marry Kata and follow all God's laws and commandments?"

"I certainly do!" William Rogers smiled down at his soulmate.

"And you, Kata, do you wish to marry Prapa and follow all God's laws and commandments?"

"Yes, yes! I do! I do!" She squeezed Rogers' hand.

"If your marriage is as strong as mine and Susan's, then you shall be happy forever and ever!" Gene winked at his wife. "I gladly pronounce you man and wife. William, you may kiss your bride!" Scott laughed and walked over to his wife and took her hand.

"Susan, you look beautiful enough for me to marry you again."

"Rev. Scott, you may kiss your wife!" Susan looped her arms around his neck as he kissed her.

Emily Robinson stood wiping her eyes and, caught up in the moment, reached over and kissed Pogo, catching him by surprise. "I hope I didn't embarrass you, Pogo. We just looked so left out."

"Better watch that, Mrs. Robinson," Gene teased. "Pogo's new girlfriend, Beth, might not approve of another woman kissing her lover boy." He smiled as he took Susan's hand and started toward the house. "Alright, everyone, let's pop the cork! We've got some celebrating to do!"

The other five filed in behind Gene and Susan after letting the newlyweds go first.

Everyone had a glass of champagne except the young teens who had punch. Gene held up his glass.

"Here's to the happy couple! May their married life prove to be as exciting as their shacking-up days!" Everyone laughed before taking a sip. "On a more serious note, Susan and I would like to give you the cruise-ship tickets to America as a wedding gift. Along with me and my lovely wife, Pogo and Emily have purchased airline tickets to TarSa, so Granddad can see his great-grandbabies and his lovely daughter, Shirley, can meet her stepmother. Then you will find two return airline tickets to Africa."

"I can't expect you kids to give up that romantic ocean liner you met on." Dr. Rogers had tears in his eyes. "It was my thank-you gift for coming all the way here to help me." He looked at the others who had given so much. "I can't expect you to spend your hard-earned money on airline tickets either."

"William, are you finished trying to sound too proud to accept our gifts? First, the ship will take too long to get us back to our twins, and second, if we leave it up to you, your great-grandkids will have grandkids of their own before you visit us!" Again laughter, this time from Kata and William. "And the airline tickets are part of the deal I made with the federal government to continue helping them get their man after Susan went missing. Besides, the check I got from them is not too shabby either. If you still feel bad about our generous loving gifts, then when you return to Africa, you can start mining that mountain and send us all a big fat diamond"—Gene teased—"or just accept our gifts, given in love."

"We accept your beautiful gifts, Rev. Scott!" Kata smiled, then kissed her new husband.

Susan moved up to the happy couple and lifted her glass, "To Granddad, the best in the world and his lovely wife, Kata! May your love blossom and bloom!"

"That's beautiful, sweet girl." Dr. Rogers hugged his granddaughter. Then he and the other adults took a sip of champagne.

Gene held up his glass, followed by the rest as he looked over at his friend and said,

"Your turn, Pogo! Then you can have a go, Jobi!" Jobi stood looking down at Randy, blushed and held up his glass as Pogo said,

"Here's to Prapa and Kata, two of the sweetest people I know. May you get to go up early to seal your marriage!" Gene reached over and slapped Pogo on the arm playfully as everyone else once again joined in laughter.

Jobi stepped up to his grandfather and shook his hand, then kissed Kata.

"Granddad, you deserve to be happy! You are the best and I'm glad Susan and I got your genes for being ambitious and adventurous! Kata, we welcome you into our family with love and thanks for making our granddad the happiest man in Africa!"

"Thank you, young Jobi." Kata returned his kiss. "Your granddad, my Prapa, make me happy too!"

"We're just one happy family!" Gene hugged Susan and opened another bottle of bubbly. "Refreshments are waiting and I'm starved!" Gene walked around filling the adults' glasses, then placed the empty bottle down and headed for the table. Susan got in line behind her husband, who was piling his plate full.

"Gene Scott, you're always starved for food! So what's new?"

"My darling devoted wife, as you noticed, I did let the newlyweds go ahead of me." Gene leaned back to whisper in Susan's ear, "To be honest, my beautiful wife, if I'd just gotten married to you, I'd take you up to bed first and skip the refreshments!"

"The man who's always hungry. I do remember on our wedding day we had a big feast before we went up to our hotel room." Susan laughed softly as she patted him on the rear, then picked up her plate.

"Keep doing that, little darling, and I'll show you I can skip the food!" Making sure no one else could see him, Gene reached back and grabbed her breast. "Sometimes dessert in bed is a whole lot more delicious and tempting!"

"Hey, Rev. Scott!" Jobi called from the back of the line. "Stop holding up the line. I thought you were starving!"

"Yeh, Scott—or are you hungry for something else?" Pogo teased, glad to get him back. He'd heard part of their conversation while standing quietly behind Susan.

Gene Scott picked up his filled plate and frowned back at Pogo and Jobi before stepping away.

"Look, fellows, if it weren't for those ladies standing with you, I might have taken everything and left you the scraps!" Placing a chicken leg on top, he walked over and took a seat.

Susan joined him with half of a pimento and cheese sandwich, a small helping of potato salad and a fried chicken wing on her plate. Gene picked up one of his sandwiches and placed it over on her plate. She stared down at it.

"Hey, buster, take back your sandwich! I've got plenty!"

Gene compared their plates of food and shook his head. "Somebody's got to feed you, young lady! You're going to need your energy to keep up with me later in bed!"

"I'll have a big piece of wedding cake, topped with ice cream!" Susan smiled as she took a drink of her champagne.

"Wedding cake?" Gene reached over and took her hand. "I thought I was your dessert, darling."

"You, lover boy, are my tasty nightcap!" Susan whispered in his ear. "The last thing I crave and the very best thing I indulge in." Susan ran her fingers up his leg as he smiled broadly. "I sip on it slowly, so it will last and the taste explodes in my mouth! Mumm!"

"Damn! You're good!" Gene whispered next to her ear as he could feel himself growing sexually excited. "Eat up, beautiful! Your nightcap awaits!"

Pogo could tell from experience that Gene was ready to take Susan up to bed. His thoughts turned to Gloria and how he missed carrying her up to his bed. William and Kata had slipped away earlier, hardly touching their food. Romance was on their mind after being separated for such a long time. As for Jobi and Randy, they asked to be excused after downing big pieces of wedding cake and ice cream. They'd found a set of cards and wanted to play before heading up for bed. Emily Robinson had collected her half-finished book and walked into the study for a quiet place to read before turning in.

Pogo walked over between the Scotts and placed his hands on their shoulders.

"Alright, you two lovebirds, off to bed! It's our last night here so get up there and enjoy yourselves!"

"Pogo, we can't leave you with all this mess to clean up. It wouldn't be fair." Susan stopped Gene's hand from moving up her dress. "Gene and I'll help you!"

"Susan, that's sweet, but Scott can't wait! Don't torture the man any longer." Pogo slapped his friend on the back and Gene looked up smiling.

"You're a pal, Pogo, a real pal!" Gene Scott stood up, not letting go of Susan's hand. "Just for this, little buddy, when we get home, just forget the housework. Let the grass grow or we'll call Freddy down the street to mow. Call Beth, go and see her. I know you miss her, pal. I've been there."

"I know, I remember! Thanks, Scott, that sounds super!" Pogo smiled from ear to ear, getting Scott's permission to call Gloria the first thing and go see her. He'd been sweating, wondering how he could see her after Gene and Susan decided to fly home instead of take the ship. "Now go and have fun, you two."

"That's the plan, pal!" Scott picked up Susan and carried her up to their bedroom where Gene had his dessert and Susan drank her sexy nightcap until they both were filled to overflowing and concluded with an explosion of colorful fireworks!

Susan and Jobi hugged their grandfather goodbye at the ship's dock where the good doctor and Kata waited to go aboard. William Rogers shook Gene's hand proudly.

"My granddaughter did well to marry you, Gene Scott! Our family has gained a wonderful son and a faithful friend."

"Thank you, William. I'm happy to be a part of such a wonderful family." Gene patted the doctor's back. "As for Susan, I love that woman more than I love life; and believe me, I'm pretty fond of that too—especially my life with Susan. I'm grateful she fell in love with me and wanted to get married to an older man." Gene stood smiling when the ship's speaker announced for passengers to board the ship.

"I guess this is goodbye for now, my friend. I hope you and Kata have a long happy life together and enjoy this ship as much as Susan and I did." Gene took Susan's trembling hand as she looked at the ship where she'd met him. "We look forward to your visit, and I know Shirley and Joan are in for a surprise!"

"At least we'll be arriving as newlyweds instead of live-in lovers!" Dr. Rogers teased. "Thank you for saving me, Scott. Now my life is complete!" Gene helped them on the ship, then stood back to wave.

"See you, Granddad! Kata!" Susan called loudly, "Enjoy our ship!"

"You're not upset that I gave them our tickets, are you, Susan?" Gene led her to the waiting taxi that would carry them to the airstrip.

"I think it was a very wonderful thing you did and who knows, if Granddad does start mining, he might just give us another voyage on the African Queen Line." Susan laid her head over on his shoulder. "But you were right, darling, we have two small children who are missing their mommy and daddy and a congregation who's gone without your sermons long enough!"

"I love you, Susan Scott!" Gene kissed her. "Let's go home!"

THE AUTHOR'S NOTES

A GIRL'S RETREAT TURNS INTO DISASTER WHEN ONE OF GENE SCOTT'S OLD ENEMIES SHOWS UP WITH REVENGE ON HIS MIND!

GENE SCOTT RELIVES HIS WORSE NIGHTMARE, ONLY THIS TIME IT IS SUSAN THAT IS INVOLVED!

POGO AND GLORIA'S SECRET COMES OUT AS THE RESULT OF THE EVENTS THAT HAPPEN ON THE GIRL'S RETREAT!

YOU WILL FIND A LOT OF ACTION, JOY, AND TEARS SPRING OUT OF BOOK #5: "LOVE NEVER ENDS" IN THE "ALL MY TOMORROW" SERIES.

www.ingramcontent.com/pod-product-compliance
Lightning Source LLC
Chambersburg PA
CBHW060922250626
47159CB00008B/3117

* 9 7 8 1 6 3 0 6 6 5 2 0 3 *